A tremor rippled through her.

Then another. Not from cold. Not when Kee cupped the back of her neck and drew her face closer to his. Not when she felt his warm breath fan across her cheek.

"I don't know what's ahead for us, Isabel," he whispered. "But I'm a man who wants to die happy. And I need one thing from you."

"What?" The shudder that ran through him acted like a caress to her body. She could feel what he was doing to her, but Kee was not hiding how he felt in return. Her breathing became labored as if she had run a long way. She cupped the side of his face, felt the roughness of his unshaven skin and then the first brush of his lips over hers.

Temptation...

Dear Reader,

In *The Bonny Bride* by award-winning author Deborah Hale, a poor young woman sets sail for Nova Scotia from England as a mail-order bride to a wealthy man, yet meets her true soul mate on board the ship. Will she choose love or money? Margaret Moore, who also writes mainstream historicals for Avon Books, returns with *A Warrior's Kiss,* a passionate marriage-of-convenience story and the next in her ongoing medieval WARRIOR series. Theresa Michaels's new Western, *Once a Hero,* is a gripping and emotion-filled story about a cowboy who rescues a female fugitive and unexpectedly falls in love with her as they go in search of a lost treasure. For readers who enjoy discovering new writers, *The Virgin Spring* by Golden Heart winner Debra Lee Brown is for you. Here, a Scottish laird finds an amnesiac woman beside a spring and must resist his desire for her, as he believes she is forbidden to him.

For the next two months we are going to be asking readers to let us know what you are looking for from Harlequin Historicals. We hope you'll participate by sending your ideas to us at:

**Harlequin Historicals
300 E. 42nd St.
New York, NY 10017**

Q. What do you like about Harlequin Historicals?

_____
_____

Q. What *don't* you like about Harlequin Historicals?

_____
_____

Whatever your tastes in reading, you'll be sure to find a romantic journey back to the past between the covers of a Harlequin Historicals novel. We hope you'll join us next month, too!

Sincerely,

Tracy Farrell,
Senior Editor

Theresa Michaels

Once a Hero

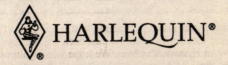

HARLEQUIN®

TORONTO • NEW YORK • LONDON
AMSTERDAM • PARIS • SYDNEY • HAMBURG
STOCKHOLM • ATHENS • TOKYO • MILAN • MADRID
PRAGUE • WARSAW • BUDAPEST • AUCKLAND

ISBN 0-373-29105-1

ONCE A HERO

Copyright © 2000 by Theresa DiBenedetto

Available from Harlequin Historicals and
THERESA MICHAELS

Harlequin Historicals

A Corner of Heaven #104
Gifts of Love #145
Fire and Sword #243
Once a Maverick #276
Once an Outlaw #296
Once a Lawman #316
†*The Merry Widows—Mary* #372
†*The Merry Widows—Catherine* #400
†*The Merry Widows—Sarah* #469
Once a Hero #505

*The Kincaids
†The Merry Widows

Other works include:

Harlequin Books

Renegades 1996
"Apache Fire"

Please address questions and book requests to:
Harlequin Reader Service
U.S.: 3010 Walden Ave., P.O. Box 1325, Buffalo, NY 14269
Canadian: P.O. Box 609, Fort Erie, Ont. L2A 5X3

To Anthony and Michael
for battles won and battles lost—
heroes through them all.

Chapter One

Kee Kincaid never set out to be a hero. His adopted family called him one. A practice he discouraged. Fact is, he found it downright embarrassing. Just as bad as calling a man a coward for not bucking odds stacked against him. Sure enough, since the time he'd lost his parents to an Indian attack he'd found himself risking his neck to help someone out. Those times, he'd figured he had just been doing what was right. Folks found it easy to hang labels like *brave* or *courageous* on a man. Truth was, he had been a mite faster doing what was needed.

He wasn't a trouble-hunting man; none of the Kincaids were. But if someone dealt him cards without his nay or yea, he'd play out the hand as it came.

Which is why he found himself hunkered down at the opening of the small branch canyon where he'd camped, rifle in hand while the echo of shots died away.

The gunfire rolled through the clear Arizona air just as he was breaking camp. His packhorse was saddled, and the four Appaloosa mares he had been hunting were strung out on the leading ropes. With a last tug the cinch was tightened while Outlaw stood sweet as a kitten under his hand. The mountain-bred mustang mix was a gelding who reacted to the shots by herding the horses to the far end of the small branch canyon. Docile to Kee, Outlaw was known to attack any man whose scent he didn't like.

Back on the Rocking K, there'd been arguments aplenty about turning the horse loose or shooting him, but Kee kept him. The mustang had shown him a lot of wild country, his hankering for the next trail as deep as Kee's own.

Kee had not seen another soul for almost two weeks. The gunfire bothered him. He glanced up at the fingers of color crawling across the night, a bright mix of yellows, pinks and purples that formed long, thin streaks in the inky sky. The spring air already held a hint of the heat the coming day would bring.

And there was a stillness that prickled the hair on the back of his neck.

Folks back East said the frontier was closed three years ago. They hadn't been riding the Arizona territory. Cattle rustlers and horse thieves, train robbers and outlaws still rode the desolate badlands.

Kee studied the rim of the canyon, searching out the shadows. The four purebred mares were a prize worth stealing. But those shots were not that close. Still he slipped the thong from his Colt. Outlaw snorted and pawed the earth.

Kee thought if he had pushed on last night, he would be snug in his adopted mother's old cabin, and that much closer to home.

But a faint cry cut into his thoughts, followed swiftly by a shout that sent itchy feet crawling up his back. Someone sure as hell was in trouble.

Kee knew he could turn back to his camp and wait out the day. Many a man would do so and none would think less of him for doing it.

It wasn't his way.

When a scream rent the air, nothing could make him leave.

He lived with a passel of females and had heard screams of outrage, delight and sheer fear.

That scream came from a woman. A woman's scream signaled trouble all its own.

No man worth calling himself one would turn his back on a woman in trouble. Not if his name was Kincaid. Even when he knew women like those in his family that could do a sight of protecting themselves.

Kee was moving as the sun rose to splash light on the upper walls of the canyon. He stood at the opening and stared at the still, murky shadows that covered the wider canyon's floor.

He carefully studied the boulders, fallen trees and brush. Again he wondered about the shots. Apache Junction in the shadows of the Superstition Mountains was the closest town. Miners hunting gold kept the place alive and these mountains were a draw to every treasure seeker and those who'd rob them. He'd hunted for color a time or two himself. So a miner could be protecting his claim.

But the silence bothered him now as the gunfire had earlier. If it wasn't for that scream he'd lay down the shots to an early hunter.

His patient search of land and rock was rewarded. Two riders at the far end of the canyon dipped into sight and were just as quickly lost behind the tree line.

A few minutes more told him they were hunting, and it wasn't animal. Their noise carried up to him.

He couldn't make exactly what they were hollering, but the two sounded angry.

Definitely trouble.

Without a sound he went back into the feeder canyon for Outlaw.

Mounted, he once more waited at the opening as light crawled into the dark. He watched the small clearing below, sure those riders would show there.

A shout from one rider to the other made Kee tighten his grip on the reins. He heard another faint cry as one rider broke into the clearing. Kee could make out the cutting motions of the rider's horse. He thought he saw a smaller figure dodging the rider.

Despite the rider swinging a rope and yipping as if he were heading off a stray, Kee couldn't rid himself of a cold snake of fear for whoever was running from them.

The gelding pricked up his ears. He sensed trouble, too.

Kee felt every muscle in his horse poised with eagerness to take out and run. His spur caressed the mustang's flank, ready to nudge him into action.

Still Kee was forced to wait. He had to know where the other rider was.

He picked out the stumbling run of the woman. She cried out and ducked the flung rope. Kee freed his rifle and sighted down the barrel. He squeezed the trigger and the bullet tore through the hand holding the rope.

Kee cursed as he saw her run from the wounded man where her best chance lay. And then the second rider appeared, and his rope didn't miss.

Burning rage filled Kee. He didn't give a damn what she had done. No woman deserved to be roped like an animal. She fought the lasso, but the rider had enough skill in roping to keep the loop tight and bring her to her knees as he took up the slack rope and closed in on her.

Now Kee couldn't shoot. And he was out of time.

His spurs raked Outlaw's sides.

The rock-strewn path offered no threat to the mustang. He'd run with a thundering herd before and behind him where to hesitate meant death.

Kee's wild yells seemed to freeze the two riders. And to his luck kept them separated. Coming at them at a dead run, Kee freed his belt knife. Every second as he closed with them saw a fluid body move as he put to use the skills learned in a summer with a Wild West show.

He ignored the shots that barked over his shoulder, hugging close to his horse's neck. He kicked one boot free of the stirrup, laying his leg lengthwise on the mustang's back. He held the reins tight and with that same hand grabbed hold of the pommel. The wickedly honed knife blade gleamed in a flash of sunlight.

"We're in for it now, boy." Kee felt the cold sweat break out on his body. He could almost feel the gunsight tracking him.

Pressing his boot into the stirrup, he slid his body to the side of his racing horse. His gaze remained on the woman struggling to her feet.

A whisper from Kee made Outlaw veer sharply to the left. Another shot went wide of them. The rider had wrapped the rope around his pommel, pulling it taut and freeing his hands for the rifle he brought to bear on Kee.

Outlaw had no more wish to be shot than his rider. And this was a game they had played out many times.

The mustang veered on his own toward the wounded rider, putting him in line to get shot.

One swing of Kee's arm and the taut rope parted. Outlaw, at his signal, nearly turned in place, his head angled down, teeth bared as he went after the shooter's horse.

Kee hit the saddle and just found the swinging stirrup when Outlaw reared, screaming a challenge as if he were still a stallion.

"Run!" Kee shouted at the woman.

His yell seemed to free the two men from whatever had gripped them. Just as Outlaw's hoof came down on the flank of the nearest horse, the wounded man tried to send his loop flying at Kee.

Without help from his rider, the mustang dodged the rope. He knew the tricks of men trying to catch him. He spun on his hocks, his front hooves hitting the earth with a bone jar to his rider, then he was moving again.

Kee despaired when he saw the woman was either hurt or too frightened to move. He swung his knife at the man closest to her and yelled again for her to run. A second swipe with the knife brought a grunt of pain as the blade sliced flesh.

He ignored their shouts as he raced past, turned and headed back. Trusting to his horse, Kee freed his hand of the reins. He extended his arm, leaned out and grabbed hold of the woman to fling her belly down across his saddle.

The one he'd shot first tried to sight his gun, but Kee slashed out with his knife barely nicking the man's horse, and forcing him to control his rearing mount.

Kee was still between the two men, Outlaw doing his best to keep their horses from closing in on them.

That little bit of safety was all that kept them from shooting him.

Blood and dust, frantic whinnies from the horses mixed with the shouts of who was to get him.

On top of that, the damn woman was struggling under his hand to push herself off the horse.

Having put himself to a hell of a lot of trouble to rescue her, Kee was of no mind to be gotten by anyone.

And he'd be double damned if this blistering female was jumping back into the fire.

"Hold still! I'm trying to save your life!"

It was all he had time to say before he gripped his knife handle with his teeth and drew his Colt.

His boot heels banged the mustang's sides. Kee laid covering fire over his shoulder as the horse took off.

The mustang wove his own erratic path toward the small branch canyon's mouth.

Kee held on to his ungrateful burden, feeling every muscle of the horse bunch and strain as he carried the two of them.

The whine of flying bullets came too close. Rock fragments were thrown high to the side. Kee emptied his gun with little hope of hitting either man. He needed two hands free to get his rifle and use it.

The woman's long black hair might once have been a braid. Now it was a cloud that entangled his hand. Her shriek of pain forced him to look down at her.

Blood welled from a tear in her pant leg. He hoped it was nothing more than a bullet graze, but the way those two behind him were throwing lead, it could be worse. And he had no time to do more than look.

The mustang was laboring. With his double burden the horse couldn't keep up this fast pace much longer, not over the rough, broken ground.

The opening to the branch canyon appeared like a gateway to salvation.

Kee knew how false the thought was. He could easily hold the men off, but the reverse held true, too.

They could just as easily keep him pinned down.

Two to one. Not the worse odds he'd faced. Still, he'd shorten them. He grabbed hold of his knife.

"Just hang on tight. Don't fight my horse," he ordered the woman.

Outlaw swept through the opening. Kee slid free and, rifle in hand, turned to meet the men that followed.

His first shot cut up dust in front of the lead horse. He barely kept his rage in check not to make it a killing shot.

The man was smart enough to jerk his horse still.

His partner drew rein alongside him.

Kee figured he was dead, coffin nailed and grave dug by their looks.

He was in a killing mood himself, but no murderer.

"You two figure on eating again, shuck the guns and rifles where I can see them."

"The hell I'll—"

"Do it!" Kee ordered and sent a bullet over their heads. "I'll bury you right here if I've got to wait."

He planted another shot between the horses to show he meant business.

"You ain't got a call to interfere," one yelled.

Kee saw the gun belts drop, then the rifles.

"She stole somethin' that's mine."

"You'll give her over if you know what's good for you, stranger."

"You the law?" Kee demanded. Then, before they answered, he motioned with the rifle. "Dismount and take off your boots."

"Like hell I'll—"

This time Kee's shot took the man's hat off.

"The boots, now. And since I don't see a badge, you're not the law. You call her a thief...get a town marshall or the territory sheriff to arrest her. Then she'll stand trial. Hear tell the truth comes out then."

Kee had shut them up with his talk about the law. He studied the two men who dropped to the ground to remove their boots. He couldn't hear their whispered talk. He had to be satisfied for now that he had the upper hand in the bluff he was running.

Kee didn't know either man. The lean, taller one who had his hand shot was doing most of the talking. A curved scar pulled down one side of his mouth. His clothing was worn, like his gear. Boot heels run-down, lank, dark hair hanging to his shoulders. Not a bit of shiny metal anywhere. A hunter, all right, Kee confirmed.

A quick look showed handguns well cared for and both Winchesters were new. With their boots tossed aside, scar mouth tugged his worn felt hat low then faced Kee.

The close-set eyes held a promise of retribution.

Kee almost laughed. The man had never faced down a Kincaid bent on extracting revenge. Still, they weren't a pair of eyes Kee wanted to face on a dark night. And he had a feeling that dark nights, in even darker alleys, were where this man hunted.

He had started to rise when the other man grabbed

his arm. He was shorter, thin as a rail post, his face covered by a straggly beard.

Kee passed men like him on every street in every town. Deep-set eyes, a broken nose and a habit of hitching up his belt when he talked. He noted the notches on the gun butt. No one but a tinhorn marked his weapon.

He'd seen a gun like this and heard tell of men who notched their kills. Hard not to when his uncle was sheriff of Sweetwater.

He figured them both for cheap hired guns, but Kee didn't lower his guard. He didn't like the sneaky looks the smaller man shot toward him. He could almost follow those thoughts of getting the jump on him.

Kee cocked the rifle. "Time's a-wasting. Start walking."

"Now just hold on…" scar mouth started to say.

"The thing is, gents, I'm holding my rifle. It speaks with a bark that's mighty hard to argue with. You boys feeling testy and want a piece of this, come and get it."

More whispers. Kee grew past impatient. He wondered if the woman was all right. He hadn't heard a sound from the canyon. Outlaw would have ridden straight back to the mares and stayed there. After all this, he hoped the woman wasn't dead. He wanted some answers.

The hell with it! He'd had enough.

He fired off three shots, startling the horses into running, and the men into backing away.

"Move out!" Kee wasn't about to give them time to grab a gun. He placed exact shots on the boulder nearest them. Then fired two shots into the earth.

Since they weren't running fast enough after their

mounts, Kee spurred them on with a few more shots. The horses were hell-bent for leather, and if this wasn't so deadly serious, he might have smiled seeing their jerky dance down the trail.

Kee figured he had five shots left. Careless of him not to have kept better count. A man could lose his life that way.

Much as he hated to do it, he lifted the rifle and sighted. They were barely wounded, and he had a feeling they'd lie in wait for him.

And he had no idea if they were riding alone.

For good measure he nicked one's belt, then creased his thigh. The man stumbled, but it wasn't enough to slow him down. The other wore a bullet crease across his shoulder. Kee emptied the rifle high over their fleeing heads.

Before he moved, he reloaded his Colt, then shoved .44s into the rifle. When he spied them down in the clearing, then and only then did he turn to find out what kind of thief he'd rescued.

Well, she took his breath away. Especially since she stood holding his spare gun, cocked and aimed at him.

Chapter Two

Slim. Taller than he had guessed. Younger than he thought, with midnight-black hair that held an unruly curl and blue eyes so dark they were nearly as black as brows arched over them.

"That's a hell of a thank you," he finally said, motioning with his rifle at the gun she held on him.

And held steady, too, he noted.

"You figure to use that on me?"

He tilted his head, sizing up the quality of her clothing, boots and belt, despite the tears and dirt that marred them. Her silence unnerved him.

"Those two could go for help. Might think about that before you shoot me."

"Do you believe I will not?"

A faint accent caught his ear. He gazed at her face. There was a bruise on her high cheekbone. Kee's grip on his rifle showed the knuckles almost white. He reached out without thought to touch her, but she backed away.

"It's all right," he said softly, understanding her fear. "You're safe now. I wouldn't hurt you. I've never hurt a woman in my life. Those men—"

"They are cowards. You did well to chase them off."

"They accused you of stealing something from them."

"No."

He waited patiently, despite the small voice of caution urging him to get away from this place. He expected more to the denial, some explanation as to why they had been chasing her.

Young she might be, but he sensed that the silence growing between them bothered him more than it did her.

He saw there was a feline cast to her features. The chin a little pointed, eyes with a slight, intriguing slant. Eyes that directed a hard gaze at him.

Kee had the answer to his earlier silent question. Not a bit of doubt about it.

She'd shoot.

"We can't wait around here."

"We?"

He had been introduced to a few highfalutin women back East, and once to a duchess. Not even she managed that raised brow and imperious tone to one word.

Patience flew by him. And he wasn't about to call it back.

"Look, lady. I saved your life down there. You don't feel like thanking me, fine. You need my spare gun, that's fine, too. Take it with my blessing. But, lady, I'm riding out of here. Now."

A flush tinted her olive skin that owed its color more to heritage than the sun. Her slim, straight nose spoiled the hard, arrogant look. The tip titled upward just a bit. But that mouth...it was worth a second look, a whole lot of second looks. Full and wide, ripe for smiling, ripe for kissing.

Belatedly, and none too soon, he noted how she shifted her weight and remembered the wound.

"You caught a bullet. Let me tend that for you." He couldn't help but glance toward her hips. Slim as a boy's but the slight curve showed off a waist he could span with his hands.

"A graze. I barely feel it."

Kee set his teeth. Obstinate, contrary woman!

He touched his fingers to his hat brim. "It's been...hell, not a pleasure, ma'am. Ain't sure what it's been, but it's over. I'm leaving."

The sun was full up, the heat already making itself felt. Kee didn't wait to see what she'd do or say. He walked by, heading down the canyon toward his horses.

"What will you do with their horses and guns?"

"Leave them." He didn't pause or turn around.

"You cannot leave them there. What if they come back?"

"Now you're talking to me, lady? I really don't care if they do. You're a mighty ungrateful woman to my way of thinking. You've got my gun, and I know you will use it."

"You are angry with me."

Kee shouted back. "Damn right I am."

"I do not know you."

"That's fine. We'll leave it that way. This is one gent who's making tracks out of here. Alone," he added with a perverse pleasure.

"I am Isabel Dolores Rosalinda del Cuervo."

The way she said her name, as if it should mean something to him, forced Kee to stop and face her.

The wind caught her hair sending the unruly curls into a wilder tangle. Kee could almost see the capital *T* for trouble branded in the middle of that slim body.

"You've got yourself a fine-sounding pedigree, lady. Pardon me if I don't scrape and bow."

"I could shoot you."

"You sure could." And with that said, he turned his back and kept walking.

"Wait! Who are you?"

He muttered something Isabel couldn't hear. She limped after him. Holding his own gun on him had been wrong. He could not begin to understand how frightened she was. But he had rescued her. She could not allow him to ride away. She needed him.

The wind whipped her hair around her face and she reached up to contain the thick mass, wincing as she pulled on the bullet graze.

The horses nickered as he neared them, all but the one he had ridden. That one snorted.

She heard the murmur of his voice but not the words as he rubbed the animals' noses or scratched between their ears. *Kind to animals, kind to women.* Her grandmother's words. Dear *abuela,* I miss you so. Help me now to know what to do.

She had been through too much, fought too long, and through it all had been alone. Trust did not come easily.

Not even for a man whose eyes and hair were the melted shades of her favorite chocolate.

She had only minutes more to make up her mind about the man who moved with the fluid grace of a born *vaquero.* She could think of no higher praise than that of the finest riders in Mexico or this vast, desolate territory of Arizona.

He did not have the *vaquero*'s flowery gallantry. His less than gentlemanly behavior was her own fault.

And he did not appear to know her name.

Isabel bit her lower lip. She had few, very few facts with which to judge this man. A skilled rider, an excellent shot, handy with the knife he wore. Her quick search of his saddlebags produced the gun she took, two beautifully handmade shirts, a pair of pants and a simple silver buckle with the initial *K* set in the open-worked oval.

No clue to who he was. He could be married; someone had made those shirts.

He is brave, Isabel. Do not forget what he has done for you.

And if she could forget those terror-filled hours.

She rubbed her arms, and realized she still had his gun. What should she do?

He had stripped the saddle and was rubbing his horse with a bunch of dry grass, already done while she tried to decide. The horse's hide was still dark with sweat from his hard ride. With an ease she envied, he lifted the heavy saddle in place, every move as smooth as the fit of his dark gray shirt.

His stance emphasized the strength of his long legs and the slimness of his hips. Muscles rippled across his chest. There was a confident set to his shoulders, to the whole of his rangy body.

The profile spoke of power and strength. He wasn't a handsome man. The features appeared too rugged for true masculine beauty in a face bronzed by sun and wind. The slightly square cut of his chin suggested a stubborn streak. His full lower lip suggested other things that she did not dare think about, for he was mounted, tying the lead rope to his saddle.

"Your horses," she said, "I have never seen such mares. The confirmation and coloring of such young-blooded stock is a thing of beauty."

Kee looked down at her. He shoved his hat back on his head. Where he found the small store of sympathy and patience from he didn't know, but he used it now.

"Look, at any other time I'd let you stand and admire these mares all you want. Maybe you're in shock over what happened to you. C'mon over here and I'll help you mount behind me. We really need to leave here."

His strong, callused hand was held out toward her. Isabel hesitated and then with a shrug, stepped closer to him.

"Where are you going?"

"Wherever you'd like," he promised rashly. Damn! Double damn! What got into him? He never made promises. Never!

The fingers she held up were long and slim, the skin smooth, the wrist delicately boned.

Kee took a firm grip, kicked his boot free for her to use the stirrup to help her mount.

But when she tried stretching her leg, she cried out and pulled free.

"I told you to let me look at that wound." Kee was down and lifting her to his saddle before the words were out.

"Scoot back. I'll need more room than you."

"I noticed," she murmured, biting her lip against the pain.

Kee didn't miss the blanching of her skin. The words *It served her right* were hanging on the tip of his tongue. He swallowed them.

Neck-reining Outlaw to walk out, Kee thought he

should have put her in front of him. Between her slender arms wrapped around his waist, the press of her body against his back and the heat of her breath sliding through his shirt, he was in for one hell of a long ride.

And not the kind he'd been looking forward to.

Like Uncle Ty said, trouble came with a scent all its own. And once Ty had been on intimate terms with trouble. Kee remembered those words when Ty defended his need to ride out when and where it pleased him. Trouble with a scent as elusive as water in the desert. Or the smell like a storm gathering, wicked and wild, striking out of nowhere.

Or the kind of trouble that drifted into a man's senses on the fragrance of a woman.

Kee figured the lady with the fancy name and capital *T* carried all three kinds of trouble for him.

At the canyon's mouth he was surprised to find the horses still standing, the guns on the ground.

He gathered up the reins, thought about leaving the guns, quickly decided against it.

"Painful as it is for you to move, you'll be more comfortable on your own horse." Kee didn't give her time to nay or yea him. He swept her up and very gently set her into the saddle.

"You do not believe one of these is truly my horse?"

"No, ma'am. I sure don't. Yours would have a mess of fancy trappings to go along with the fancy name." Kee kept a sharp lookout while he looped both holsters around her saddle's pommel. He set the rifle in the boot, then grabbed the reins of the other horse. He led the animal back to the end of his own string, and secured him to the packhorse. He checked the spare rifle, saw it was fully loaded and carried it back to his own saddle.

"Their boots, you will not leave them."

He glared at her. Took himself a deep breath, and huffed the air out. He tried telling himself that the lady was accustomed to giving orders, and what's more, having them obeyed. He lived with women like that. And while it rubbed every bit of him the wrong way to be subservient to anyone, he merely nodded, told himself to be charitable to the contrary, obstinate woman. He shoved the boots into her saddlebags, smiled and touched his hat before he mounted.

This was one piece of baggage he was going to ditch at the first ranch, or town he came to.

Instead of taking the trail down to the canyon, Kee headed Outlaw toward the rim, letting the mustang pick his own way.

"Wait," Isabel called out. "We must go back to where my camp is."

"That's asking for trouble if those hombres have anyone else waiting for them."

"They were alone."

"We're still heading out this way." Kee's voice was hard with a finality that brooked no more argument.

Outlaw topped the rim and it was a breathtaking piece of country spread out before him. A blue bowl of sky with pillow-soft white clouds, sun-gilded mountaintops and deep, shadowed canyons. Off in the distance a thin ribbon of blue river. A pair of red-tailed hawks floated high above.

At any other time Kee would have sat and thought about the next mountain he hadn't climbed, the next canyon to be explored. He had a slight sense of all the places he hadn't yet been, but surprisingly, his companion's silence began to grate on his nerves.

He wondered what she was scheming.

From the softness of her hands, her imperious manner and her name, he guessed pure *hidalgo* blood ran in her veins. But if that were true, he knew no Spanish nobleman worthy of the name would allow a woman of his family to travel without a heavily armed escort.

And a *duenna*.

In his considered opinion, Señorita del Cuervo was in dire need of a chaperon.

Preferably one with a good stiff hairbrush. Lord knew he had comforted his nieces when their mischief making proved too much for the household.

As Outlaw chose a way down the loose scree, Kee thought about Reina. At twelve, Ty and Dixie's eldest didn't care much for rules. The Kincaid princess from her birth, she had run away once or twice when a spanking was looming.

Run away…

Maybe that's what his Spanish lady had done.

Or maybe…

He yanked on the reins, causing Outlaw to slide. He managed to hang on, but jerked around to look at the woman.

"You running from a husband?"

"Do you look for a reward?"

"What kind of an answer is that? Did I say any damn thing about a reward? Did I?"

The tumbled boulders made for treacherous footing and Kee had to pay attention. He'd wait. Once they were down on level ground, he'd have his answers or he wasn't going another foot.

The lady was fast going beyond contrary, obstinate

female all the way to mule. After a moment he amended that. She'd gone straight to a stone wall.

Once off the rim, Kee headed for the towering cottonwood he spied from above. He had guessed there would be water, and while he wished for a wider and deeper stream, this one would do.

He led the horses in and rode upstream a ways, then headed downstream without leaving the water. He tossed the lead rope to Isabel, who, he absently noted, caught it with a deft hand. He rode farther down, came out of the stream on one side, made tracks along the bank, then once more entered the stream.

When he rode up to her, she handed over the lead rope.

"Do you believe what you have done will hide our trail?" she asked.

"Not for long. Not if one of them can track, but it'll sure confuse the hell out of them. You wanted to go back to your camp. Where is it?"

"I am uncertain. When I ran this morning it was still dark. My only thought was to get away from those men."

Kee took a hard look at the towering walls around them. "South should be Phoenix and the Superstition Mountains. Over east we'd cross the Salt River and hit the Sierra Ancha. I don't think you or anyone could cross that in the dark. The trails are rugged, box canyons and high walls that are nearly impossible." Kee led off, heading downstream, keeping to the center. "Did you notice anything about the place where you camped?"

"There was a stream."

"Lots of those around. I was thinking more of a landmark. We need something to point the way." He thought of the Sierra Ancha's ancient cliff dwellings. If she had a guide crazy enough to take her into that wildness, she would have seen them. Or maybe the man would have told her a few stories about Devil's Chasm or Aztec Peak.

"You never said if you were traveling with anyone. Come to think of it, you haven't said much about anything." He neck-reined Outlaw up the bank where a thick stand of cottonwoods were just leafing.

Kee made sure she had followed him. He sat a few moments, staring at her, not backing down beneath that very direct gaze of hers.

"You know something, lady—"

"I told you my name."

"So you did, and truthfully, that's really about all you've told me. Oh, I forgot. You denied stealing anything from those two hombres. Right? Or did I miss something?"

She looked away first, and Kee was struck again by the delicacy of her profile. But he wasn't going on until she told him more.

"You should know that I've heard some tall tales. If you're sitting there contemplating telling me one, better make it good. If I don't like what I hear, I'm riding on. Alone. Despite—"

"Despite your promise to me?" She glanced at him, and found his implacable expression unnerving. "I— I came here to find something." She heard the underlying note of resignation and could do nothing about it. For in truth he was asking her to trust him, and she had no choice. To a point. But there was no need for him to know that.

"Go on. I'm listening."

"What I seek men will kill for."

"Hold it right there, lady. Tell me no more. You're hunting gold, right?"

She was hurt by his scoffing tone, more by the look in his eyes.

Her chin lifted and she fixed a cold, hard stare on his face. "What if I am?"

"You and every other damn fool. Oh, I'm not saying there isn't any gold in these mountains, there is. But you, a woman alone—"

"I have a map."

"Right. And the man that sold it to you was dying or something. I don't believe my luck. I just don't believe it. I wish you luck." He nudged the mustang out from under the trees.

"Wait! You do not let me finish." *Calm. Be calm,* she warned herself. "The map I have is very old. I knew the man who made it. My grandfather. From the time he was a boy he had come with others to work the mine in these mountains. The last time, he had hurt his leg and felt something was wrong. He urged the others to leave. They would not listen to him. He took the gold he had mined and left them."

Isabel took a deep breath and released it. She searched his face for a sign that he was listening, and more, believing her. Better she should try to read the bark on the tree.

"Later," she continued, "he heard most of the others were killed by the Apache. Two escaped. They met with a man. A Dutchman. Some say that he killed the two after they told him about the mine."

"Jacob Walz," Kee said, shaking his head. "You know, I thought my luck was bad. Lady, just forget about this map. More men have been killed hunting that mine than anyone really knows. Any map you have is worthless.''

''That is not true!'' She heard the desperation in her voice, could feel it in every nerve of her body. ''Why do you say this? You cannot know. My grandfather—''

''Listen!'' Kee walked his horse closer to hers. He grabbed hold of her arm. ''You just listen up and it might save you grief. The map's no good. Six years ago there was an earthquake here. Every landmark is changed.''

''No!''

He had seen what news of death could do to a person and she reacted as if he dealt a death blow. Her face blanched, she closed her eyes, tears leaking through black lashes, and he barely managed to catch her before she fell.

Chapter Three

The press of a cold cloth brought Isabel out of her faint.

"You're a deceiving woman," Kee murmured as he cradled her upper body against his chest. There was a sudden fear in her dark-blue eyes, and he hurried to finish what he started to say.

"What I mean, is that you handled yourself like a real strong woman this morning with those men, and I wasn't expecting you to faint."

"I never faint."

"A man once told me there's a first time for everything under the sun."

She read the concern in his gaze.

"I feel foolish. I have never done this."

"Too much happening. Bet there's something else. You said it was still dark when those men found your camp, you couldn't have had anything to eat. I've got a fire going and now that you're awake, I'll fix you some grub."

She shivered as a smooth move took the warmth of his body from hers. His words came rushing into her mind and with them, an unbearable pain.

Worthless.

He claimed the map was worthless.

Everything she had done was for nothing.

Isabel wrapped her arms around her waist and rocked. His look filled with compassion only added to her misery. No man could understand what this meant to her.

The fire he had going was so small that he could cover it with his hat. She watched his deft moves to slice bacon into a pan. In moments it was sizzling, sending out an enticing aroma, but she didn't think she could eat.

She closed her eyes, pressing against the tree trunk. What was she going to do?

Although there was no sound, she sensed him near and opened her eyes to find him hunkered down, holding out a cup of coffee.

"Be careful, it's hot. And start with these."

He unfolded a square of fine bleached linen. What held Isabel's gaze was not the two biscuits but the tiny, even stitches that hemmed the cloth. Mother? Sister? Wife? The last sent a faint disturbing ripple through her. She was sure that somewhere there was a woman.

"Go on, take one."

"Thank you. You truly are a kind man." She gazed at him, watching the slow smile form, softening his features, even if his eyes held a hint of devilry.

"Don't be so sure. Better wait until you taste those."

"It would not matter. You have been very kind to me." She hesitated, then in a softer voice added, "I— I have little reason to trust anyone. I have treated you badly. My grandmother would be ashamed of me. I am ashamed."

"A grandmother, huh?" Kee's smile deepened as he attempted to ignore everything else she said. "I have one of those. She rules the house with a pair of black snapping eyes that can bring a man to his knees, but her heart is so full of love that you want to do anything to make her happy."

He found a small reward in her smile and caught himself leaning closer. He jerked back. Grandmothers. They were talking about their respective grandmothers. And he knew what his would do to him. Young women were to be respected, protected, and never, never seduced.

Kee always calmed his conscience by letting the young lady take the lead. What his grandmother didn't know couldn't hurt him.

Besides, what the hell was he doing thinking about her lips and kissing and seducing. The lady had problems. Big ones. He was not getting involved beyond seeing her somewhere safe. No way was he helping her hunt for gold. He had his horses to get home. He had...

He had been staring into those big, dark-blue eyes for too long. Hints of secrets, of pain, a plea and more swirling in their depths. Looking down didn't help him. Her lips were slightly parted, soft and full. His fascination increased the moment the edge of her white teeth worried her bottom lip.

Temptation. Pure and simple.

The small hitch in her breathing coming at the same time as his didn't help him one bit.

They were too close. He was going to take what was being offered in another second.

"I know you are kind and brave, but I still do not know your name."

Where had that husky, seductive whisper come from?

Kee felt gut-punched. *Sweet heaven!* Every nerve ending ruffled where her breath caressed his face.

Those eyes weren't all dark blue. There were tiny flecks of gold that enticed his gaze.

Then she touched him.

Sizzle. His blood pumped heat that spread through him. She would burn him alive.

All this from the light skim of her fingertips across his unshaven cheek.

He dipped his head down, lashes half veiling his eyes. He needed this kiss.

She tilted her head back and to the side of the tree, but upward, leaning forward just enough.

He could feel the tension that gripped both of them. He could smell the burning air. With one fingertip he lifted her chin, bringing her mouth a little closer.

His thumb touched the corner of her mouth and now he was ready to...

"The bacon is burning."

"It sure as hell is," he murmured back, wishing he had thought to open his bedroll.

Her hand pressed against his chest, and he felt branded.

He went for her mouth and the kiss he now needed.

His long fingers cupped her neck, his lips barely brushed her mouth. A moment to savor the slight shiver of her body, the quickening breath. That oh-so-special anticipation.

He'd learned a lot growing up with a father and two uncles who never turned from a boy's curiosity.

Then he learned a lot more by putting all those frank answers into practice.

Now.

But the hand on his chest wasn't caressing. She was pushing him back.

And those lush lips weren't waiting for his kiss, but angled away and her voice...something about burning.

And the smell...

He jerked around to see the bacon grease on fire engulfing the whole pan.

Things had heated up. Right to burning, all right.

All the wrong things.

With a swift move he was on his feet, running to the stream. Dipping his hat in, he started tossing water at the fire, catching the lovely lady who had wrapped the linen around her hand and attempted to remove the pan.

In moments he stood close, kicking the sandy earth over the fire.

He felt like a six ways to Sunday fool. He could think of only one time when he felt worse. He and Missy Gardner left a dance to celebrate the new school and headed back to the old one-room schoolhouse. They had been studying a history of kissing and felt a powerful need to explore what came next, only someone had beat them to it.

Her father. And he wasn't just kissing the store clerk's wife.

Isabel knelt with head down, her hands gripped together. One look and she had no choice but to hide. Laughter rolled through her, she could feel her body shake with it. But she knew enough about men's pride to keep her face hidden. He stood towering above her, the wide-legged stance, hands on hips and scowling face reason enough for her to bite her lip hard. If he thought she was laughing at what happened, he would likely stalk off and leave her.

But she was not laughing at him. She had been as caught up in the moment as he. The unexpected warmth that turned too swiftly to heat shocked her.

Especially coming now, after his devastating news about her worthless map.

The thought sobered her faster than anything else. With a graceful motion she rose. Using the folded cloth she pulled the blackened pan out and turned toward the stream.

Kee didn't say a word. He was still fighting down the heat of embarrassment. Nothing cooled a man quite so quick. He did not want to watch the dip and curve of her body kneeling by the stream as she used the sand to scrub the pan.

So lost in his own thoughts, it took a few moments to realize that she was talking to him.

"I didn't hear you." His harsh voice made him look upward. There wasn't any help coming, but it served to calm him down.

"I asked you what your name is. You never told me."

"My name? Now you want to know my name. You almost, well, we just…ah, the hell with it. Kee. My name's Kee Kincaid."

She nodded. That explained the belt buckle. "I do not believe I have heard a name like yours before."

"You don't have to dance around it. Just say it's odd. I won't take any offense."

"From your voice, your very testy voice, I believe you take offense quite easily."

He rubbed the back of his neck, heaved a heavy sigh and decided she was right.

"Look, you're right. And I'm sorry. It's just that a man's feelings hog-tie him to one thing and then…"

He stopped because she turned to look over her shoulder at him. And he saw that he hadn't been alone in the heated feeling that sizzled between them.

He was sure he was not mistaking her look. She wasn't bold enough to say a word about it, but the knowledge was there in her eyes.

Suddenly he felt like smiling. And talking.

"My name is a family nickname. Short for Kenny. Short for Kenneth. The children shortened it down when they were learning to talk, and before you know it, everyone was calling me Kee."

"Children? You must have a big family. And are they yours?"

"Yes. Yes. And no. Not so I know about them."

She sorted out his answer. Scrubbing hard on the pan as a little devil of envy for his big family and note of increased warmth in his voice once more reminded her how alone she was.

"And you? Do you have family worrying about you out here?"

"Only my grandmother waits, and she knows where I have gone."

Isabel was not really thinking about what she said. *Not so I know about them.* There might not be a wife, but there had been women. Again, that faint disturbing ripple went through her. She had no reason for it. She did not know this man. And if he made her heart beat a little faster, or left her feeling flushed over a kiss that did not happen, it was her own foolishness.

She had a mission to complete. Nothing must stand in the way.

Again he took her by surprise. She had heard no

sound, but he was there, hunkered down next to her. He took the pan from her.

"Scrub this any more and I won't know it's mine."

Kee took hold of her hand. "We got off to a real bad start. You're still hungry and…" *So am I*. He had to look away from her penetrating gaze and swallow those unspoken words.

He rose to his feet and offered her his hand. "I suggest we go back and find your camp. That is, we'll find it if those two hombres left anything. I assume you had a horse and a pack animal."

The top of her head touched the tip of his nose. Kee hadn't realized how tall she was. Just the right height to… Stop it! he warned himself and stepped away from her to help him do it.

"You never said if there was anyone with you," he said, turning away to repack his saddlebag. He tossed out the remains of the coffee, noted the crumbs of biscuit and promised himself that he'd feed both of them shortly.

She was glad his back was toward her when she lied to him. "I am alone."

"Don't figure you for a stupid woman, but you come mighty close. How did you think to travel in these parts by yourself?"

"I came alone, Kee, because there was no one else to come. I managed."

He turned then. "Until this morning."

"Yes, until this morning when providence sent you."

Providence? She figured the Lord looked kindly on her and sent him?

No!

"I'm no angel. The Lord may have given up on me.

Leastways that's my mother's opinion. She figures the devil is gonna roll out the red carpet for me when my time comes.''

"That is because you are a good man and the devil will have won."

"No. You've got that part all wrong. The red carpet is for the celebration in having one of his own back.''

Isabel's smile had a bitter cast. She doubted Kee Kincaid knew what true badness was. He could not have lived with evil such as she had known.

She had to stop herself from delving into the past. She hurried over to her horse. A cold shiver crawled down her spine. Tension gripped her until she wanted to scream to release it.

About to mount his horse, Kee glanced over and saw the way she hung on to the saddle. "Are you all right?" he called out.

"Fine. I am fine."

Kee didn't believe her. He started toward her, thinking she was too weak to mount by herself.

Outlaw snorted and pawed the earth. Kee murmured to the mustang, wondering what suddenly bothered him. The horse lifted his head, ears pricked forward.

"Hey boy, what's wrong?" He lifted his hand to scratch between the mustang's ears, but Outlaw shied from his touch. Kee took the horse's warning seriously.

Something or someone was close by and Outlaw didn't like the scent. He tossed the lead rope to Isabel.

"Keep the horses quiet and bunched up," he ordered. "Outlaw won't let anything or anyone near them."

Kee slid his rifle from the saddle boot, then he

slipped off the short rawhide thong that held his Colt secure in its hand-tooled holster.

Anger tightened the line of his mouth. He'd let his concern for the woman overcome good sense. Dead faint or not, he should have kept riding with her.

Well, if those two hombres wanted more of what he'd given them, Kee was of a mind to oblige them.

Only this time he wouldn't waste time talking.

He shot a last warning look at Isabel, then disappeared between the young cottonwood trees.

Chapter Four

Isabel quickly took each of the guns from their holsters and reloaded them. She swung one holster over to the other side, put the guns back, and then took Kee's gun from where he'd stuck it in one of the boots.

Holding his gun made her feel less alone.

She hoped it was no more than an animal that had disturbed his horse. But the deep chill that shivered over her body warned that the animal was human.

Her look was anxious as she searched the brush across the stream. She kept glancing back at Kee's horse. The animal's reins trailed on the ground. She walked her horse over and tried to grab the trailing leather, but the horse backed away from her.

She stared at the place where Kee had disappeared. If he was hurt or killed, they could follow his tracks back to her. She could not be found again. The guns made sure she would not be helpless this time.

She could ride away and leave Kee his horse.

But when she glanced over toward where the horse stood, he was gone. Standing in the stirrups, she caught a glimpse of the dark-brown tail heading in the direction Kee had disappeared to.

The choice to stay or go churned through her.

Hands damp, heart thudding with fear, she had to make a quick decision.

She owed Kee Kincaid a debt for saving her.

Debts. There were too many of them.

All were older than the one she incurred today with a stranger who almost kissed her.

Whom she wanted to kiss.

Decide!

Kee made his way through brush and tumbled boulders. He found a gap about fifty or sixty yards wide and maybe a little longer. Water pooled at the bottom. There was a little grass and a few cottonwoods. He sat and waited, studying the place.

A sound caught his ear. He turned fast, rifle ready to fire, only to swear to himself when Outlaw headed toward him.

He grabbed hold of the trailing reins and cupped his other hand over the mustang's nose to keep him quiet.

"Stay," he whispered.

Kee stepped out and circled the water hole. He found what he was looking for. Footprints.

The ground was too muddy to show the print clearly, just deep and man-size.

As he circled back the way he had come into the gap, there came a questioning nicker from a horse. The sound was quickly cut off.

Kee knew it wasn't Outlaw.

He moved fast in the ensuing silence to first stand then crouch in the shadow cast by one of the older trees.

And he waited.

The minutes passed slowly. Heat seemed intense in this small hollow.

The mustang stretched his neck, nostrils flaring at the scent of water.

Kee knew the horse would remember the days when he ran with the wild herd and they watered whenever they could. He did nothing to stop the horse as he took a few steps forward. The mustang kept his head off to one side to keep from stepping on the reins.

Kee spared a thought to Isabel. The sound of gunfire would have traveled back to him. Yet he was bothered that Outlaw had abandoned the mares and the pack-horse. Unless the mysterious lady had taken off to parts unknown.

The way his luck was running, all away from him, he figured losing her would be the perfect ending to one hell of a morning.

Kee thought he'd tracked the two men from this morning, but the presence of another horse changed his mind. Those two wouldn't have had time to go back to wherever Isabel's camp was and then trail him. He knew how rough the ground he traveled was, knew, too, how to leave almost no sign.

Odds, and not in his favor, were that someone else was out there.

Outlaw was all mustang. He stopped well before the pool of water. Tossing his head, stopping with ears pricked forward to whinny a bit, he drew forth an answering whinny. Once more the horse started for the water and stopped.

There was only one reason Outlaw stopped. Someone was close to him.

Kee wished he could see through the thick tangle

of brush and rock on the opposite side. But he went
back to watching his horse.

Outlaw kept tossing his head, a habit he had when
someone other than Kee talked to him. Kee smiled.
Whoever that fool was, he'd be working up a thirst
trying to coax that horse near enough to grab hold of
the reins.

The mustang wasn't having any. He suddenly shied
away. And that's when Kee caught a glimpse of a
hand.

He had had enough.

"Just hold it right there." His low voice carried and
he made sure the man heard the cocking of the rifle.

There was a rustle in the brush, and Kee put a bullet
into the earth. "Stop there. You ain't got a chance of
leaving here without carrying away lead."

"Who the hell are you, mister?"

"Never you mind who I am. That's my horse you're
trying to grab."

"Figured him for a stray."

"If I hadn't walked around out there I might buy
your story." Kee stood up, but kept to the protection
of the tree trunk. He didn't like the smell of this. Not
one damn bit.

"Show yourself," Kee ordered. "And you should
know I've had me a bellyful this morning. I'm not in
a charitable mood."

The brush parted and Kee tracked the man's moves
with his rifle barrel. The hat was pulled low, hiding
his face. The barrel chest and stocky body hit a note
of recognition for Kee but he couldn't quite place the
man.

He glanced up. "I know you. You're Kee Kincaid."

"Unbuckle the gun belt and step away from it."

"Like hell I will. I ain't done nothin' to you. You got no call, Kincaid, to take my gun."

"I've got a Winchester aimed at your belly. That gives me the might and the right."

"You know me. Alf Dennis. Met you up in Denver. Played poker a time or two. Why, I recall that winning hand of yours. Took yourself a mighty big pot with four of the sweetest little ladies. Stood me to a round of drinks. Was working for McCutcheon. Hunting a—"

"Shuck the gun." Kee was getting that awful feeling of being set up. The man was talking too much, not too loud, just running on and on about that meeting in Denver.

But saw he was finally unbuckling his gun belt.

"Step away from it. No, not back, over to the side." Kee had to keep his eyes on him, despite the hair prickling on the back of his neck. He moved in quickly, took up the belt and slung it over his shoulder.

"Let's go find your horse." Kee motioned with the rifle for Alf to lead off. He remembered him now. Knew he'd been fired from McCutcheon's for selling off feed and pocketing the money. Money that Kee unknowingly had won that night. There was some talk about a shooting, but nothing could be proved against Alf. What the man was doing out the backside of nowhere was a question that itched and needed scratching.

If Kee had just left Denver and found Alf on his back trail, he would suspect the worst. Robbery of his horses and maybe a bullet in his back.

But Denver had been months ago. And all his speculating wasn't giving him the answers he needed.

"Mighty lonely place to find you, Alf."

"Jus' driftin'."

Kee thought back to the morning. He tried to recall if he had ever seen either of those two men with Alf. In a way, he'd feel better knowing they were together. A nagging sense of worry for Isabel made him step closer and prod Alf in the back.

'Where'd you tie your horse? Up on Tonto Creek?"

"Not far."

The very absence of fear warned Kee he was walking into a trap. But why? And who? He saw the small clearing up ahead, and the smell of coffee tantalized him since he never had any of his own.

At the edge of the trees, Kee paused. Alf went right to the fire and helped himself to the coffee.

A lone bay horse was staked out away from the fire on the other side. One bedroll tossed near a saddle. One cup that Alf was filling from his pot. For a man who just lost his handgun and had a rifle aimed at him, Alf's grin smacked of satisfaction.

Kee took another quick look around the clearing. Something wasn't right.

"Strikes me strange, Alf, that you had coffee brewing and found time to scout a far piece from your camp. You didn't, I wouldn't have known you were around."

"Could swear I heard somethin'. Almost sounded like a cry. Figured someone might be in trouble." He sipped at his coffee and looked across to Kee. "Man travelin' alone these days can't be too careful. Know what I mean? Hey, want some coffee? Only got my cup, but there's enough to share."

Kee remained beneath the shelter of the trees. It still didn't add up for him. An edgy feeling was taking hold. Trouble was coming faster than an old mossy horn that had been in the brush too long.

"Hell, Kincaid, you got my gun. What more do you want?"

"What he wants and what he's getting ain't the same."

Kee spun and ducked to his left. His fast move was all that saved him a blow to the head. He didn't know the man, but his gun butt came down hard on Kee's shoulder. His arm went numb and he dropped his rifle.

A tuck and roll took Kee into the brush just as a bullet hit where he'd been standing. Kee fought the pain in his arm and drew his Colt. He fired at the unknown man, then turned to find Alf. He was gone.

Kee was not waiting around to be shot. He backed away from the clearing, using every trick he had learned to move quietly.

Not a breath of air stirred. He was not drawing their fire. Either they were waiting for a clean shot or they were already gone.

He moved again, waited, and then circled back to where he had dropped his rifle.

Gone. Kee spent a few minutes searching for a good boot print. He wanted to know that man if he came around again.

He whistled for Outlaw, who came not from the water hole but the opposite direction. So someone had tried to grab the mustang again.

The whole thing was a ploy to get him away from Isabel. And she had to be the reason. His mares were too well marked for a horse thief to chance stealing them.

Where before he had used caution, now he raced the mustang to get to the stream.

And found about what he expected.

Isabel and the horses were long gone. But the churned earth had a story to tell and before he set off after them, he would read every bit of every sign.

Chapter Five

Isabel lost Kee's mares and packhorse. Perhaps *lost* was not the right word. She knew where they were. Only she was not the one guarding them for Kee.

He had been gone awhile when the feeling of being watched came over her. She remained in the saddle and kept looking around, gun ready for any threat.

Minutes later she heard gunshots. Her first thought was to try to find Kee. The second to run.

Torn again over what to do. Her grandmother had entrusted her with finding the mine that belonged by right to them. Kee risked his life to save hers.

The restive movements of the horses added another layer to her fear.

Her gaze was drawn to the brush across the stream. She could see a rider coming closer. Isabel recognized the horse as one from her camp. She knew the men that Kee had set afoot would get mounts from there. What surprised her was the rider. Clay Benton was one of the men from this morning. How could he have tracked them so quickly?

And then she saw his face. He was every bit as

surprised as she was. But Isabel had had a few moments to see and understand her danger.

Isabel fired at him and missed. The horses shied, pulling at the rope attached to their halters. Her own horse half reared trying to get away. She fired another shot, knew she had missed. The next thing she knew the ground was coming up to meet her. The jar to her wrist sent the gun flying. The horses bolted.

By the time her vision cleared, she found herself on her knees, crawling to the trees where Kee had disappeared. Every part of her ached. She heard the splashing from behind her, knew Benton was crossing the stream. She composed herself as much as possible.

She had to get away. She grabbed the tree trunk and struggled to her feet but everything around her was moving in circles. Benton wanted the map. She knew he had been sent after it.

And she was just as determined that he would not get it.

She pushed off, running blindly.

The brush was thick, she tore her shirt free and felt the sting of a cut. Her mouth was cotton dry. There did not seem to be enough air for her. She heard the sounds of pursuit and forced herself to move faster.

Small branches snagged her long hair. She broke the wood, turned and tried to find an easier path.

There was noise up ahead. Thinking it was Kee she called out. Only her intended yell was more of a parched whisper.

She ducked beneath a low-growing limb, glanced back to see how close Benton was, and slammed into a hard chest. Seconds before she lifted her head, she knew the thick barrel chest did not belong to Kee Kincaid.

The stocky man, his breath foul in her face, had surprisingly powerful arms. He wrapped them around her so tight she could not move or breathe.

Desperate to get away and save what she had, she kicked him.

Isabel had the brief satisfaction of her pointed-toe boot connecting with his shin. His howl of pain made her try for another one.

The sharp yank on her hair caught her off balance. She attempted to twist away, but Benton held her fast.

"Come along real quiet an' you don't get hurt, missy. There's someone waitin' to see you." Benton pulled on her hair just as the other man let her go.

Isabel fell to her knees.

"Took you long enough to get in place, Alf. Thought for sure I was gonna lose her. There'd be hell to pay if she got away again."

Isabel felt the cold press of Benton's gun barrel against her temple. Isabel, too frightened to pray, could not even draw a breath.

The anger she felt from Benton made a small knot form in her stomach. Would he kill her, and then search for the map? He had to know it was not with her things left behind at her camp.

When he grabbed her arm and pulled her to her feet, the relief was so great that she did not fight him.

She had gotten away from them once.

She could do it again. She had to.

The image of Kee Kincaid's face formed in her mind. She saw the smile that curved his masculine mouth, the light of devilry in his eyes; she felt the warmth of his touch and clung to her own heated response to the almost kiss they had.

She was not alone. As sure as the sun set on this

night, Kee would come after them. Isabel was a realist. He might not come after them for her. But he would for his horses.

If he was unhurt.

She had to bite her lip to keep from demanding to know what they had done to him.

They rode hard for most of the day through lands more desolate than those she had seen. The heat robbed her of strength. They were generous to themselves and the horses with the water. She had one mouthful to their three. She turned aside the bitter thoughts of whose orders those must have been.

The lack of water stole from her the chance for a few moments of privacy. Not even these men who sold their guns for money would deny her that.

But they rode through the day and she had no chance to escape. The shadows lengthened as the sun started its descent and they finally made camp. Anger served to help warm her, for even near the fire, the desert night cold made itself felt. She should not complain. The blanket Alf threw over her concealed her working on the ropes that bound her feet. Every now and then she dipped her head and used her teeth on the rope that held her wrists. She had to thank whatever providence made them tie her hands in front.

Benton was pouring himself another cup of coffee. He and Alf sat opposite from her. She was alone with the two of them, and that had her worried. Where was the man that had been with Benton this morning?

Muley Cotton. A name she would not forget. He was her guide and he'd betrayed her.

Her horse, the last of the palominos her family had bred, was not here, nor was her packhorse. She strained to hear the men's whispered talk, needing to know if they were waiting for someone, or intended to ride on come daybreak. The Lord was not in a granting mood to answer her plea.

Or perhaps He was in His own way and time.

A few minutes later, Alf stood up and stretched, then took up his rifle. "I'll stand first watch. Wake you in two hours. Best you keep an eye on that one," he said, pointing with the rifle to where Isabel leaned against a boulder. "I don't wanna be chasin' after her in the dark."

"She's not goin' anywhere. Stop all your worryin'. Gonna git you into an early grave, Alf. A few weeks an' you an' me'll be rich enough to set San Francisco on its ear. Gonna buy me a fancy saloon, an' get me the prettiest little gal—"

"Clay, jus' you remember that we've got to find the mine first. An' when we do, them nuggets ain't gonna be lyin' around awaitin' for you to pick them up. The way I see it, we're gonna do all the work. Come time to divvy up, I ain't so sure we'll see a fair share. An' don't you be countin' Kincaid out. You know him. He ain't gonna let you get away with takin' his horses or his woman."

"She ain't his woman. Go on an' keep watch. You jawin' that old woman talk is gratin' on a man's body. We's gonna be rich. Rich, I tell ya. Ain't no one gonna pull no double cross."

"Jus' you remember, Clay, rich is mighty fine so long as I ain't dead."

"Fool talk," Benton muttered once Alf moved off.

Isabel seized her chance to sow doubt, and if she was lucky, a little fear. "You do not believe the stories that all the men who have tried to find the mine have died?"

She leaned forward, and under the concealing folds of the blanket worked harder on the rope securing her ankles. With only Clay Benton to watch her, this could be her best and only opportunity to get away.

"There's always talk," he answered in a surly voice, and then in a whisper, "You know what's good for you, you'll hand over that map to me. Sort of a private deal. Before the boss comes. Leastways I won't kill you."

"But you will stand by and watch someone do it?"

"Ain't said nothin' 'bout standin' around an' watchin'."

"Ah, I understand. If you do not see this thing happen, then you will sleep easy at night."

"You shut up now. Man's got to get some sleep." He tossed out the last of the coffee, set his cup aside and rolled himself in his blanket.

Isabel glanced over to the picket line where Kee's horses were tied along with the others. Benton had been pleased to have both his old smelly boots back along with his gun.

If there was any mercy for her, he would have left the other holstered gun hooked over the saddle. In the dark she could barely make out the packs from Kee's horse and the extra saddle.

She desperately wanted to look down and see why the knots were proving to be so stubborn to her fingers. The moonlight didn't penetrate deeply into the dry wash they had chosen as a camp. She knew fear kept her gaze pinned on where Benton moved restlessly. Just when she thought he was asleep, she would hear him muttering.

The minutes passed with agonizing slowness before he was finally still.

Alf had tied a series of triple knots, but her renewed effort soon had her ankles untied.

Isabel heaved a sigh. She held on to the blanket with her hands, leaning against the boulder at her back and got to her feet.

Benton snored. The fire died down a little so she stood in shadow.

Ideally she would grab both a gun and the horses. Time was against her. Alf could be coming back at any moment. Keeping well back, she inched her way around to the other side, speaking softly to the horses so they would not shy and give her away.

She managed to find the packs and saddle. There was no holstered gun. Her search was too hurried. She could not even find a knife.

Anger would serve no purpose. Frustration even less. She had to think, and act.

Fear had never left her, and now reared up when she thought to linger. Her breathing sounded loud to her ears, her heart pounding as she neared the horses. She needed her blanket for warmth, but it hampered her attempt to untie the picket rope. Every few seconds she looked over her shoulder at the still-sleeping Benton.

Hurry! Hurry!

The one word, the only thought in her mind.

She nearly gasped aloud when the last knot gave way. The lack of food and water, and her effort exhausted her. She hurried along the line, thankful the reins were in easy slipknots. All but Kee's mares. Their lead rope had been looped and tied.

A scream of frustration welled in her throat. She would never get them free, and yet she could not leave them behind. Without horses Benton and Alf would have trouble following her.

Isabel heard a faint noise and dropped to the ground. She yanked the blanket over her head. She curved her body tight, hoping that if someone looked she would appear no more than a dark shadow.

If the horses stopped their restless movements.

If one of them stopped nosing the blanket.

If she could stop shaking so her teeth would not chatter.

The noise was closer and a little louder.

She broke out in a cold sweat of panic. What if Alf had come back early? Or had the two hours passed?

Her mouth and throat were desert dry. She tried to stop imagining what was out there, tried to stop thinking about being caught. The blanket's inky smothering protection only added to her fear.

Kee had watched the bull's horns of the new moon rise slowly over the harsh mountainside to give enough light for him to pick out small features of the land immediately surrounding him. The dry wash on the other side was his goal.

He had an easy time finding their trail. For one thing, they had done little to conceal it, the other was Outlaw's fondness for those mares. He wasn't about to let them ride off without him.

Kee left the mustang ground-tied below while he climbed the rock face siding the deep wash. The smell of a fire grew stronger as he neared the top. He was sure he had caught up with Alf Dennis and his partner. Just as he had been sure when trailing them that there were only three riders, Isabel being the third. It nagged him that the other man from this morning had gone missing. Unless these polecats had a falling-out and killed him.

There was more at stake than the stealing of his horses. Even more than his stung pride for them playing him like a newly arrived pilgrim.

There was the woman whose face would not leave his inner sight. If either one of them had laid a hand on her, he would skin him alive.

Kee found the last handholds needed to bring him over the top. The rock beneath him was nearly flat. A perfect place to scout the camp below.

But what caught Kee's eye was movement on the opposite sloping bank. A large slab of rock protruded itself into the night sky. To one side was a bulky shadow that moved even as he watched. The moonlight picked up the gleam of a rifle barrel.

Alf was standing watch. Benton was a tall drink of water compared to the stocky man. It had to be him.

Where Alf stood his watch he could see everything below. That meant he would spot Kee if he moved down to their camp. Kee saw the fire had died to coals, he made out the form of one body but could not spot Isabel.

And something was spooking the horses.

Not an animal. The horses would be more restive and whinnying to get free if it was a mountain cat.

He spotted his own packs, two saddles nearby.

What he wanted to see and didn't was any sign of where they had Isabel. Kee scooted back. He'd have to enter the wash farther up, well out of Alf's sight.

Kee absorbed the brooding quiet of the night. He felt carefully for every rough-edged handhold as he made his way along the rocks. He ignored the chilled breeze that sprang up. He heard the small, restless sounds from Alf's position.

Overhead a nighthawk dived and veered off before attacking its prey. Kee's head came up like a wolf's and his nostrils flared, scenting the air. Drawing his knife, he scanned the rock outcrops, every low-growing bush below that could offer a hiding place.

No scent came to him. Instinct hadn't flared with alarm that someone else was out there. Yet the day had enough lessons of almost being trapped so he moved cautiously until he was satisfied Alf could not see him.

Kee saw that Alf was watching the nighthawk, too. And he huddled back against the thick slab of rock to ward off the chilling air. He blew on his hand, switched the rifle and repeated it. Kee imagined that all Alf could think about was hot coffee and his bed-roll. He heard him muttering about Benton letting the fire die down. A small bit of gravel grated as it slid down into the wash. Alf came away from the sheltering slab and searched the darkness below.

While Alf peered over the edge to the camp below, Kee made his run across the wash about fifty feet away. He scrambled up a sandy slope, quick as a cat and just as quiet. He could come up on Alf's blind side now.

The moccasins he wore instead of his boots allowed him to close the distance to the slab of rock without alerting Alf that he was near. What distracted Kee to look down at the camp at that moment, he couldn't say, but look he did and a prayer sprang to mind that Alf was not seeing the same thing.

There was Isabel near the horses, rising out of dark. He wanted to warn her, and couldn't. Any sign he tried, from throwing a pebble to any noise, would only alert Alf. And there was no promise that she would understand that he was there. Shooting was the one thing that Kee hoped to avoid.

Especially now, with Isabel between the sleeping man and Alf.

But the damn woman was messing his plan. Her moves were awkward. That much he could see. She was spooking the horses and it wouldn't take much for Alf to hear, then look down.

Kee was not going to do this quietly, in his own way and time.

He drew his gun.

Chapter Six

The night exploded with sound.

Kee shot down into the fire. Isabel flipped off the blanket and waved it at the horses she had freed. Alf saw movement below, aimed his rifle and thanks to his cold hands missed his shot.

Kee scrambled around the slab and came up behind Alf. A swipe with his gun butt saw Alf go down, out cold.

"Run, Isabel," Kee yelled when he spotted Benton take aim at her. Kee fired and Benton's gun went flying.

"Hold it right where you are. I've got an itchy trigger finger and you're the one who's going to scratch it if you move." Kee caught hold of Alf by the collar and half dragged him over to the edge. With a push of his foot, Kee sent his body rolling over.

He followed him down, refusing to look for Isabel for she'd only distract him. He was riled. Mean riled at the woman. The horses were scattered to hell and gone. Kee knew his temper, knew how to control it, but this woman had tested its limits.

Benton was moaning about his bleeding hand when

Kee stopped across from him. He was in no mood to be charitable.

"Stop the bellyaching. I hit what I aimed for and you haven't got more than a bullet graze across your knuckles. Get a piece of that picket rope and tie up your friend here. And do it fast. I'm a man whose patience is drier than this wash."

"Kee!" Isabel called out. She started toward him, only the bark of his voice ordering her to stay put shocked her into doing just that.

With Kee's gun trained on him, Benton made short work of tying Alf hand and foot. Kee stopped him from tying the man's hands in front of his body. Even with his arms bound behind him, Kee wanted more rope run from ankles to wrists. Alf was not getting free until Kee had the answers he wanted.

Benton sat beside Alf, holding his hand up. "You gonna let her bandage this for me? Likely to bleed to death if I don't get somethin' on it." He shot a look of pure venom at Kee.

"Use your bandanna. After I hog-tie you, we're all going to have a talk."

"Ain't got nothin' to say to you."

"You'll talk. I learned ways to blister your skin that you never heard about."

Benton shut up. These were the lands of the Apache, and although most of them had been forced on the reservations, he knew plenty of white men who either saw firsthand what they could do or had learned their ways. Kincaid was young, but that didn't mean some old Indian hadn't shown him a trick or two. Being cooked over a slow fire wasn't the way he planned to die.

"Roll over on your belly." Kee had to cock his gun

before Benton did just that. He made short work of tying him like Alf.

All this time Isabel had stared at Kee. His hard, cold voice threatening Benton had shocked her. She took another long look at Kee. There was nothing of the gentle man who almost seduced a kiss from her. He looked hard, and cold, and very dangerous.

Kee poked at the coals, adding a few small sticks and when they flared up, threw on some wood. He took the coffeepot that had been warming on the edge of the coals and drank from the pot. Anger only carried a man so far. Tension helped, but now he felt exhaustion seeping through his body.

And he still had to deal with the woman.

Kee noted to himself that he called her by her name when fear for her ran high. Now, to distance himself, he refused to use her name.

He could not stop the doubts creeping in. The tracks back at the stream told him she had run and a man had waited. No, he had to fight them off for now. He had to remember she was trying to free the horses when he showed up. But there was a nag that troubled him about her.

He turned slowly and found her watching him. She was as safe as his presence could make her. He was surprised to see her looking at him as if he were a total stranger, and one she was not sure she wanted anything to do with.

With a rough shake of his head he fought off tiredness and these fanciful thoughts.

"Did they hurt you?" Kee meant the words to be soft and lulling to show his concern. Instead, he heard for himself the harsh command that smoked with the violence of his temper.

Isabel, mouth still dry, started toward him. She held out her still-tied wrists. "Please, could you—"

Kee set the battered enamel coffeepot down with exaggerated care. As he drew his knife, he saw Benton's eyes widen as firelight flashed against the blade. In the softest, but coldest voice Kee condemned them.

"You gully-raking bastards. Hanging's too good for you. Men would horsewhip you for touching her. I could skin you alive for this."

In contrast to Kee's continued swearing, his touch was gentle as he examined the rope burns that marred her skin. A cold fire of rage burned in his eyes.

"Stay here near the fire. I've got some salve in my pack."

Kee was back in a few minutes and first washed, then spread a thick salve over her wrists. He cut up the linen napkin hemmed with the fine stitches she had admired. He cut off her protest.

Isabel rested her hand on his arm when he started to move away. Both their gazes lit on her hand. She felt the sinewy strength of arm beneath her fingertips. And the sudden warmth. She fought off the answering response that shivered through her.

"There are no words to thank you, Kee. But I will repay—"

"Don't say another word. I'm not asking to be paid. Not in any way."

The last acted like a slap. Isabel never meant that she was offering herself but the sharpness in his voice and the cold glare in his eyes confirmed his thought. She realized that she still held his arm and snatched her hand away as if it burned.

From an inner core she found the strength to hold back the tears that threatened. The innocent interlude by the stream had to be buried. This was not the same man.

She shoved aside her tangled hair and lifted her chin. "I am very sorry about the loss of your horses. I did not want Benton and Alf to follow me so I set the horses free."

She wondered if he heard her. Kee moved around the campsite, gathering guns and rifles which he piled near his packs.

The feeling that he blamed her, despite what he had said to these men, came and took root inside her. She was not sure what to do or say to him. Being so uncertain was not a role she enjoyed.

Kee's whistle cut through her thoughts. Within minutes there came the clatter of rocks falling, and then his horse trotted into the wash.

All this time Benton had listened and watched. When Kee loaded his packs on the mustang—who did not take kindly to being used for a pack animal—Benton started whining.

"You ain't gonna leave us here. You can't do it. We're helpless hog-tied like this."

Kee offered his canteen to Isabel. "You carry this and one rifle. Think you can manage?"

"I will manage." And she glared a silent message with all her womanly pride that she would manage through hell if necessary.

Kee took their canteens and hooked them over his saddle. He eyed the extra saddle and knew if he tried loading that on Outlaw, he'd have a fight on his hands. Grabbing the pommel with one hand, and taking up his own rifle with the other, he started toward the sandy slope as the easiest way out of the wash.

"You can't leave us!" Benton yelled over Alf's awakening groans.

"Watch me," Kee answered.

"You're a cold-blooded bastard, Kincaid."

"Use one of the sharp rocks to cut yourself loose and be damn thankful I don't just shoot you and be done with it. You cut my trail, better turn and run. That's all the warning I'm giving you."

"We'll die here."

"No." Isabel stared at Benton. "You will not die. Your partner will find you."

Kee stared a hole in her back. A few moments later she faced him. Too much had happened with little time to think things through. His doubts that she had told him the truth came rushing back. And now he put them into words. "This whole setup struck me as strange from the beginning. Now, it sounds like you know more than you told me. And I don't mean about these men working together."

She did not need to see the mistrust in his eyes. She heard it in his voice. She had no choice. She told him the truth.

"His partner's name is Muley Cotton. He was the other man this morning."

"And…" Kee prompted, reading reluctance in every line of her slim body.

"And he was hired to be my guide. Only he betrayed me. Muley and Benton stole my horse and pack mule. But they did not get what they had come for."

"The map," Kee concluded. He glanced over to see Benton's face lit by firelight. There was avid greed in his eyes at the mention of the map. Gold fever and treasure made damn fools of men. Looking back at

Isabel's rigid stance, Kee amended his thoughts to include women, too.

"So finish it, Isabel," Kee prompted once more.

She threw him a puzzled look. "You know the rest. You were there. You saw what they were trying to do to me. What they intended doing if you had not stopped them."

"I figure there's more to this story. A lot more. Like the truth of why you came here alone with only one guide and no trusted *vaquero* to guard you. Why did Muley and Benton attack you? Where did this Muley disappear to? You sounded sure that he's expected. So you see, *Doña*—" and Kee deliberately used the Spanish title alone "—some things just don't add up for me. There is more."

He was not asking her, and Isabel did not make the mistake of thinking he was. This tall, dark man with the courage of a mountain lion, and the deadly force of lightning, demanded the truth from her. And one thing more. He demanded her trust.

She nodded, but more to herself. She tossed her head back and motioned for him to go.

"Once we are away from here I will tell you all of it."

Kee held her gaze a few moments longer. "Fair enough." He started out of the draw, hauling the extra saddle, Isabel behind him with the mustang trailing them.

Earlier, while daylight had lasted, Kee had taken his bearings from the peak of the nearly six-thousand-foot Iron Mountain. To the north lay an old Indian trail that some claimed was used by the Salados, long before the Apache used it to raid the Pimas. The land was rugged, forbidding at times, and held scant water. But it was a land that held a fascination for him, too. Nowhere else did the mountains hold such color, nor test a man to his limits.

But Kee was not heading north. He struck out for the south where he knew there was shelter and water.

Using his own rough judgment of time passing, he stopped every hour or so with the excuse of checking on his horse and to scout around. Without her knowing it, he checked on Isabel's condition. Her steps were dragging, but she didn't complain. His admiration for her grew.

He knew he pushed her, and himself as well. But he wouldn't stop until he had a good defensible place to camp. Those men would be out for his scalp and a little blood-letting. Twice now he'd stolen their prize away.

A faint light showed at the edge of the mountains. Daybreak wasn't far off. Kee figured they had about another hour to walk. He went back down to where she waited.

"You are worried." Isabel shivered in the still, cold air. She had nearly emptied Kee's canteen as they plodded on for hours. She was beyond weariness, and knew if they stopped much longer, she would not be able to go on.

"We have about another hour's walk. There's a spring up ahead and some old cliff dwellings. You should be safe there and able to rest up most of the day."

"I will be safe there? You will leave me?" She hated that he heard the panic in her voice, but she had so little strength left that she could not control her fear.

"I'm not abandoning you, Isabel. I need to find my horses, and with them, a spare for you to ride."

"They will be looking for the horses, too."

"I know. That's why I want you out of the way. I can move faster and easier if I don't have to worry about where you are."

She shook her head as he started to walk. There was no point in arguing with him. He was not about to listen. And she still had to shake off exhaustion to think clearly. How much should she tell him?

All, a little voice of reason warned. *But the gold...* she argued with herself. No man could be trusted with so much gold at stake. He did not know that the very direction he headed was where she wanted to go. More lies...

There was a thought to stagger the strongest woman. He had done everything to earn her trust. What more did she want?

He walked ahead without faltering, and she knew the heavy weight of the saddle he had been carrying for hours.

She had told herself that Kee would come, if not for her then for his horses. But he had not gone after his precious mares. He had stayed with her, was still with her and would be until she was safe.

Had she ever known such a man?

Her grandfather was one, the only one she could name.

If only she had met Kee before she had set out on her own. With such a man beside her she could have ridden straight to the old mine. She would have offered him a share, not had to pay him for his help.

Was it too late? How deep did his pockets go? Those horses cost more money than a cowhand could make. Where, then, did he get them? The thought that Kee had stolen the horses crossed her mind. She quickly chased it. The man had a depth of character unlike the other men she had known.

Isabel, lost in her thoughts, stumbled into Kee's back. She followed his gaze upward and gasped. "Do you truly believe to go up there?"

"I told you the old cliff dwellings are the safest place around here to rest throughout the day. It's a climb, I admit, but we can make it. Just give me a minute or two. I could swear there's a game trail nearby."

The mustang, his head hanging, did not shy away when Isabel leaned against the saddle. After a minute she roused herself. Using her hat she poured out the last of the water for the horse. Kee had said there was water nearby, and while she normally would have waited until she saw the water for herself, she had given him her trust.

Kee suddenly appeared beside her. She felt his hand cupping the back of her neck, his long fingers gently easing the tension that gathered there.

"I'll take you up first, get a fire started and then bring up the packs."

"Yes." She turned only to find him still there, far too close. She wanted nothing so much as to rest against him, just for a little while. Just time enough to pretend that she did not have to be the strong one.

"You'll feel better soon. I promise." He took the rifle from her, and holding her hand led her to the narrow game trail.

The rock-strewn path made for a rough climb. Isabel could not have made it without Kee's help. Most of the dwellings had crumbled into ruins from the rock slides. But where Kee led her, the room was nearly whole. She stood near the opening, searching out their back trail for a sign of dust. There was nothing but broken rock and the shadows slowly deepening as morning light spread over the land.

Using a pack rat's nest, Kee got a fire started. Others had camped here and there was wood enough for a day or so if they were careful.

"Come and sit, Isabel. Take off your boots, too."

She heard the grind of stone against stone as she walked toward the welcome fire. In the far corner Kee had removed a large round stone that had covered a well.

"All the comforts of home. Our own well. I need to get Outlaw up here, but while I'm gone I want you to bathe your feet. If I don't find those horses we've got a lot of walking ahead. 'Sides, it'll make you feel better."

She heard small scurrying sounds coming from the tumbled rocks and listened to the rising wind. She glanced over at him, seeing the play of firelight and shadow over his hard-cut features and remembered vividly the moments when he had held her.

"Come closer to the fire," Kee invited. "I can see from here that you're shivering." Her reluctance to turn around had him adding, "Don't worry, I won't bite. That is, I don't, unless invited."

As soon as the words were out, Kee regretted them. The air was charged with an intimacy that had been absent. He felt the tension as he slowly rose to his feet and started toward her. From the tips of her dust-laden boots to the wild tangle of her hair there should have been nothing to attract or arouse him.

But the stirrings of need and wanting were there. Stronger than when he was about to kiss her. With her arms wrapped around her waist, dark eyes watchful and wary, Kee knew he could not, would not take advantage of her.

As she started toward him, drawn to him by what she read in his eyes, she barely realized that he veered away from her. Without another word he left her. And she looked after him going down the path, wondering how she would deal with this new threat.

Too weary to stand, she sat near the fire and stared at the flames. How many other women from times past had sat like this and pondered the intentions of a man?

She felt no fear of Kee Kincaid. He would never force himself on a woman. *He would not need to,* a little devil's voice supplied.

Isabel wrapped her arms around her raised knees and watched the flames. She caught herself nodding off. Her thought was to close her eyes for a few minutes and rest, but the exhausting day had taken its toll and she slept.

That is how Kee found her, curled like a bedraggled kitten near the fire. What he never expected was the rush of protectiveness for her.

Wanting to share a kiss with a pretty woman was one thing. This feeling welling up from deep inside him was quite another.

And he wasn't sure he liked it one bit.

Why this woman? She'd lied to him.

So his blood pumped a little harder and a hell of a lot hotter near her; that didn't mean he was ready to settle down.

Whoa! Where the devil had that come from?

Like a rope-shy colt, Kee found himself backing away from her. He set about unpacking his bedroll. But his backing away physically only lasted a few minutes. He had to pick her up, and there was no way he could mentally back off from where his thoughts were taking him.

Isabel's sleepy murmurs, the trusting way she curled against him, her head resting against his heart, all seemed to conspire against him. He couldn't set her down fast enough. Then he stood there, looking down at this black-haired woman, as he absently rubbed his chest where her warm breath had slid beneath the cloth and heated his skin.

He wasn't sure he trusted this woman. He had made himself a promise to protect her and get her somewhere safe. That was it. He'd ride on.

That easy, huh?

Kee softly swore with disgust. He didn't know. He just didn't know the answer to that.

Chapter Seven

Isabel awakened to the harsh cry of a hunting hawk. Sunlight splashed the walls and floor of the stone room. Grandmother would say she had slept the sleep of the dead. She snuggled deeper beneath the warmth of the thick wool blanket and inhaled the scents of horse and sage from its folds.

Kee's scents. Her eyes opened wide. What a strange thought. But it was true. They were Kee's scents and she had taken them in without knowing.

Stretching and yawning she sat up, and everything came rushing back. All the danger of yesterday, and what she still faced. She tossed aside the blanket. As she started to stand she caught sight of the message scrawled on the earthen floor: "Eat. Rest. Gone for horses. Don't go out. K"

She glanced over to where the fire was contained within a ring of stones. The coffeepot sat on a large flat rock. On another rock, the pan rested with crisp bacon curled on top of a pan-size bread that had baked in the drippings.

The note was so like the man. Nothing wasted, all

orders, expecting to be obeyed. She looked with long-ing at the jagged-shaped window.

Contrary to what Kee thought, she did have the sense to know she should not be seen outside. Benton and the others would be hunting for her. They would never be paid unless they handed her over.

Her stomach rumbled a protest as the aroma of the coffee reached her. First eat, and then take advantage of these minutes of privacy which had been few since she started on her quest.

She ate quickly, then refilled her coffee cup and went to stand to one side of the window. The day was clear and hot, yet this high up, a slight breeze made itself felt. She wondered how many times a woman had stood in this very place and watched the trail be-low for the sight of her man or her children.

She glanced around, drawn to the dark doorway on the far side. Last night's gloom had not revealed this. And today, even with sunlight in the outer room, it did not penetrate here. Perhaps a place used for stor-age, or a place for retreat when danger threatened. She stepped forward, dawn by some need to do so and kicked something that rattled. Afraid of snakes, she backed away to return to the sunlight. Outside in the stone room a long stick caught her eye. She could light it and explore the inner room.

Where or why the idea came from she did not know. The feeling of being pushed to do this was strong enough that Isabel obeyed.

The thin wavering light revealed little of the whole inner room. She discovered that what she kicked was not a snake but shells. Tiny clamshells strung together to make a bracelet. It was a thing of little value, yet Isabel lifted it carefully. Long ago some other woman stood in this place and lost this. Had she, too, been fleeing an enemy or had she been taken captive? This room, then, was not a good refuge from danger, but a trap.

Yet as Isabel turned to go, the faltering firelight showed something against the back wall. Closer inspection showed it to be a wooden ladder. She held the lit stick high, but no trace of daylight showed. But if there was no opening, why put the ladder here?

She was not tall enough to touch the roof, and while the ladder appeared sturdy, she was not going to attempt it alone. Cupping the shell bracelet, she once more went back to the sunlight.

There was no telling how long Kee had been gone, but she guessed he would not be returning soon. The stone well beckoned with its supply of water. She could use the coffeepot to heat water for bathing. And while she hesitated about opening Kee's saddlebag, she had no choice. She had nothing of her own to wear if she washed out her shirt.

The late-afternoon sun slanted across the earthen floor when Isabel spotted Kee on the sloping trail below. She hurried to button his shirt that she still wore. A closer look and disappointment flooded her. He had not found his mares.

As she stood to one side of the window, watching Kee, he led his horse about halfway up the trail, slapped his rump and then Kee returned below. He walked out, bending to grab handfuls of sand, then backtracked, letting the sand drift from his hand to cover the horse's tracks.

A careful man. She must not forget that about him. He would be tired and hungry. The hunger she had taken care of. Beans and bacon simmered in the pan, a flat rock served to bake the hoecake, made with the cornmeal she found in his pack. Coffee was ready, too.

She waited for Kee to come, staring at the man who made her heart beat a little faster, despite his dusty appearance. Her nostrils flared like those of an animal suddenly scenting danger. Watching his long, powerful legs eat up the distance between them sent excitement rippling through her.

All this time a little voice warned that she must not get involved with him. She had no place in her life for a man. Not one like Kee. He would take all she had, all she was, and absorb her into himself. She had to remind herself that she was not free until she completed what she had set out to do.

But primitive forces stirred in this place. She'd felt their hovering shadows ever since she had found the shell bracelet.

Once a woman's home, now another woman's refuge.

The earth and stones provided the basic shelter necessary for survival.

The fire offered warmth and comfort against the coming darkness.

Food to still one hunger.

A woman.

A man.

When his shadow melded with those the dying sun left behind, she turned to stare at him. A dark, powerful force made its presence felt. She named it to herself. Need. A compelling need to go to him, to offer Kee every solace that was hers as a woman to command.

Kee stood there after he ducked through the doorway, his breath caught somewhere for a few moments. Isabel, framed by the sun's rays in the open window, stared at him. Was she truly unaware that her eyes were wide and dark with passionate curiosity, or that her lush mouth had parted with invitation?

He looked his fill. Her black hair a braid of dark silk that beckoned his gaze to follow its fall from her shoulder across the curve of her breast down to her slender waist. He absently noted that she was wearing his shirt. The cloth had time to absorb her warmth and scent.

How long he stood there, he didn't know. Every bit of the frustration that twice he'd found horse tracks and twice he'd lost them was put on hold. His gaze drifted back to her face. She hadn't lost that almost breathless, waiting expression. He studied the delicate refinement of the angles and planes of her features.

Here was a woman a man would never tire of looking at through all the seasons, through all his life. He found that tiny claws of need had hooked themselves inside him.

Isabel stilled, as a fawn hiding in a thicket would still when a predator was close by. A very elemental womanly fear asserted itself. The wrong move, the wrong word…she could not understand what had happened, but she felt Kee aware of her, as she was of him. With every nerve ending alive, every beat of her heart speeding up, and the blood flowing hot and sweet as wine.

Kee broke the spell with a muttered curse as he turned away from her. What the hell had gotten into him? He had to use his iron will to control the need that urged him across the distance to where Isabel stood with bated breath.

For a moment he saw a flicker in her eyes and he couldn't tell if it was relief or disappointment.

"I'm glad to see you made yourself useful. You go ahead and eat. I've got my horse to tend."

And he was gone.

If it were not for the instinct that she trusted above all else, Isabel would swear these past minutes had not happened. But they had, and they changed things.

She had not imagined Kee's hot look, nor the husky tone of his voice. Her passionate culture precluded lying to herself about when a man was aroused and very interested. Yet Kee had walked away from the taut heat between them.

Kee Kincaid was no simple cowhand; he was complex male creature, every bit as contrary as most men claimed women were.

That decided, Isabel looked at the food she had prepared with thoughts of sharing the meal with him. Disappointment quickly became anger. Somehow his male thinking had turned things around and he blamed her for what transpired.

But nothing had happened. A shared long look. A tense feeling of heat building and...poof...he was gone like the cool breeze she'd enjoyed all afternoon.

And he whistled.

He dared stand a few feet from the doorway and whistle while he brushed dry grass over his horse.

She bit her lip. Everything happened for the best. She did not want to kiss him. She did not want to be near him now, either.

As if he could divine her thoughts, Kee whistled a little louder. He had a fondness for women, raised as he was in a household where their wants, their imaginings, even their direct and explosive anger were freely expressed. He knew a great deal about women's little tricks to get the men in their lives to do what they wanted. He had had some of the best teachers to show him how to avoid a woman's snares.

But even as the thoughts formed, Kee wondered why he'd gone off in this direction. Isabel had not done one darn thing but stand there by the window.

With a body so delicate she moved like a shadow.

He couldn't forget that.

Or her eyes that seemed to look inside a man and demand everything he was or could be.

And that mouth...

He stopped his brushing and leaned against Outlaw.

Isabel's mouth was worth at least an hour or two of the deepest, and most serious male contemplation.

The taste, and the feel, fast heat or cool passion.

Damn! He gave himself a mental shake. He knew exactly what had gotten his back up.

All day long he could not keep her out of his thoughts.

Kee stroked his mustang's neck. "This is bad, boy. Real bad," he whispered with a hard look toward the dwelling. "I've lost my horses. I'm entangled in who knows what. I should be demanding that she tell me her story, only the truth this time, and all I can think about is how that mouth of hers would fit to mine."

Outlaw tossed his head and Kee's hand slipped off. "All right, boy. There's a lot more about how we'd fit that clouded my head today. And it's going to stop."

Kee led the horse into a broken-walled room where sparse grass fought to grow through the cracks in the rock. He had already watered him down below at the springs where he had found the second set of his horses' tracks. With a light slap, Kee left the mustang. He took a long look around as dusk covered the land, noting where the shadows fell, and the deeper pockets that could provide concealment.

There was no sign that he had been followed.

But then, he reminded himself as he slung his saddle over his shoulder, he had not cut any rider's sign all day.

Isabel looked up as he came inside. She wore a carefully schooled neutral expression. "The food is still warm, if you want to eat."

"I owe you an apology."

She twisted fully around, her hands clasped in her lap. "For?"

"For that crack about making yourself useful. It was uncalled for, and I apologize."

"I see. Accepted." And she turned back to the fire.

Kee dropped his saddle opposite where she had spread out his bedroll. He shot one long, regretful look at the blankets that would be sleeping one for tonight and maybe awhile to come.

He settled himself across from the fire that Isabel stared into.

"While I eat," he said in a voice that brooked no argument, "you can tell me the truth about this gold mine and those men."

If Kee had expected a protest or some other feminine ploy to put him off, her direct gaze quickly disabused him of that. The woman, he decided, had the damnedest way of keeping him off balance. Just when he figured he had her all figured out, she changed into someone else.

"Yes, Kee. It is time for you to know."

Chapter Eight

Isabel closed her eyes for a moment, praying for courage. When she opened them, she found that Kee watched her with his dark, steady gaze that she thought saw too much of her.

"Kee, I owe you an apology, too, for I have lied to you about where the mine is."

"And that's not the only lie," he snapped.

The hot flush of color tinting her high cheekbones made him mumble that he was sorry for jumping on her. He was just having trouble keeping his mind where it belonged—on facts and the truth. Words and his own trusted instincts.

But sane reasoning had to fight Isabel, lovely and mysterious, lit by the firelight, caressed by the play of shadows. That hot, restless feeling that he'd tried to deny from the first time he saw her was back. With a vengeance.

And it was his problem to deal with. As Isabel began, Kee leaned forward to hear her soft voice.

"To understand, I must tell you of what happened at the time Coronado came to this land. It is then that my grandfather's family began this quest. In his search for the seven golden cities of Cibola, Coronado came north from Mexico in 1540. The lands here were the golden heart of the Apache Thunder god. It was their belief that here is where storms are born, and it is home to an evil spirit that will kill any who try to find the trail to the treasure.

"Superstition Mountain. An apt name for a place that began and ended in legends so colored by truth and lies, few will ever know the whole story. It is a secretive place, dark gray with its jagged peaks so forbidding to a child."

Her pause drew out as memories seemed to hold her. And Kee filled the silence.

"Is that how you saw it, through the eyes of a child?"

"The first time, yes. My grandfather took me there. Not to the mine, but to stand at the foot of the mountain. It was there that he told me what befell the soldiers with Coronado. Two brothers of my grandfather's family had accompanied him. One went with a small band to search up the mountain. After a storm they were found. It was days later. The bodies were—" here her voice broke and she looked down "—they were headless. The brother wished to take back to his mother the golden cross like his own. And he wished to bury his brother and the others. There was a fight with the other soldiers. They wished to flee the place quickly.

"The story is told that he found a gold nugget the size of an egg in his dead brother's fist. He took it, and he said nothing about the gold to the other men.

"You need to understand that these men with Coronado were very superstitious. They were afraid and fled to the north. The story of the fierce Indians and their god who protected the mountain kept everyone away for almost two centuries.''

Kee scooped up the last of the beans with a bit of bread and chewed slowly while he searched his memory for something he had heard. Setting down his plate, he reached for the coffeepot only to find that Isabel anticipated his desire. She handed over the cup.

''I seem to recall that Miguel Peralta came up from Mexico hunting silver when the mines played out. I know I heard some story about Justin Kincaid meeting the man when he went down there to buy cattle. Justin had a claim or two at the time. It was how he started. My grandmother told me the story of how they met then, and she decided Justin was the only man she wanted. She comes from an old and respected family. It was she who brought the Spanish land grant to the marriage. And they had their troubles when Mexico sold off this territory. Men came and claimed the land didn't belong to them. Kincaid fought, and filed on the land. He made improvements to every water hole he could find, and claimed more land. I know Peralta visited their ranch a time or two.''

''Yes,'' she said with a nod, ''Peralta came and with him my grandfather and his brother. They looked for silver when the mines in Mexico were exhausted. Miguel was given a land grant here. And he did not find silver, but a rich vein of gold. Richer than he had dreamed of. My grandfather was very young, but he remembered Peralta named the hat-shaped peak that rose above the mine as Sombrero. Now I hear they call this place Weaver's Needle.''

''After another prospector. Isabel, there are so many stories—''

''But this is not one more. I have come to claim

more than the gold, Kee. I promised my grandmother that I would find my grandfather's body. She wishes to bury him on the lands of his family since the *padres* came.

"I have seen the gold. I have touched it. When my grandfather first came here, he made a map. He knew the Apache watched the men work. He even warned Peralta, for at the time there was an Apache woman who worked around their camp. She told him that the Apache had no use for the gold. It was not this that they grew angry about. But the place was a home of their god, and they believed the men desecrated this place.

"Before you say anything more, yes, it was true that they forced the young Indians they captured to work for them. Peralta used them harshly to labor in the mine."

"And this was a time for Indian troubles," Kee said, then finished off his coffee.

"Yes. What my grandfather told me was that white trappers invited the chief of the Mimbres Apaches to a fiesta. Mangas Coloradas barely escaped with his life when the trappers massacred the Indians to procure scalps. It is a shameful piece of Mexico's history that they paid bounty on Apache scalps regardless if they were men, women or children."

"Everyone, Isabel, who lives in the Arizona territory knows how the Apaches were betrayed. Cochise, another chief of Chiricahua was shot while attending a peace talk. They claim his mountain spirit helped him escape. After that, things fell all to hell. Every white was fair game, every Apache hunted to be forced onto the reservations."

"What you say is true, Kee. This Apache woman

and my grandfather were lovers. He warned Peralta that the Apache were growing angry for their continued presence. He begged him to move everything to a high camp, secure the mine and hide its entrance. After a night of such talk, Peralta agreed. The men worked feverishly to load as much gold ore as they could onto the mules. They were to head back to Mexico and await a better time to return.

"But it was not soon enough to save them. The Apaches attacked the train as they left the mountain. My grandfather said the very air was filled with arrows like the flights of swallows. There was hand-to-hand fighting, the Indians using pointed stone hatchets against the unarmed men. The pack animals bolted. All were thought to be slaughtered that day. Those who found the bodies later put up a marker there."

She stopped and without thought took the cup that Kee handed her. She sipped the cool coffee, shuddering with remembrance of the horror in her grandfather's eyes.

Kee rose from his place by the fire and grabbed hold of his blanket. He knelt by Isabel's side while he wrapped it around her.

"Thank you, Kee. I forget how cold the mountains become at night."

Kee settled in beside her. He wanted to hold her close and banish the painful memories that lived in her eyes.

"Maybe you've told me enough for tonight."

"No. I want to finish telling you what happened. Some you may know, for after that attack, the stories began. My grandfather and one other young man survived. They hid in a small cave while the burros fled into the ravines and washes, their saddles packed with gold ore. The Apache, as I said, had no use for the gold. They hunted the mules and pack animals for food. The saddle packs were thrown aside.

"My grandfather managed to catch one of the burros and escaped. The other man refused to go with him. He wanted more of the gold to take home. He was never seen again.

"Then," she continued with a sigh, "a few years later, my grandfather heard that two prospectors had found a few of the dead burros with full saddle packs. These men were smart. They took out the gold and did not try to return. They did not go near Apache Junction where the news of the gold would likely end with their deaths. My grandfather learned later that they pounded the ore and went to the mint in San Francisco to collect their money.

"And a few other prospectors have found saddle packs. Some lucky enough to get away, and others have died. Not all their deaths can be laid at the feet of the Apache."

Isabel shifted her seat on the ground. She reached out to add another piece of wood to the fire, but Kee grabbed it first.

"No more wood tonight. The scent of wood smoke carries a long way. The last thing we need is company. Sit closer to me if you're cold."

He made the offer without thought until he caught her slant-eyed gaze. "I'll behave. Promise. Just lean close and I'll put my arm around you. Comfortable?" he asked a moment later when her head came to rest on his shoulder.

He took her murmur as assent. He wished he could say the same for himself. But he had asked for this nearness, and promised he'd behave. Sometimes, he told himself, a man ought to have his tongue twisted before he said more foolish things.

"Isabel, what I don't understand about your story is the long wait before coming here. I mean, you claim to have a map, which likely is no good, but still, you're sure there's a gold mine. So why wait?"

"Simple," she answered with a slight shrug. "The Apache were on the warpath. You must know of the terrible raids on both sides of the border when the renegade bands stole everything from animals to children and sold them to whoever had the money or they traded for guns. When we heard that General Crook was being sent here to hunt them down, we could only wait and pray that he succeeded.

"And now they are on the reservations and the land is open."

Kee didn't say anything, but something rang false to him. It was not so much that he believed she was lying to him now, but that she was leaving something out.

Something important.

Isabel grew alarmed at his pensive stare and his silence. She covered his hand with hers about to ask what was wrong when he jerked his hand away.

"What have I done? Or said to make you—"

"Sorry, Isabel. All the talk about the Apache brought to mind the way they killed my folks. But that's another story for another time. You still haven't told me how those men got involved with you."

She wanted nothing so much as to have him tell what happened to his parents, but something about his voice warned her off. She stared at the shadowed wall, and sorted her thoughts, then continued her story.

"This part gets a little confusing, Kee, even to me.

My grandfather heard of Jacob Walz. That he, with an Apache woman named Ken-tee who worked at the Vulture Mine near Wickenburg, stole ore from the mine and hid it here in the mountains. My grandfather knew that was only part of the truth. Do not ask me how this is so, I do not know. Not with any certainty. I do know that Ken-tee's Apache family believed that she betrayed them and told of the mine's location to the Dutchman.''

''Funny about Walz calling himself a Dutchman. He was German.''

''You sound as if you knew him, Kee.'' At her side, Isabel clenched the blanket. She looked at Kee, but he had turned to look outside the darkened doorway. She wanted to see his eyes. They were the windows of truth, or so she had been taught and believed. What was he hiding from her? Had she been foolish to trust him?

Isabel examined the thought, and found that instinct said no. She had not been foolish. Trusting Kee Kincaid was not a mistake she would live to regret.

Not that it would matter. She had withheld the most vital piece of information about the finding of the mine.

And that she would tell to no one.

Isabel lifted her hand and pressed it against her upper chest where she felt the reassuring shape of the carved disk. She closed her eyes and thought of her promises. She would carry this through no matter what stood against her.

Kee suddenly came to his feet in a controlled rush, and motioned her for silence. He kicked earth over the dying coals. His long legs ate up the distance to the doorway where he snatched up his rifle and disappeared.

Isabel sat stunned. She had not heard a sound.

The only thing that saved Kee from a bullet was his quick move to a crouch as he came out the doorway. That and the fact that he had been staring at the darkness so his vision was not impaired by the fire. He could hear Outlaw snorting. He had to set him free. There was no chance that he and Isabel would make it out of here with the horse.

The way things looked, they might not make it out of here at all.

Stone chips flew as he darted and dived for the broken-walled room. He whistled, and quickly dropped to his belly as shots went wild overhead.

He felt the mustang's hot breath at the same moment he whispered an order to go. Using the cover of the horse moving down the trail Kee ran back to Isabel.

"Stay down. Those aren't warning shots they're firing, Isabel. I don't know for sure how many are out there. We've got two choices. Make a stand here or we find a way out."

He threw a look over his shoulder at her. "And I'll be damned if I can figure out how they found us."

She turned away even as he did, hiding the haunted and very guilty look in her eyes.

Chapter Nine

Guilt drove Isabel to help find a way out. And then she remembered the inner room and the wooden ladder. She snatched up a thin piece of wood and poked at where the fire had burned. There were still a few coals and she fanned them until the end of the wood caught fire.

Kee kept up a measured cadence of return fire and did not see her disappear, only to return and call him.

"I'm here, Kee. I am not tall enough to see if there is an opening in the roof."

Kee ran back to her. "Take this and just fire a shot every few minutes to let them know we're here."

He took the burning wood from her and quickly found the ladder. The firelight showed no immediate opening above. But Isabel was right to think there might be another way out.

Kee was desperately weary. He'd had less than three hours' sleep and faced another long night of running. It went against his grain to run, but he had to think about Isabel. Alone he would have fought it out.

But she trusted him.

Kee quartered the small room, getting a crick in his

neck from looking upward. He heard Isabel firing just as he had told her, one shot to their three or four.

He planted the burning stick in the ground and climbed the ladder. He pushed against the roof, turning his head just in time as earth fell. No matter how hard he pushed, he could find no opening. He wasted time to move the ladder and try again. No luck. The best he could figure was that a rock slide had covered over the opening.

But there had to be another way out.

In disgust that he had somehow been at fault so that they'd been found again, Kee kicked the wall. Small stones tumbled free. He was just desperate enough to try again and was rewarded with larger rocks falling to the earth.

He grabbed the torch and fell to his knees before the small opening. The draft of air stirred the fire. Once again he planted the burning stick and started to widen the hole. Some of these mountains were riddled with caves. The air wasn't all that stale. Somewhere up ahead there was an opening feeding the air in. He worked feverishly to pull the larger rocks away and never felt the cuts on his hands.

When the opening was large enough that he could squeeze through, he tossed the burning stick inside.

The light was too feeble to allow him to see much. A black cavern, leading who knew where. As he backed out, he realized that Isabel's shots were longer apart.

"Kee," she whispered moments before he reached her. "I think someone is coming up the trail. I heard what sounded like a boot scraping against rock. But I cannot see anything."

"I found us a way out. Trouble is I don't know

where it leads.'' He drew his Colt and fired a few shots to keep heads down. ''Reload the rifle. We can't take much with us. You go first. Light another piece of wood. Grab the canteen and a blanket while I give those boys something to worry about.''

Kee belly-crawled to the doorway. He needed time to find where each one was shooting from. Time they weren't giving him. Someone down there had a damn good eye. Bullets sprayed all around him. Rock fragments stung his face. Still he fired back. He had to give Isabel time to hide.

Her frantic calling of his name made him begin a backward crawl. He felt her hand on his leg, heard her whisper to hurry. He was half in and half out of the doorway when someone called her name.

The shock was great enough for Kee to come to his knees. And he heard it again. That husky voice calling out for Isabel. That very feminine voice that no man could pretend to imitate.

The distraction proved deadly. The bullets slammed to the side of him, and someone down below got lucky.

Kee felt the rocking pain in his shoulder. He emptied his gun, and with Isabel giving him covering fire, got back inside.

''Kee, your shoulder, you're bleeding.''

''Yeah. But we're going out. Now.''

''You need—''

''What I need and what I'm getting these days ain't riding the same trail. Let's go.''

He pushed her ahead of him. And that voice called out again. Closer this time. He wanted to know who it was. He wanted a lot right now and settled for getting clear of here.

Isabel was crawling through the hole when Kee smelled something burning. He turned to look and saw someone kick burning brush inside the stone room.

They may have found them, but they didn't know too much about these cliff dwellings. Kee pushed the saddlebags closer and saw Isabel grab hold of them. He dropped down.

"You go. Don't turn around. Don't wait for me. Find us a way out." He gritted his teeth against the pain in his shoulder and reloaded both his Colt and the rifle. He heard Isabel for a few seconds, then the black cavern swallowed all sound.

He crawled in backward, laying the rifle beside him. He ignored the pain, though he still felt it. While he was alive and able to do something to stop the pursuers, he started piling the rocks back. Time. He needed more time.

Shots fired simultaneously echoed in the other room. Kee was nearly deafened by the report. To him it sounded like eight or ten guns, but he knew it was close confines that made it sound like that.

He had built up the rocks until he had enough room for his rifle barrel and half his face. Just enough to squeeze off his own round of shots at the first man to appear.

"Alf's shot! Get that bastard!"

Kee didn't know or care who yelled. He had one down and kept firing to keep them back. The more time he bought for Isabel the better the chance she could find a way out.

Suddenly Isabel was back. 'Come on, Kee. I found an offshoot cave. There are ancient steps cut into the face that lead upward. I did not go far, but I think it is a way out."

Kee got to his feet, caught himself swaying and might have fallen if she had not braced her shoulder under his arm.

"Lean on me. You are hurt because of me. I will—" Her voice was lost as the full range of guns arrayed against them were fired into the storage room. She heard shouts, knew there was too little time, and hurried him along.

The wood she had left burning was almost down to coals. They needed light and she had found none.

"This way. Do not be afraid to lean on me, Kee. I am stronger than you think."

Kee didn't answer. He was saving his breath, and his strength for what lay ahead of them.

"You start climbing," Isabel ordered. "I will hold them off."

So much for saving his breath. "Just like a woman to start arguing now. It's you they want, not me. I'm already shot. You've got a chance. I'm buying that much for you. Go."

"Kee, I—"

"Now!" Despite the near killing pain, he lifted her up. "Go. Hurry." Kee handed up the bundle she had made with the blanket. "Don't stop for anything or anyone."

With his forearm he wiped the sweat that dripped from his forehead and stung his eyes. Isabel had disappeared up the carved stone steps into a black hole.

And they were coming for him.

Kee had had his back against the wall before. Not quite so physically, he thought, ready to shoot the first person through the opening.

But instead of a body, smoke came drifting into the cavern. Within minutes he was coughing. Seconds later, he braced himself for the climb. They'd given him no choice but to run.

He had trouble from the first. The distance between the steps had been carved for shorter people. Kee had to stretch his arm to find a handhold; twice he almost slipped off the ancient rock steps.

And the smoke was drifting up right after him.

Kee couldn't see worth a damn. He hoped he'd called it right and this was an escape hole, not a grave. Not that it mattered now. He had pushed himself and Isabel into a course from which there might be no escape. But without taking this chance, there would certainly be none.

Kee reached upward for another handhold and found emptiness. He had climbed as far as he could. The edge crumbled beneath fingers.

"Hell," he whispered.

"Here, Kee. Take my hand."

The smoke had not come up this high yet, and he took a few deep breaths and handed her his rifle.

"Stay back, Isabel. The edge's unstable. I'm not taking you with me if I go down. Not after all this."

"Stop being a man," she whispered back, latching on to his wrist.

Kee didn't think he'd have reason to smile, but that is just what he did. "Honey, in case you ain't noticed, a man is what I am. Kinda hard to just up and quit in the midst of things."

Her furious mumbling served to distract him from the growing pain in his shoulder as he hoisted his body over the edge, then scrambled for all he was worth to roll his long legs over as pieces of the rock fell below.

Kee scooted back a little. His breathing was harsh

and heavy, but in minutes he was ready to blister her a new hide.

"You don't listen worth a damn. I told you to keep going. Talk about me being just like a man about accepting your help. Hell, you got me beat six ways to Sunday with a woman's stubbornness."

On her knees beside him, Isabel, like Kee, did not think she would have reason to smile. She touched his cheek, thankful that he had not been shot again, thankful, too, that he was with her. She handed him the canteen and while he drank sparingly, she packed her folded shirt against his wound.

"If you would stop talking, Kee, you would see I cannot go farther without you."

"See? Can't see my hand in front of my face."

"There are two tunnels leading off from here. I had no way of leaving you a sign to follow me. And, if you must hear it, I feel better that you are with me."

In the dark cavern he heard the underlying fear in her voice. "Come here, Isabel."

"I am here."

"Closer. I can't see you, remember?"

"Yes." But the word came out all soft and hesitant as she leaned forward. For the moment they were safe. For a few minutes she could pretend there were no men down below ready to kill Kee and capture her again. For a stolen bit of time she could indulge this man who risked his life for her.

By some sure instinct her hand found the thick lock of his hair that fell over his forehead. It was damp with sweat and she gently brushed it aside.

She wished for light to see the cause of the sudden change in his breathing. She knew the cause of hers.

This close she could smell him, the animal heat of

his body, dark and potent. A strange, frightening excitement knotted her stomach and set her heart pounding.

The danger that surrounded them extended to Kee. A tremor rippled through her. Then another. Not from cold. Not when Kee cupped the back of her neck and drew her face closer to his. Not when she felt his warm breath fan across her cheek.

"I don't know what's ahead for us, Isabel," he whispered. "But I'm a man who wants to die happy. And I need one thing from you."

"What?" The shudder that ran through him acted like a caress to her body. She could feel what he was doing to her, but Kee was not hiding how he felt in return. Her breathing became labored as if she had run a long way. She cupped the side of his face, felt the roughness of his unshaven skin and then came the first brush of his lips over hers.

Temptation.

Everything she had been warned against from the time she was too young to understand. But there was no thought of sin when she wanted to taste the reckless slant of his mouth against her own. For without a word desire was there, between them, sizzling the very air they breathed, heating blood and skin and the lips that met and clung as if to the very essence of life itself.

Kee incited a hunger to taste the forbidden, and she could not summon the will to fight him and herself.

His hand splayed out, rubbing up and down her back, bringing her closer to his body until she was half lying on him. His fingers tangled in her hair, tilting her head toward his shoulder. She had never felt such a wild, exploding assault on her senses. The low hungry sound he made before his tongue swept her mouth, all hot and fierce desire as if he could not get enough of her, made her cling to him, trembling helplessly.

As softly as the kiss began, it ended abruptly with a groan torn from Kee. It was not pleasure, but pain in his voice.

Isabel pulled her body away from his and then to her horror realized her hand pressed against his wounded shoulder.

He overrode every protest, every sound she made with soft, satisfied masculine laughter. "Honey, I'm going to die a happy man."

"You are not going to die at all, Kee Kincaid. Not if I have anything to do with it." Realizing what she said, Isabel leaned back, tears helplessly falling. "Oh, *Dios,* what have I said? You were shot because of me. Only your skill saved you from being killed. How could you want to kiss the woman responsible for this and the loss of your horses?"

"Guess you don't look in a mirror much," he said with a hint of laughter, then turned serious. "Isabel, I've wanted that kiss since I first saw you. And now, lovely lady, now I want to get the hell out of here."

With her help Kee stood up and braced part of his weight on the rifle.

"Isabel, do you trust me?"

"Yes," she replied without hesitation.

Kee knew that for here and now she told the truth. The other parts…no, that would have to wait.

"I want you to pace off about ten feet since we can't see anything. Go slow. While you're moving, wet your finger and hold it high. If there's air coming in from the outside, you'll feel it stirring. Then count back and I'll meet you here."

"Why must you move? Stay and rest. I will do this."

"No arguments. If you take a deep breath you'll smell clean air. I was in a mine cave-in once and believe me, the air is stale. But I've caught the drift of smoke once or twice." He sniffed. "Can barely smell it now. They must have discovered the cavern and the steps. Won't take much for them to figure on smoking us out. 'Course, they don't know if we have another way out."

"But Kee, we do not know that there is a way."

"Even odds, Isabel. When you're up against a stacked deck, they're the best you're going to get."

Under their feet lay the dust of centuries. And without light, there was no way to tell where the walls were. What concerned Kee the most was stepping into another hole. He had matches, but had to save them. Thankfully, Isabel wasn't afraid of the dark, enclosed place.

Something rolled beneath his foot. Kee bent down to pick it up. The dust stirred and he coughed, but his hand closed over an ancient ear of corn. None of the kernels remained, but he could feel the individual rows with his fingers. Small cob, no more than ten rows. Yet the feeling persisted that this was not a place where people lived.

"Kee, Kee, come here to me. I think I have found something."

He turned at the sound of her excited voice and hurried toward her. He could barely make out where she stood.

"Kee, it is another opening."

"Clever woman. So it is." Yet Kee hesitated to go forward.

"What is wrong? This could be the way out." Impatience marked her tone.

"For all we know there could be a maze of these caves. Or you could be right and it's a way out. I'm figuring the odds, that's all. So keep your shirt buttoned."

"It is your shirt, Kee."

"Let me go back and get the bundle." He did so, tossing the corn cob in the far corner where it bounced and rolled and then Kee heard it fall. "Sweet hell, I knew there had to be another one of those black holes around here. If you didn't call out when you did, I'd likely stepped into it."

Taking hold of Isabel's hand, and using the rifle in front to poke at the ground, Kee started off. They had gone about seventy feet from where they started when the walls narrowed enough that his shoulder brushed against one side. But it was the faint gleam up ahead that drove him forward.

Within a few feet Kee felt the sudden openness around him. He stopped and looked at the rifle-barrel width of faint light that stretched across the floor. Above there was a crack in the rock roof. Kee judged it to be at least fifteen feet high, far too high for him to see out, far too high for them to climb up there. But the cool air stirred around them, and hope renewed itself. Hope that had been diminishing by the minute.

"It is a good sign, Kee. This must be the right way," Isabel said, squeezing his hand tight. She had not said a word of worry to him, but she thought of being entombed in this place, and it frightened her.

Now he reached into his pocket and pulled out his match safe. He struck one and the tiny light was swallowed by the darkness around them. Kee lit another match and this time he smiled. The air stirred the flame.

"Straight ahead now, Isabel. We're getting out."

But straight ahead led into a tunnel where Kee had to bend low to pass. "Isabel, count our steps. I'll give it to a hundred. If we don't get into a wider passage we turn around." He said nothing of the hot stale air that filled this tunnel. Hot and close, just the way a man wanted to be with someone like Isabel, but along with that went a feather-soft tick and sweet-smelling air that was easy to breathe. He swiped at the sweat beading his forehead, forgetting about his wound until his upward stretch pulled the flesh. Kee couldn't stifle his groan in time. Behind him he felt Isabel's free hand reach out to touch him.

"It's all right, Isabel. A stupid move on my part. Keep going."

There was no change in the tunnel. His breathing as well as Isabel's was labored. As near as he could figure, they were a couple of hundred yards into the mountainside. How much farther did they have to go? Or was this another blind tunnel that would lead nowhere?

"One hundred, Kee," Isabel whispered, crowding closer to him as he stopped. Her breaths were gasps for oxygen.

Kee's were no better. He faced her. Touching her face, he found her cheek streaked with dust and sweat.

"Isabel, we go on or turn back. Your decision."

She leaned her head against him. Her instincts were silent. "We can't...stay here, Kee. I can hardly breathe."

"Let's go on. Another hundred feet."

The tunnel narrowed almost immediately. Kee had

to turn sideways to pass a few sharp protrusions of rock.

"The tunnel is turning. Maybe this is the way."

"I am praying, Kee."

"That's good. We need all the help we can get."

There was another tight squeeze for Kee as the tunnel took a hard, sharp turn. But he struggled, ignoring the rip to his shirt for he felt the cool air. Isabel's soft cry told him she felt it, too.

"Come on," he urged, stumbling a little as once more he felt the vast space around him. He fumbled to get two matches lit and immediately cupped his hand around the tiny flame to protect it from being blown out. Cool, fresh air stirred against his heated face. "This way, Isabel. Hold on a little longer."

"I am with you no matter what." She pinned her gaze on the dying flame, but hope flared, bright and hot, even as the matches burned out.

Kee led her across the vast space. And there was moonlight spilling down upon them, revealing another set of ancient carved steps. Neither one urged the other, but both hurried outside.

"Never saw such a pretty sight as that night sky," Kee whispered. He cradled her against him, absorbing her shudders of relief. He felt a few of his own.

"We made it, lady. I don't know where the hell we are, or how we're getting down, but we made it."

"Together, Kee. We make a good team." Isabel hugged him around the waist. Her cheek pressed against his heart.

"We'll rest here tonight, and then," he added in a soft, but warning voice, "and then, my sweet, tempting little liar, you—" he cupped her face with both his hands so there was no escape ''—are going to tell me who the woman was that kept calling your name.''

''Kee, I—''

''No.'' And he silenced her with a brief, hard kiss. ''In the morning.''

But in the morning, Isabel was gone.

Chapter Ten

The last thing Kee remembered was Isabel cleaning his wound. Luck had been with him. The bullet went clean through. He couldn't recall just when he fell asleep.

Now, in the cold gray light of morning he discovered that she had left him his rifle and canteen.

He supposed he should be grateful that he still wore his money belt. But Kee wasn't feeling grateful at all. A little betrayed, a whole lot foolish, maybe downright surly. Grizzly mean sort of surly. The one thing he wasn't, was worried about Isabel. Still he felt ready to shoot the first one of that bunch that crossed his path.

Sure he would, he laughed to himself. With his arm so stiff, he'd be lucky to hit the broad side of the mountain if he tried to fire his rifle.

Kee stood and looked at the rock ledge that spread wide from the cave mouth. He saw where Isabel had found the way down.

It was a good thing they had not tried to leave in the dark. The way was steep, loose rock and over-grown brush made for slow going, but Kee was determined. He ignored hunger and pain, just about everything to get himself down below.

Well, not everything. He made plans. Plans that made him argue with himself over how pilgrim-green he was to even think about going up against men ready to kill him.

And he couldn't forget the other woman.

Or Isabel. Sweet—trembling—lying—blue-eyed witch.

He couldn't seem to bury thoughts of her.

Do you trust me?

And her *Yes* said without a moment's pause.

A smart man would find his horses and head for home.

To hell with gold, women and shooting men.

Every ounce of horse sense told him to cut and run, but he found himself studying the earth to find Isabel's tracks.

He just couldn't leave her alone with that pack of wolves. Walking away from her just wasn't in him.

Kee spent most of the day following Isabel's tracks. A part of him knew that she hadn't tried to hide them. It was almost as if she knew he would come after her.

What did surprise him was where the trail led him.

Right to the base of the cliff dwelling. He found where horses had been tied, and scuffed footprints of men moving around. He found one perfect smaller boot print, too. The deeper heel impression told him this belonged to the other woman who had called Isabel by name.

Dusk covered the land. He wasn't going to find them by trying to track in the dark. Not afoot. He looked upward. It was worth a chance to see if his gear was still up there.

The stench of burning brush filled the stone room. He was surprised to find his saddle and bags intact. What he needed was his horse.

Kee settled for a small fire, just enough to make coffee and fry bacon. It was a quick supper, but a welcome one.

He needed sleep, but his mind wouldn't let him rest.

Had Isabel gone willingly with them? Or had she been taken against her will?

And where would they have gone? That question plagued him the most. Plagued his restless sleep when it finally came. Plagued his first thought upon awakening in the morning.

Kee sorted through his pack, taking only what was necessary since he would have to haul his saddle with him. He swore and cursed as he worked, knowing why they still hung horse thieves. A man on foot in the middle of nowhere needed every skill he possessed to survive.

Then he remembered the springs where he'd last seen horse tracks. Odds were with him that the horses would come back there. It meant wasting a day at best, two or three at the worst, but he wasn't going to catch up to that bunch without a horse.

Even taking only what he needed, the saddlebags and rifle proved a chore to carry with his bad arm. He walked, drank sparingly from his canteen, rested and then walked on.

Late afternoon found him at the spring. There were fresh tracks, all right, including those of Outlaw. Kee almost smiled. If that mustang caught his scent, that horse would bring those mares and his packhorse right to him. Kee refilled his canteen, washed his wound and then hunted a spot to wait.

He found a thick slab of rock tilted just enough to provide a hollow shelter for his fire. But after he'd eaten, he doused the fire, scattered the ashes and settled himself on the warm earth. Once the sun went down, the temperature fell right along with it.

While he waited, Kee's thoughts kept returning to the story Isabel had told him. When he came right down to sifting through everything, the facts weren't much.

If they had a little more time, he might have had a more solid picture of what had happened. He had a gut feeling that the Apache woman Ken-tee was involved somehow with Isabel's grandfather.

Kee took that idea apart and it kept coming back together like the perfect fit of gun to hand, man to saddle.

He racked his mind for any talk he'd heard over the years about the old Dutchman. But then, he'd not been interested in the mining end of the Kincaid holdings.

Give him his horses, and cattle if he had to. But breeding stock was his first love and one he'd been lucky enough to indulge.

Isabel loved horses. He remembered hearing it in her voice when she admired his Appaloosa mares. His stud was a blooded Morgan, gentle as a baby, more cow sense than any other horse he had ridden and he could outwalk, outrun and outrace any horse put against him. Coal-black with a long narrow band of white from his forehead down to his muzzle, the Prince was Kee's prized possession.

And he had every intention of bringing him four of the best mares he could find. Just as soon as he helped Isabel out of her troubles. And he had a few scores to settle of his own with Benton, Alf and Muley Cotton.

Kee had his palm on the ground to help him rise when he felt the vibrations of the horses. Slowly, he moved to a crouched position. The very last thing he wanted to do was to spook the horses.

There was just enough daylight left for him to see that he'd been right about the tracks. Outlaw came in first, circling the spring, sniffing the air before he nickered to the other horses and then trotted back to stay with them with all the innate caution bred into the mustang.

Kee whistled.

Outlaw's head came up. His whinny blended with Kee's voice.

"Easy boy. Easy now. You've had a rough time, you and these pretty ladies." Crooning softly, Kee worked his way around the spring and ever closer to where the horses bunched together.

He wasn't worried about the mustang bolting, but those mares were fresh off wild range and would run.

Outlaw trotted toward Kee, offering his nose first for petting before he butted Kee's shoulder. "Take it easy, you rangy coyote. While you were sparking these here gals, I was getting shot."

The mustang tossed his head and nickered. Kee smiled for the first time that day. It was almost as if the horse was laughing at him for not having his horse sense. He rubbed the animal's neck, all the while he kept talking softly to put the other horses at ease.

Despite an inner urgency, Kee forced himself to be patient. He approached each horse, let them smell him, and made sure every one got a good scratching between their ears.

But he had a problem now in what to do with his animals while he went after Isabel. There was no place to leave them, and running loose they were sure to attract some lone rider's attention. In the end the decision was taken from him. Outlaw wasn't going anywhere without them. And Kee knew he had too much invested in the horses not to take them.

At daybreak he found the trail he'd been hunting.

About midmorning he discovered that one of the horses carried double. He paid special attention to that horse's tracks. He also noted their general direction headed toward Weaver's Needle. Kee spurred his mount and pushed him for all he was worth. The chances of losing them in the twisting canyons was too great.

Off to the west was Superstition Mountain. The Pima Indians called it *Kakatak Tamai,* Crooked-Top Mountain and others just named it Killer, for all the lives it claimed.

Kee spied a game trail heading upward and on impulse took it. Nothing scared off the mustang and Kee was glad he was riding him, for the trail cut through and over rock, in some places no more than a foot wide.

But he made the top and was able to see for miles around in the clear desert air. No sign of a fire, no sign of dust. He'd either lost them, or they had made camp for the night.

Water. It was the one thing they needed, and the one thing that would lead him to them.

While there was light enough he studied the land, looking for cottonwoods. When that failed, he racked his mind for every bit of trail talk that he had heard of the area. Most times he picked up information over a drink in a saloon from some cowhand who rode over the area. Word was passed along in cafés, the bath-houses or the general store.

He knew about the spring, and farther north were lakes, but there was something…

He neck-reined the mustang to turn when he spotted two horsemen coming out of a draw. Too far to identify them, Kee thought of the odds that it wasn't the men he trailed.

"Let's go. We got to get lucky this time."

Kee used every skill he possessed to move unseen to the mouth of the draw, and even then he made no direct approach to enter it. The two riders were long gone, but he didn't know to where or when they would return. If they did come back.

He staked out the horses far enough away so they would not be seen or heard. Swapping his boots for his moccasins, Kee made his way back to the draw and climbed to where he could see below.

The last rays of the sun slanted across the land, creating shadows. He quietly studied the brush and rocks, sniffing the air for a hint of wood smoke, but there was nothing. Discouraged, he went back to his horses.

Whoever those riders were, they didn't leave Isabel behind in that draw with anyone to guard her.

But then Kee thought about Benton and Alf. Muley he didn't know, but he was the one who betrayed Isabel.

Would these men worry about building a fire for her? If they had what they wanted from her…

Kee raced back to the draw. The need to find her had built a fever in his blood, yet survival instincts made him move with caution. He listened to the sounds of night-prowling animals, the slight rustle of brush as a breeze sprang up. It was a trick that his uncle Ty had taught him. To listen with all senses, identify what was naturally there. Less surprises for a man that way.

As he worked his way inside the draw, Kee felt a change come over him. He knew Isabel was near. Nothing cried out to him, only the sharp sense that he was right.

Then he heard what he'd been listening for…that one out-of-place sound. Like cloth rubbing against rock or brush. The sound a man makes when he has been in one position too long.

Kee had no use for his gun now. He wanted his knives. He slid out the one he wore down the back of his neck inside his shirt, and lifted the one from his belt. There could be one or two waiting for him.

Trouble was, he didn't know if one of them might be the other woman.

He circled where he heard the sound, most of the time crawling on his belly. Tension gripped his body. This was going to be close and tight. The very absence of all the little night sounds told him how close he was to his quarry. He had not heard a sound from Isabel, but the feeling that she was close persisted.

Kee had one knee under him ready to rise. There was a solidness to the bulk shadow a few feet in front of him that resembled a seated man.

''Did you hear that?''

The whisper sent Kee to his belly again. It did not come from in front of him, but off to the side. Two, then.

And the one closest to him was the smart one. He didn't answer, didn't make a move or any sound.

Kee stretched his hand out in a search for small

rocks. He found three. Slowly rolling over so as not to make a sound, he threw them quickly in different directions.

He was already moving when bullets flew, all away from him. He grabbed hold of the man sitting on the rock, his knife pressed against his throat.

"Move and you're dead." Kee breathed the words into the man's ear. To make sure the man understood, Kee nicked his skin. "Call your partner over here."

Kee had his head pulled back, and couldn't see the man's face clearly. He saw the reflected gleam of his eyes darting from one side to the other.

"Do it!" Kee ordered. "Now."

"Muley," came the man's whisper.

"Louder," Kee demanded, his eyes searching out the darkness before him for any sign of movement.

"Muley, get out here."

Kee yanked the man's rifle free and swung the butt at his head, knocking him out in one smooth move.

There was silence then, the edgy, dangerous silence of the hunt.

Then Kee was rewarded.

"Benton?"

Kee grunted, hoping to draw Muley out in the open.

But the silence grew, and Kee knew this Muley was not one to be easily gulled.

Suddenly Kee heard something off to his right. He crouched down. He caught a glimpse of a dull gleam, then it was gone. The man was moving, trying to circle around him. Kee gauged where the rifle fire had come from. He was directly across the draw from the place. Where the man had been might be Isabel, and that was all he really cared about now. Finding her.

And Muley gave him the opportunity. He had just found Benton.

Kee saw him stand and threw his knife. His long legs ate up the distance and nearly tripped him when he stumbled over a body. He never heard the man's grunt.

"Isabel?" He reached out with one hand to touch.

A mewling noise came in response.

Kee found the gag and cut it free. He wasted no time talking, found the rope that tied her wrists to her ankles and sliced through them.

"Wait here," he told her. He was going back for his knife. He understood her sudden grip on his arm; she must be frightened out of her mind.

He didn't understand why she knocked his hat off. He didn't understand why she grabbed his hair and yanked it.

But he sure got the message that this wasn't Isabel when her teeth sank into his knife hand.

Chapter Eleven

"Muley. I've got him."

"Like hell you do, lady." Kee shoved her away from him. She'd torn his skin and his hand bled.

"I'm hurt. Caught his knife in my shoulder. He's all yours."

If Kee had expected teeth and nails, he got a surprise. She drew a knife on him. And the way she slashed toward him, he didn't have time to be shocked.

Served him right. He bowed his body to avoid her wicked thrust. He'd spent so much time wondering about the other woman that some devil decided to show him what he'd been missing.

Kee jumped back. He didn't want to use his knife against her, but he was damned if he was going to let her slice him like some dumb rabbit.

He feinted to his right, weaved left and caught her wrist in his powerful hand. "Drop the knife or I'll break it." He barely missed being kicked. Still holding her wrist, Kee spun her around and locked his other arm around her. He kept her pinned to his body, her arms useless, and ignored every backward kick that she landed.

"Where's Isabel?"

"She rode off with Alf."

"I'll just bet she did." Kee had never hurt a woman in his life, but his temper was close to breaking. He couldn't let her go, and he wasn't going to kill her.

The strain of holding on to the twisting, spitting woman set his wound to bleeding. She was still gripping her knife and he didn't trust her not to use it on him if he turned her loose.

But the blood dripping down his arm said time was running out. Kee moved fast. He loosened his armhold, turned her toward him and clipped her chin with just enough force to put her down. He disarmed her. Working quickly, he used the piggin' strings he always carried to tie her up. It had been a while since he had roped and thrown a calf after roundup in competition with other cowhands. He still had the skill to move fast.

He left her, staggering a little as he hunted Muley.

"You will die for this."

Kee ignored this threat and the ones that followed him. He tore off his neckerchief and tied it around the pad on his arm. The fight, the tension, the fear for Isabel, all took its toll on him. He felt himself weakening.

Muley wasn't hard to find. His moaning led Kee right to him. Here was a man, and Kee had no desire to be charitable.

"You want that knife out? You tell me who that woman is, what she wants with Isabel, and where Alf took her."

"You're a real bastard to stand there and watch me bleed like a stuck pig. You know I can't pull this knife by my ownself. You up to living with killing a man for doing the job he's paid for? Huh? You gonna just stand there jawing away at me?''

Kee had never knowingly killed a man. He had never wanted to cross that line until now. And he was smart enough to understand he wouldn't live easy with that decision.

But Muley couldn't know that. Must not, Kee warned himself.

''You want the knife out then start talking and don't stop until I say so.'' The threat was enough. Muley talked.

Kee could barely sit the saddle when he rode away, taking their horses with him. For the woman's sake he left the three of them two canteens and their guns. They weren't going far on foot in this rough country.

The trap in the draw had been laid for him. All the planning of the woman who claimed to be Ken-tee's daughter. Everything had been set with Isabel as bait, but she confessed that she had buried the map back at the cliff dwelling. Something about that smacked false to Kee.

That gold was so important to Isabel, he couldn't see her willingly giving over that map. Worthless or not. There was something else, something he'd missed.

And the only way he was going to have all the answers was to head her and Alf off.

What he needed was a place to wait. Outside the draw, he pulled up near his own horses. He stripped the three saddles and covered them with brush. Not quite hidden, they would slow their owners down. He couldn't turn their horses loose, so he added them to his string.

Riding Outlaw he hunted his place.

And when he found it, all he wanted to do was close his red-rimmed eyes and sleep. He couldn't even chance taking care of his wound, afraid he'd be caught and unable to help Isabel. But it hurt like somebody stomped a mudhole in him, then stomped it dry.

The moon rose shiny as a new ten-dollar gold piece. While the spread of light made it easier for Kee to observe the land around him it also revealed the dry wash that barely concealed the horses. But no one could approach the draw without passing him.

All he had to do was wait and not pass out.

He kept thinking back to Muley's claim that the woman was Ken-tee's daughter. He worried it over like a tongue probing at a sore tooth.

Isabel told him that the Apache believed Ken-tee betrayed them and told Walz about the gold. If this woman was Apache, she wouldn't touch that gold. Not when the place was home to their Thunder god.

Yet Muley swore a blue streak that it was true.

Since Kee had been pulling his knife free, he tended to believe Muley's screamed words.

Kee roused himself. He took a long, careful look around. Deadly as the desert land could be at night, for him it held a certain beauty, too. The gilding on the rocks, the play of shadow, the soft rustling night noises, the whisper of the wind. He caught himself nodding off. The far-off yipping of a coyote snapped him alert. He walked among the horses, his own calm, the others restive. But Kee had a way with them, none shied at his touch or the soft sound of his voice.

He wished he could take the chance and ride back to the cliff dwelling. Isabel had escaped them once on her own. She was smart enough to look for another opportunity.

But what if she couldn't get away from Alf? His wound was slight, he had lost her once, so he'd be wary.

The sudden appearance of a hard-ridden horse off in the distance held Kee's attention. He searched for the second rider. There wasn't any.

"I'll kill that bastard if he hurt Isabel." Only Outlaw heard the furious words as Kee mounted and raced out of the hollow to intercept the other rider.

He had to admire the other rider's skill for pushing his horse over dangerous terrain at night. But he cursed under his breath in the next moment for forcing him to do the same.

They closed, and as they did, Kee realized that the stocky body of Alf was not the one on the horse.

Before he could call out, believing it to be Isabel, the rider veered away. That damn woman was going to get him killed yet. He shouted her name, swearing when she didn't pull up. Urging the mustang to give all he had, Kee went after her.

Isabel tasted the bitterness of defeat. She rode blindly, whipping the reins back and forth over the animal's neck, desperate to get away from the rider that approached her.

Terror for Kee was her constant companion. Had been since she had left him. She knew what they planned for him. Knowing Kee, he would walk into their trap in the belief that he was rescuing her.

The tense knot in her belly suddenly expanded to encompass her body. Blood pounded in her ears, just like the horse's hooves thundered against the earth.

She could barely hear the rider's shout as he raced to close in on her.

Tension, fear and resolve stiffened her spine. At any moment she expected warning shots to be fired. He would not shoot to kill her, but he would shoot her horse.

She could not stop. She had to stay free. It was the only way she could help Kee after all he had done for her.

Her horse stumbled. Only Isabel's skill saved her from a fall. She would either kill the animal or herself if she kept up this pace.

The cold desert night wind slapped her face. She sensed rather than saw how near the other rider was to her.

She realized he was attempting to pull ahead and box her in. Flecks of foam flew from her hard-ridden animal. Kee! she cried silently. She had no choice.

Isabel did not slow a bit as she turned her horse. She still hoped for a way out. Fear had dried her mouth and throat. Her heart pounded like a small captured songbird beating its wings against the reed cage.

Where to go?

Massive rocks loomed ahead. She swung her horse away. The animal's stride faltered.

Panic was the one thing she could not give in to. But all she felt was the utter hopelessness of getting away.

The horse went through a scattering of boulders. The animal's stride was broken, and Isabel knew she would not have more than a few minutes. This was not her golden horse whose great heart would carry her like the wind for hours. She kicked free of the stirrups and attempted to slow the crazed animal who had given her all he had.

He went down in soft sand and she tumbled free. Then she was up and running.

Only the rider was there, his horse cutting off her every dodge. Wild-eyed she stood still, chest heaving, body shaking.

"Isabel? What the devil were you thinking of leading me to hell and gone?" Kee kicked free of the stirrup, and swung his long leg over to dismount. She hadn't moved.

He hated seeing her head bowed in defeat. He called to her again, almost afraid to touch her. She suddenly seemed vulnerable, swaying like a slim, delicate blade of grass, but sealed off in a place that he could not reach.

Kee's emotions ran a swift gamut from fear to anger edged by more than concern for her, more than caring for a woman alone fighting against too many. And what he was feeling scared him.

"Isabel?" His voice was harsh, not at all what he wanted. Suddenly he understood a little of what scared him. He needed to hold her, to drink in the scent of her, he had to know that she believed herself safe with him. The why and how of the importance of these feelings didn't matter to him. They were there. He felt them.

"It's Kee, Isabel," he whispered and took a step closer. "No one is going to hurt you. Not while I'm around." She didn't seem to hear him. Kee shoved back the brim of his black, flat-brimmed hat.

"Hey, lovely lady, do you hear me?" She made a soft sound, but it made no sense to him. He reached for her arm and she backed away. "That's it! Don't

move, Isabel. I'm damn well not going to hurt you!''
He was shouting and didn't care.

She flung her head back, revealing the taut line of
her slender neck and then her gaze fastened on his
face. She closed her eyes for a few seconds. Her silent
prayers had been answered. Then she looked at him.

"Kee? I thought—"

"I've been trying to tell you—"

"You don't know how I feared—"

"What in tarnation—"

Isabel silenced him by throwing herself at him. She
grabbed hold of his shirt with both hands. "Kee! Listen! I was so afraid. They have set a trap for you. You
must ride away. She is out of her mind. She killed my
horse, Kee. My beautiful golden mare. She hates me.
I do not know her anymore." Sobs threatened. Her
fingers dug hard into him. She was shaking, saw his
mouth move, but she could not hear him. "She promised to kill you. You—"

"Hush!" Harsh still as his own fear reigned, then
he found softness. "Hush, Isabel, it's all right." He
hugged her tight, fighting off the wave of pain from
his wound. He rocked her with his body.

"I'll get you another horse. I know it won't be the
same. But I'm glad it wasn't you. I managed to learn
a little from Muley." She tried to pull away then, but
he held her fast. "I need this. I need to hold you."

There was such a rightness to this, holding her,
feeding each other warmth. The fear and tension in
him dissolved. Her heated breath seeped through the
cloth of his shirt, and with it, came the hot wetness of
her tears. He felt the slow hammering of his own
pulse, the race of blood building when she whispered

his name and pressed harder with a stir of her body so hungry desire flared to life.

A little voice of sanity whispered this was not the time or the place to satisfy his need.

With his fingers entangled in her silken hair, he tried telling himself to be thankful they had both escaped.

But words of thanks fled from his mind with the feel of her hardened nipples pressed against his chest. He tried telling himself that she was unaware of the invitation of her body, that every sigh, every snuggling move closer to him was only a woman seeking comfort.

But Kee was only flesh and blood and not a saint. He could tell himself all the right things from hell and gone, and they didn't hold a candle to the hunger Isabel ignited.

"Kee, oh, Kee," she moaned against his chest. "They want to kill you. She believes I told you where the gold is. She will not allow you to live."

Those words acted like a dash of cold water. Not enough to put out the fire, but enough to bring it to simmer.

"I do not want her to kill you, Kee. I will not let her kill you."

The way she clung to him, he knew she believed that. It didn't go halfway to explaining why she had taken off on her own, but he figured that question could wait.

There was one that couldn't. "What happened to Alf?"

"I hit him with a rock. He was not dead when I left him, but he was bleeding."

"Listen to me now." He tried to set her away, but she held him fast. "We need to get out of here. I've got their horses so no one is going to follow us easily.''

He ran his hands down her back, intending to reassure her. But as his daddy told him many a time, the road to hell is paved with good intentions.

Kee rested his hands on her slim hips and pulled her tight against him. He made no apology for his aroused state and Isabel would need to be dead not to know it.

She looked up at him, her dark eyes holding his and Kee could no more stop himself from claiming her lips than he could stop breathing at that moment.

Kindling and match.

The taste of her ignited a fire that burned down to blood and bone. Sweetly given, her mouth was his with all its womanly promise and the soft, soft sounds she made drove him wild.

Wild. The thought, the taste of Kee, the feeling streaked through Isabel. She had his scent, the ones she had marked without knowing, of leather and horse, of smoke and sage, of power and passion. All very masculine. All intriguing. All Kee Kincaid. And very heady to a young woman tasting the first bite of desire.

The involuntary tremors of arousal began and quickly shattered the hard shell she had built so carefully over the years. The heat and strength of him was intoxicating.

He stole all rational thought with the seductive ply of his mouth against hers. He held her head between his large hands, but there was no fear with him. Kee would never force her to give more than she wanted to give. The belief, so strong it shocked her, was there, rooted deep inside. The softness of his lips wooed her as he skimmed her mouth, pressing tiny kisses to the corners, using the edge of his teeth to send shimmering sensations rioting through her. He teased her into needing more. She shivered when his fingertips rubbed the delicate skin just behind her ears.

A sudden stillness filled her. She was on the edge of a cliff, afraid to move, almost afraid to draw breath and lose the glimmering anticipation that trembled to life.

Molded from knee to chest, sealed with heat and hard-pounding pulses. She felt the softening of her body, the need to give to this one man all that she had, all that she was, and would be. She knew nothing of men. No man had ever kissed her like this, or held her against a body so hard, the only giving softness to be found were his lips. Her breasts swelled, heavy with wanting. Her hands slid upward, knocking off his hat as she drew his head down.

"Open your mouth, Isabel. Yes, sweet lady, just like that."

His dark whisper. Her own helpless response. Then his mouth claimed hers in a kiss that told of hunger, of dark and heated passions. Dangerous. Like the night, he called all that was dark, forbidding and unknown from her.

Isabel ignored the warning that tried whispering to her. It held no place in this dizzying longing to answer the hunger in him. Every place their bodies touched was hot, sharp and soft, pulsing with life. She was shocked by the trembling that seized her and the flood of warmth that followed a soft, deep explosion that rocked through her.

She was overpowered by the storm that assaulted her. Too many sensations rushing through her at once. No time to savor, to understand why the heated thrust

of his tongue sweeping her mouth intensified the shivers that began so deep inside her. Or why she followed
the silent coaxing he offered to tutor her to do the
same to him. In a small corner of her mind she tucked
away the knowledge that she brought a shudder to his
body with the tentative play she made. Womanly
power. A heady wine to drink from Kee's lips.

And she wanted more.

But Kee tore free of the kiss. His breath sawed in
and out as if he'd been running a long way. His body
hard with need, he shook for a few seconds, battling
to get some control back. He slipped his hands to her
shoulders and roughly held her away from him.

"Hot enough to scald a man and have him not give
a hoot. Sweet and giving. Enough to make a man
crazy," he whispered more to himself than to her.

The moon's bright light revealed her dazed look.

"Sweet purgatory, woman. You don't even know
what the hell you've done to me." Crazy. That's what
he was. Standing like some greenhorn in the middle
of nowhere with gunmen hunting their hides, and him
barely able to keep his pants buttoned. And she didn't
know. The look of her...Kee closed his eyes briefly,
shuddered and fought to wipe out the taste of her, the
feel of... No!

"We've got to get out of here. Now."

The words were bitten off, and suiting action to
them, he lifted her up to the mustang's back.

Isabel could barely speak. She did not understand
what had happened. She reached for his arm and he
jerked away from her. Hurt filled her.

"Why, Kee?"

"Why?" The word was choked. Innocence shone
from her eyes, but his gaze slid down to her mouth,

reddened from his lips, slightly swollen and parted as if she waited for another kiss. The image of taking her beneath him, right here, right now, surfaced and with it came a rush of anger.

Cold and hard, his voice lashed her. "If you need to ask you're too damn innocent to be out here alone without a dozen men to protect you. Stay away from me. I'm no damn saint. I'll take what I'm offered. And lady, you offered it all. You never said no. You never even tried."

She thought about defending herself. She could plead that fear had turned to thanks that he was alive, that they were together. She should tell him the truth. She never wanted a man to kiss her like this, or hold her, or be willing to follow where he led, despite all the teachings that it was wrong outside of marriage. There were many things she could tell him, but she bit her lip and kept silent. And shivered in the aftermath of the passion he stirred to life.

"That horse you rode is done for. We'll leave him. Now scoot back so I can mount."

But Isabel was still gripped by the turbulence of her emotions and Kee's anger. She moved all right; she heard the command in his voice that brooked no arguing. But she moved forward, her hands clenched around the saddle horn in her desperate need to hold on to something solid. Because of Kee. Because of the dizzying world he had shown her. And just as abruptly torn away.

Kee knew he made a mistake to ignore her move the moment he settled in behind her. He was so hard he ached and his body accommodated hers like a glove to hand.

He wanted to turn her around and ride the night with his flesh joined to hers.

Innocent!

He might not trust her completely, but he had to trust his own senses. He didn't want to. He didn't want to calm down and think with logic. He wanted her. Isabel. All sighing passion and... No!

The devil, he thought, had all different ways of riding with a man. But that old Beelzebub knew the true tempting of a man. A black-haired, blue-eye witch, all virginal passion. A slim-hipped handmaid who made his flesh ache.

And in the battle not to be outdone, the good Lord gave Kee a conscience, with a sharp pitchfork's worth of pricking to ride along with him.

Isabel trusted him. He had sworn to her that nothing would hurt her. Well, hell, he told himself, he didn't want to hurt her, he just wanted to bed that body rubbing against his until he needed to climb out of his skin.

Trust, Kee, remember.

Yeah, he remembered.

"You stiffen up anymore, lady and you'll break. You don't want that," he coldly reminded her. "You don't want that at all. I'd have to put my hands on you then, and there'll be the devil to pay if I do."

His coldness cut through the web of numbness that she surrounded herself with.

"Do not worry, Kee. I will not break. And the devil is already collecting his due."

"How's that?"

"He let me find you," she snapped. *Only he will not let me keep you, Kee.*

"True enough, lady. Guess that works both ways."

He spoke the words but he didn't believe them. He wasn't going to leave her alone to face what that other witch had in store. He couldn't live with himself if he did.

So riding with her bottom snug in his lap was killing him by inches. There were worse ways to die. And he fanned his anger to keep her safe. How else could he protect her from this need she stirred to flame?

All Kee heard was silence in answer.

Chapter Twelve

Nearly an hour later Kee stopped long enough to put Isabel up on one of the horses he had taken. He rode the other, giving Outlaw a rest.

He forced himself to stop thinking about Isabel and the heated length of her slim body pressed against his. No time. No place. Belatedly, he remembered the night-hunting snakes. The deadly coral, and the spotted night snake. Kee couldn't stop an inner shudder. He hated snakes. Just recalling how someone tried to kill his uncle Conner by locking him in his own jail cell with a sackful of rattlesnakes was enough to make his stomach muscles clench and taste bile.

He pushed the horses hard, riding through the night with the moonlight to guide him. Twice he rode back to ask Isabel if she could go on, and twice she roused herself to mumble that she could keep up with him. He doubted that, but accepted her word.

Kee wanted to put distance between them and the bullet marked with his name.

And he refused to lose Isabel again.

She caught his twisting move to look back at her again. She forced herself to sit up, but the moment he faced front, she slumped down in the saddle. Exhaustion had wiped out all thought. She had no reserves left to fight it off. In a way this numbing fatigue was a good thing. She could not think about Kee or his kisses or how he made her feel. She would not have to remember his sudden anger. She should not recall the warmth of him.

By the dip and sway of the saddle she knew they had been climbing steadily for some time. Dawn blanketed the land when Kee called a halt. Isabel barely roused herself to look around. Her eyes burned as if she'd collected the sand of the desert in them. She was tired, hungry and thirsty, and no closer to her goal. She saw Kee dismount, but she was not getting off this horse unless he planned to camp in this desolate spot. She knew she could never climb back on the horse if he only meant to rest for a few minutes.

Kee barely spared her a glance. It was the only way he could keep himself moving. If he allowed the concern and sympathy he felt for her to surface, they would never get down the trail.

And as he walked off and rounded a boulder that was nearly twice his height, he knew this was a killer trail.

Isabel grew alarmed as minutes passed and Kee did not return. The horses were bunched together on their lead rope so she could not ride past them.

Clinging to the saddle horn with her left hand, she forced the screaming muscles of her right leg in a wide swing over the horse's rump. She grabbed hold of the raised back edge of the saddle seat and hung suspended for a moment until she kicked her left foot free of the stirrup. All she wanted to do was collapse in a heap on the ground. Instead she leaned her weight against the horse, telling herself she had to move, had to find Kee.

The intense heat of his body warned her he was near before she saw him. A shiver passed through her. She had not heard a sound.

"Must you sneak up on me?" she snapped, pressing her head against the saddle.

"I see that riding all night didn't curb your tongue any, lady."

"You curb a horse, Kincaid, not a woman."

"Well, I guess that depends on the man."

Isabel dragged her head up and stared at him.

"You can tell a lot about a man by the way he handles his horse."

"Can you?"

"Sure."

She wanted to wipe that cocky grin from his lips, but the action was beyond her. She shook her head. "I think you have something mixed up, Kincaid. The way a man handles a horse has nothing to do with how he treats a woman."

"Wanna bet?"

The way he stood there off to one side, his hands planted on lean hips, long powerful legs spread apart, and those eyes watching her every breath made Isabel want to do something violent. He confused her. And she was too tired to battle with him. But he waited for an answer. She could see that in his eyes. Baiting him in turn was tempting. She strove for dignity.

"I will not make such a bet. I would not want to see any man *handle* a woman. I would never allow a man to *handle* me." She almost spat the word at him.

Kee smiled at the flare of temper in her eyes and inched the brim of his hat back. Anything was better than the dull dazed look she had when he first came near.

"But you already did, Isabel. Remember?"

"I wish to forget. I will forget." The words were mere whispers. The curl of heated awareness surged deep inside her. For she could not forget. She wanted Kee to hold her, to kiss her like a storm, wild and furious without end.

"Why have we stopped here?" she asked in an effort to distract herself from the sensual turn of her thoughts.

"We need more light before heading down this trail. I want to switch that saddle to Outlaw. You'll be riding him."

Some vague alarm made Isabel look around then back at Kee's face. He gave nothing away, but she sensed he was not telling her something important.

"Where is this trail?"

He stopped her attempt to go around him by moving in front of her.

"Let me by. I want to see it."

'Don't go all contrary on me, Isabel. You've trusted me to get us this far. Trust me all the way."

She heard the words, and knew he meant the long ride through the night, or thought she did. His serious mien, the darkness of his eyes, all silently spoke of another trust that a woman gives to a man. All the rigid bands that had governed her life fell away. She almost murmured yes to him. Some barb of pride held her silent.

"Let me see the trail for myself, Kee."

"And I'm just to obey?"

"Yes."

She never saw his smile as he turned his back on

her. That arrogant pride he had first encountered was back. Maybe not as strong as it had been, but she had shaken off the stupor that had cloaked her through the night.

Without turning he said, "Let me warn you that it looks worse than it is." What Kee didn't add was that he'd only heard about the trail. He had never been this way.

Isabel followed him, waited until he stood aside and then she looked. She blanched. Her empty stomach found bile and she swallowed hard as it rose to burn her throat.

The little she could see of the trail was narrow and twisting. It hugged the canyon wall on one side, the other dropped away. One misstep, only one and both horse and rider would plunge to their deaths below.

"You cannot believe we will ride down this."

Kee ignored the trembling fear he heard in her voice. He tried and failed to see the trail through her eyes. The rocks were rugged and massive. A wild place. In the canyon below threaded the stream like a sliver of silver ribbon. Hawks soared above them. And there was the silence. Not one sound, not a breath of life, or so it seemed to him.

And he turned to her, wanting her to understand how he felt. "One reason to go down this way is that they won't be able to follow. If they do, it will slow them down. But for the other, I don't know if I can explain it to you, Isabel. Few men have stood in this place, less have made that trail. It satisfies something deep within me to be one of them."

"You have a home and a family. If you died here they will never know. How can you desire something so dangerous?"

"You're right. I do have a home and family. But I'm not going to die here and neither are you."

"You like the danger of it, Kee? Is that it?"

He looked away. "Partly. Have you ever been in a place and found that all is peace within yourself? Each new challenge this land presents is like that for me."

"Kee, listen to me. This trail is too dangerous. I have too much at stake to risk—"

"That trail is manageable," he stated with implacable calm. "You'll be riding Outlaw. That mustang was born on these trails. I'll ride one of the mares. They've known them, too."

"You'll ride Outlaw. I'll take the mare."

"No. You'll do as I say. The mares are only green-broke. I won't risk your life that way, Isabel. I asked you to trust me. Once you said yes. Say it now."

She stared at him, noting the lock of hair that fell across his forehead, the steady weight of his gaze, the lean strength that was Kee. She knew there was no choice. She could not go back. She would not leave him.

But Isabel had trouble swallowing past the lump that lodged in her throat. She felt a cold sweat break out on her body when she looked again at the twisting, narrow trail. It seemed impossible for them to attempt it.

"Isabel?"

"I will ride Outlaw."

He walked away to go among the horses, and she watched him, trying to detach herself from her fear to understand him better. Some balance between them had shifted. She had lost a little of the determination that had carried her to this place. Because of Kee Kincaid. Because she did not want to see him die.

Yet he could not hide his excitement in pitting himself against this trap of nature that had likely claimed many lives. He moved with confidence as if fear could find no place within him. This was part of Kee.

She understood that, but it frightened her, too.

She stood there, off to one side while he turned all but his own horses loose with a hard slap that sent them running.

She knew she should help him switch the saddles. She could see where his wound had bled again. But she seemed unable to tear her gaze from the abyss below. Her breaths grew shallow. Fear built minute by waiting minute. She wrapped her arms around her waist as if to hold it inside herself where Kee would not see it.

While she understood a little of what drew him to attempt this trail, she knew she could not ride down that piece of hell no matter how much she trusted Kee.

In the end when he called her to mount the mustang, she went. There were killers waiting behind them, she had to go on.

Kee stripped the lead rope from the mares and the packhorse. One by one he started them down. Isabel kept her gaze pinned to the black splashed across his mare's rump as he led off.

She held the reins loose in her hands, letting Outlaw have his head and pick his own way. If she looked away it was to the rock wall. At first the ledge was wide enough so the horse's footing was solid and she took hope from that. But the trail narrowed and she had to lean back as the descent angled sharply downward. Terror seized her every time the trail took Kee out of sight, and never really let go of her.

The sun rose and painted the wall with a golden

light. Isabel fought the temptation to turn around and look back. She was not sure how far they had come, only the sense of space to her side told her they had a long way to go. She continued to refuse to look down.

She jerked in the saddle hearing the clatter of rocks falling.

This was one of the times when Kee was out of her sight. She swallowed repeatedly. Her mouth formed his name but no sound came out.

Without realizing what she was doing, she pulled back on the reins. Outlaw tossed his head, ready to go on, but he stopped on the narrow ledge.

Isabel leaned against the rock wall barely feeling the sharp crevices that dug into her shoulder.

''Isabel? What's wrong?''

''Coming, Kee.'' She set her heel into the mustang's side and he took a few steps forward, then stopped. She remembered what Kee said about the horse. She had to trust him to pick his own way. Up until now Outlaw had not hesitated. She urged him forward again.

She felt as if death waited below. Its call was so strong, wanting her to look down below. She closed her eyes briefly and thought of Kee. She needed a little of his strength.

Again came the sound of stones falling, rattling as they hit the walls of the canyon. The horse rounded the jutting rock that blocked her view of the trail. Straight ahead, Kee waited.

And then she looked down when Outlaw stopped again.

There was a gap in the ledge. Below it, a black crevice without end.

"Come across, Isabel. Just let him have his head and he'll take you across." He spoke softly, swearing under his breath when he saw that she was freezing up. If he'd been riding the mustang, Outlaw would have jumped just as the mare had.

He couldn't dismount. Couldn't turn around. There was no way to go back and get her. If he tried leading the horse when he had to jump back they would all go over the edge.

"I cannot do this, Kee."

"Yes, you can. You have to. You can't go back. And every minute we waste gives them time to get closer. I don't want to be on this trail with a rifleman up above."

He knew trying to reassure her was more time wasted. She had to trust him. And he knew they were a long way from being safe. He had no time to be gentle with her.

"I cannot cross this."

"Then stay there. I'm going on down. You either make the jump or stay." His voice was as hard and cold as his eyes. He forced himself to look forward.

"You would leave me here?" Disbelief colored her voice. "There are no names vile enough to call you." Anger flooded her. His horse was moving. He really intended to go on and leave her.

"Get out of the way, Kincaid." She gathered the slack in the reins, still allowing the mustang plenty of room to stretch his neck for the jump.

Furious with Kee, Isabel still waited until he was well out of her way before she whispered and urged the mustang to jump. She wore a cold sweat at the jagged landing, and heard more rocks falling below.

Now she wanted to hurry. Kee would only laugh or

ignore her fear. But it was real to her. They were not safe here. Would not be until they were gone from this place.

They were halfway down when she came to a shallow overhang and found that Kee had dismounted.

"Why are you stopping?" she asked, swiping at the sweat on her brow.

"We need to lead the horses a ways."

Something odd in his voice caught her attention. "What is wrong, Kee? And do not lie to me."

"I haven't lied to you. It's a rough spot, that's all. We can't ride and I'm a little worried about your making it."

Still flushed with the anger over his earlier threat to leave her, Isabel glared at him. "Stop all this worry over me. If you can make it, then I will, too."

"Go on, then. Ladies first. I wouldn't want you to think I'd been raised without manners."

Isabel stepped down. She almost hated the teasing light in his eyes. Was he daring her? If so, she would show him. She stepped out, holding the reins tight and faced the wall. Her free hand found tiny crevices to hold on to as she inched her way on the ledge. Perhaps she should have waited to take a better look, but it was too late now. Her cheek almost scraped against the rock wall when she turned to look back at Kee. He still stood in the shadow of the overhang, not looking at her face but downward.

She forgot her anger. There was an intensity to his gaze that made fear grow. What was he looking at?

She felt with one foot for safe purchase, found it, and took another step. The warm breath of the horse blew against her face. With each step and handhold she became more sure. Her breathing eased as she worked her way around another protrusion of rock. Now Kee was out of sight.

Small stones were in the way. She kicked them, then stilled. She heard the small rocks fall away, but the clatter did not stop. If anything the rattling sound of falling rocks grew louder.

"Kee, what—"

"Keep going!"

She obeyed his command. This was no time to let fear petrify her, or to think about what was happening behind her. If she did not keep moving forward, there was no place for Kee to follow, and she sensed that he was in some danger. That was why he made her go first. She knew that as if he had told her so. He had seen something that she did not, and rather than argue with her, he made her go first to safety.

She looked down and ahead as far as she could see.

Nowhere did the ledge widen enough to allow the mustang to pass her.

Unless…Isabel glanced upward. There were cracks in the rock; she was clinging to them with her hands.

"Kee, please tell me what is wrong. I am going on, but I feel you are not safe."

For long seconds she waited, then he answered.

"The ledge is crumbling. The weight of the horses must have loosened the rocks. Go as fast as you can."

She scrambled ahead, wanting to see him, wanting to wait, but knowing she would only endanger him.

Kee eyed the crumbling ledge, then looked at the mare. She rolled her eyes, nostrils flaring, but those were her only signs of agitation. She had sense enough not to toss her head or shift her footing in this precarious position.

He was in trouble. Capital kind. And he had no one to blame but himself.

The only crevice that was deep and wide enough to give him a handhold to swing over the gap was a little high and to his left. His wounded arm would have to support him. If he could hang free for a minute or two, the mare could get by without him.

He spared a thought to putting his back against the rock and trying to reach up with his good right hand, but that was too dangerous.

The left hand it was. Whether or not he'd have any footing left after the mare made the jump remained his problem. And if he had to hang suspended for any length of time he was in more than trouble.

He could be dead.

His boot crumbled more of the edge. He couldn't wait a second longer to decide.

Chapter Thirteen

Kee jumped and slammed his bare hand into the crack, swinging his legs high and to the side. Trickles of gravel fell. Sweat stung his eyes. Pain shot from his hand to his arm and pierced his shoulder. He thought he would pass out if he had to hold on much longer.

His hoarse shout got the mare moving. He closed his eyes and prayed she would make a clean jump. He hoped she did not panic and crowd Outlaw. That could put Isabel in danger.

He opened his eyes. Slowly. Then, he looked down. There was no solid footing left for him.

With his face pressed against the rock he again searched his immediate field of vision for some other handhold. He angled his head to the side and looked up.

There was a crevice. Only it was too high.

His arm muscles were screaming with pain. He felt blood soak his shirt from the wound that had torn open.

Kee was weakening. The rock was cutting into his hand.

He pressed his boot against the rock wall, praying for a foothold, anything that would allow him to relieve his arm of his weight.

He had to move. The ledge wasn't that far away. A good solid jump. With his long legs he could do it in his sleep.

Once more he had no choice. It was do it now or lose his hold and fall.

Kee chose the jump.

His mind went blank for a few seconds as he scrambled to keep his balance.

Suddenly something warm and strong and very solid grabbed hold of his hand. He couldn't believe it was Isabel. But she had somehow gotten back to him. He gripped her hand hard as she helped steady him. But Kee couldn't trust their footing.

"Go. I'm all right. Just go as quickly as you can." He wanted to ask ten questions, but asked nothing now. She nodded, but did not let go of his hand as they inched their way down the ledge.

Kee opened his eyes to see light filtering through the thickly woven branches of a young stand of cottonwoods. His head felt thick with too much sleep. He vaguely remembered mumbling orders to Isabel about making camp, then he collapsed.

The shooting sparks of wood on fire drew his gaze to that fire and the woman who sat across from where he lay.

Isabel watched him with a narrow-eyed gaze that spelled trouble for him. He closed his eyes to block out the sight of her lovely face with those dark-blue gunslinger eyes fixed on him.

He knew what she was angry about, and knew, too, that she had every reason to be so.

The rightness didn't make it any easier for him to swallow.

Right now he wanted to see her eyes in the sunlight, eyes that would grow darker still and smoky with passion. The kind of blue eyes that poets wrote about. She would laugh if he told her as much. Kee peeked through slitted eyes. Yeah, especially now, when anger flushed those high cheekbones and thinned the line of her luscious mouth.

Kee took a deep breath, and then wished he had not. He wasn't fully awake, or he would've been aware of the pain shooting down his arm. But pain or no, he was going to get his apology out of the way first thing.

He opened his mouth, but Isabel beat him to it, erupting with the anger that had built as she thought he would die.

''Yes, I found a good place to camp in this canyon's bottom. Not too near the stream, not too far. Yes, I gathered up the horses, and yes, I found this young stand of saplings. And to your surprise, Kincaid, I knew how to weave the branches together so our fire's smoke would dissipate through the leaves and not easily be seen.

''And I managed to picket the horses where they could have grass and water and not easily be seen, either. I also, to your great surprise since you grumbled and swore at me, found the salve in your pack and used your last spare shirt to dress your wounds. I even cooked. I also stood watch. And you, you stubborn, mule to stone-headed man, could have killed yourself. And for what?

"To say that you survived that trail, that devil-made piece of hell. You almost died up there. You almost died up there," she repeated in a voice devoid of anger, but rich with those last terror-filled moments. She was unaware that she used the back of her hand to wipe at her eyes, brushing away tears that would not stop. She blinked, hating to show him this weakness, then abruptly stood up with her back to him.

Kee struggled to sit up.

Isabel, alerted by some sense she could not name, knew he had moved and spun around to face him.

"You must be thirsty."

"Isabel, I'm a lot of things, but mostly I'm sorry. Sorry—"

"For getting involved with me," she finished for him. She closed her eyes, her arms wrapped around her waist as if to protect herself from what was coming.

Seeing the way she stood as if braced for some verbal blow, Kee pushed to his feet. He swayed for a few moments, but forced himself to move around the fire to her. What he had to say needed some closeness. He needed that.

He touched her shoulder and felt the shudder that trembled through her. "Isabel, I said I was sorry for a lot of things, but the one thing I'm not sorry about is meeting you. I'm not sorry I got involved in your problems. What I regret is that I acted like a damn fool kid and nearly got you killed. I'll live with that for the rest of my life. I've taken risks, but I never put someone else's life at risk. I did that to you. I can never make that up to you. I only ask that you forgive me."

Kee kept his hand on her shoulder, but raised his

wounded one to lift her chin with the tips of his fingers. One look at her eyes, still bright with unshed tears, and the physical pain of his wound disappeared, buried beneath the knowledge that he had indeed risked both their lives. Words tumbled from his lips.

"Forgiveness isn't enough, Isabel. I couldn't live with myself if I caused you injury or—"

"No." She silenced him with her fingertips. "Do not say the word. We are here. We made it. Do not punish yourself. You did not hold a gun on me and say I had to follow you. I made that choice. I was frightened."

She studied his face, wanting to brush back that one unruly lock of hair that fell across his forehead. In his eyes she read the truth of his words. There was something else for her to see. Humbling himself was not easy for him. His hand kneaded her shoulder and his warmth enveloped her. Just his touch was enough to distract her from everything.

"Kee, please. When you touch me…I have trouble with these feelings between us."

"Passion, Isabel," he whispered, touched by her honesty. "Desire. Me for you. And I believe you for me."

With a desperation born of a strong will, she closed her eyes, and her heart, against him. "It cannot be. Not now. I must do as I have promised. I cannot allow that Apache witch to win. For her winning will mean our deaths."

"Isabel." He feathered her name over her lips, touching them with his own for a brief, all too brief, moment. "I want you." He nuzzled her ear, inhaling the sage-clean scent of her hair. The thought of her bathing alone while he was out of his head, unable to protect her, provoked a devilish feeling of possession. "You're mine. And I'll wait," he whispered, cupping her satin-smooth cheek with his slightly rough palm.

"Know this for the truth. I'm a very, very patient man when I want something. And I'll be very gentle with you."

Her senses all exploded. There was no mistaking the promise of his words in his steamy gaze. She shivered like a small leaf caught by a storm wind. He drew her like no other man with his gentle touch and his bold promise that took nothing from her but what she wished to give.

And Isabel knew she wished to give to Kee Kincaid the very passion she had just denied him.

A hot, tense knot formed deep inside her. She had only to lean a little closer and he would kiss her. Kiss her into a world where only desire ruled, where promises and obligation had no place. But afterward…what would there be for her?

Kee knew enough about women to understand the sudden turbulence of her unfocused gaze. He sensed her inner battle and knew she wavered. One little push and he'd have what he wanted. Isabel. All sweetly heated, giving and taking, no holding back. Her eyes drew him in, tempted him to whisper the right words, but never a promise of tomorrow.

But the good Lord, who watched over fools and innocents, used His own branding iron to sear both conscience and a few painful places that quickly disabused Kee of any idea to seduce Isabel from her choice.

For now, he allowed.

"You, lovely lady," he muttered, turning away and raking one hand through his hair, "must ride with a whole bevy of saints' protection. Just as well, too. I'd hate loving you in a rush.''

Low as his muttering was, Isabel heard him. She struggled to keep the hurt from her voice.

''You would never give up your freedom to love a woman, Kee. Your spirit is too restless. And a woman would buy herself a world of hurt to love a man who could not settle down with her. A woman, Kee, needs to make a home for the man she loves. She needs to see her dreams in his eyes. She needs to know that her dreams are in his heart. And she would want to work beside him, loving him, as he made his own dreams come true.''

She had succeeded in hiding the hurt, but not a touch of bitterness. She saw his back stiffen.

''You're talking about marriage, Isabel.''

''Yes,'' she whispered, sealing her fate with that one word. And when his continued silence frayed already strained nerves, she added, ''I need to give my body to the man who will treasure my love, Kee. The women in my family love but once.''

Kee grabbed hold of a limb above his head to steady himself. Marriage! Why, of all the females in the territory, did he have to find one holding out for marriage? And why had she said that about the women in her family?

She couldn't know what was said about the Kincaid men. There was only one woman for them. His adoptive father, his uncles, all three had escaped the wedding noose until that one special woman had come into their lives. Then there was no stopping them from having that woman as wife, mate, heart's love.

But he didn't have the Kincaid blood in him although he carried their name.

The same couldn't be said of him.

Could it?

He wasn't ready to settle down. There were too many trails he hadn't ridden, too many places he had not seen. He'd even avoided the marriage trap a time or two. But here came this black-haired, blue-eyed witch with all the feminine tempting wiles...

Hold it! a sane voice whispered.

When did Isabel tease and tempt?

She breathed, Kee thought. For him that was all the temptation needed to arouse him into an ache that would not quit.

How the hell had he gone from apology to this far too serious and undesired talk of marriage? He needed a distraction, and fast. Real fast or he'd be saying something he'd likely regret in the morning.

"You should rest, Kee. There has been no sign of them. We should be safe here until morning."

Her soft voice so full of concern for him sliced through him like a heated knife. Anger would be good right about now. He couldn't summon a spit's worth for her, or against her.

Without being conscious of it, Kee had taken in every aspect of the camp she had chosen. It was a good one. He had a field of vision of the stream, but not the horses. He could also look up and see the canyon's top. If he'd been awake and working, he couldn't have chosen a better place.

"This Apache woman, how did you get tangled with her?"

"I spent a good part of the night trying to sort out Clarai's desire to kill."

"Clarai her name?" *This is good,* he told himself.

Don't look at Isabel. Keep your mind on that Apache and her wicked knife.

"Her Apache name," Isabel said. "I believe it means *moon*. She was always a troublesome child, angry all the time, and she hated Walz. He did not want her, and Ken-tee wanted him, so she left the child behind."

Isabel moved to the fire where she had kept coffee warm at its edge. She poured out a cup and asked Kee if he wanted any.

Kee hunkered down near the fire, taking the cup from her, careful not to touch her. The coffee was just the way he liked it, thick enough to float a horseshoe.

"You told me that the Apache believed Ken-tee betrayed them. What happened to her?"

Isabel hugged her raised knees and stared at the fire. "They came in the night and raided Walz's home. They captured Ken-tee. There were people around. They managed to rescue her, but not in time to save her life. The Apache had cut out her tongue and she died within the hour. So Clarai had two reasons to hate Walz. Of course, all this happened years ago. He took up with a Mexican woman when he moved on."

"Isabel, I can understand her hating the man, but he is dead. Almost two years now. And that doesn't explain why she is after the gold."

"To keep me from having it. My grandmother will lose her land if she does not have the gold needed to fight the claim that it is not a legal grant."

Kee refilled his cup. "I know what it's like to fight for your land. The family that adopted me went through their own hell fighting cattle rustlers, outlaws robbing their mine payrolls and dodging more than a few hired guns who wanted them dead. But getting back to this Clarai. You speak of her as if you know her very well.''

She heard his unspoken question. Isabel toyed with the end of her braid, and wondered how much she should tell him. Would Kee still look at her with that hunger in his eyes if he knew the truth?

''Look, Isabel, if I'm probing where I shouldn't, tell me. But this woman tried to kill me, and she's obviously after you. I think I have a right to know just where this vindictiveness comes from.''

She tossed her braid behind her shoulder and looked at him. She was not ashamed. If it mattered so much to him, then he was not the man she thought he was.

''The relationship is complicated.''

''Try me.'' He was pushing, but wasn't about to stop. She had been hiding things from the beginning. Things he needed to know if they were both to stay alive.

The words were dragged from her. ''My grandmother and Ken-tee's mother were sisters. Clarai is my cousin.''

He studied her, thinking of his own assessment that her olive gold skin came from heritage and not from the sun. He gazed at her black hair that gleamed like a raven's wing, and noted again, the delicately drawn features. And then he smiled.

''Isabel, complicated or not, the combination however it came about, resulted in one very beautiful woman.''

Her mouth parted in surprise as she stared at him. Where was the scorn she had feared?

''What did I say?''

She could not stop the blush that heated her cheeks. ''You just surprised me, Kee. I know how most whites feel about those of mixed blood, especially here in the territory.''

''So I won't sleep so easy because you're part Apache? It's a little late to worry about that. I don't care.''

''My grandmother is the beautiful one. She is not a full blood. Her father was a Spanish soldier who fell in love with her mother and the land. When my grandfather first saw her, she was still a child, but he swore even then that he would marry her one day. His father disowned him, and then, when the older sons died one by one, he finally welcomed my grandfather back to his house.''

''You've never said anything about your parents.''

''They died when diphtheria swept through our village.''

''You were young, weren't you?'' He tossed out the last of the coffee and set his cup aside. Then stood up.

''Yes, I was young. A little while later Clarai came to live with us. My grandmother felt sorry for her and begged to have her.''

''Hell of a way to repay her kindness.''

''My grandmother was kind and understanding to her. But Clarai always wanted more than she had. She was insanely jealous. And vicious. I remember once when we were having a fiesta and grandmother made new gowns for us both. Clarai was happy enough with hers until she saw that mine had more lace. The next morning I found my gown cut to pieces.'' She shook her head over the memory and others that came quickly to mind.

Kee prowled outside. The afternoon sun was bright and he shaded his eyes as he studied the canyon's rim.

''Isabel, I think we should eat and then ride on. I

don't want to give them time to circle around. There is only one way out of here. It would be a good place for them to ambush us."

He turned and saw that she was digging close to the fire.

"What are you doing?"

"I knew you would be hungry. I found a small pocket of clay and baked the fish I caught in it. They should be cooked now."

Kee looked bemused. "You continue to surprise me, lovely one. When we're done, you'll have to tell me exactly where we need to go to get your gold."

Isabel paused and leaned back on her heels. "Kee, I do not want you to come with me."

He spun around. "Not come with you? If you think I'll let you ride out with those hombres ready to kill, you've got another think coming, lady."

"Do not snap at me. I mean it. Clarai swears she will kill you. Do you think I want your death on my conscience? You have done so much for me. I can never thank you enough. I will find a way to reward you, Kee."

"Hold it." He came to stand beside her, looking down at her with all the pent-up fury of a very confused man.

"I thought we had this settled, Isabel. But just think again. You're not going alone. I don't care about what that Apache witch swore. I'm not so easy to kill. You're not going alone. And I don't want to hear one more word about it. And forget your damn reward, too. I'm doing this to help you." He took a deep breath, then another for good measure. It hissed out from between his clenched teeth. "You're a contrary

She was ready to argue with him, but his face appeared as intimidating as a clenched fist. Now, she had lost her chance. But only for now.

"Where are we going, Kee?" She struggled to guide her horse around the boulder-choked canyon floor and keep him in sight.

"There's an old man I want to see. We should reach his place by nightfall."

"But I thought you wanted to head to the mine?"

"We'll get there. I want some supplies. I'm running low on bullets. Besides, no one knows these mountains like Old Man Reavis. He is a cantankerous old coot. Lives like a hermit."

Isabel rode alongside Kee. She turned back a few more times, but there was no one to see. Yet the feeling they were being watched persisted.

"If the man lives like a hermit, how can you get any supplies from him?"

"That old man makes more money selling vegetables to the miners than they do panning or hard-rocking for gold. Some say he's got quite a stash buried somewhere on his ranch. I've heard that one year he made almost five thousand dollars, and in any man's language that's a mother lode strike. But more important to me, Reavis can tell us if anyone else besides those four are prowling these mountains. The Indians leave him alone. They believe he's crazy and has the protection of the gods. And he, well, I can't explain more. You'll have to see for yourself."

Isabel did not answer him. Kee said there were only four, but that could not be true. She had seen one more. The one man Clarai would not be without, for Vasa was truly all that was evil, a man without conscience, who killed for sport.

Struggling to remain calm, Isabel thought of her terrifying escape from Alf, then finding Kee and the passion that exploded between them. The harrowing trail and Kee's open wound had chased thoughts of Vasa and his whereabouts from her mind.

She had to tell Kee. Had to ask him where the man was. As soon as they stopped at this man's ranch.

But Kee had neglected to tell her that the small ranch cleaved into the side of a canyon with walls thousands of feet high. There was only one entrance, and that almost as terrifying as coming down that mountain trail. She was exhausted by the perilous climb but followed Kee.

Nearly asleep in the saddle, Isabel jerked awake when a bullet spat rock too close to their horses.

"Reavis," Kee called out, "we're friendly. Need to buy a few supplies. Hold your fire, I'm coming in."

Kee turned to Isabel. "I know you're tired, but wait here for me. I don't trust that old coot not to take a notion that he needs a woman if he gets a good look at you. I'm not about to lose you to him, or to anyone else."

He set his spur to Outlaw then pulled up and turned back to her. "I meant what I said, Isabel. Wait right here for me. Bury any fool thought of going off by yourself."

His voice took on a low, dark, almost threatening tone. "I'd follow you to hell if I had to."

"Kee," she whispered when he was out of sight, "why is it you do not see that hell is where you are going if you stay with me?"

Kee rode up to the ramshackle house. A lantern glowed near the doorway but there was no sign of Reavis. In the corral the burros moved restlessly, and

Outlaw snorted. The horse pawed the earth, tossing his head as if to warn his rider that he didn't like this place. Kee ordered him to settle down and waited while Reavis took the time to size him up. Kee would have done the same to any man riding out in the dark.

The old, dry voice came from behind Kee. "You sit mighty easy, stranger."

"Ain't got no reason not to. Kee Kincaid's the name. Like I said, I need supplies. Hear tell you make a practice of helping out a man now and again."

"No charity, mister."

"Ain't asking for any. Need two sides of bacon, coffee and flour if you can spare some. Wouldn't mind having a few potatoes, too."

Kee heard the odd shuffle as the old man moved around to stand in front of him. His clothes were in shreds, his hairy chest nearly bare and he held a Sharps .50 buffalo gun pointed at Kee. The gun would open a hole in a man as big as a fist. Kee paid no mind to his slight build; he watched the coldest pair of eyes he'd seen study him.

After a few tense minutes, Reavis scratched his long white beard. "Fetch your horse over yonder. Water's sweet mountain cold. Don't get much company. Don't want any. But you look like a decent sort. That your woman waiting down below?"

"My wife," Kee snapped. "Bringing her home to my folks over by Sweetwater."

"Goin' the long way?"

"Going until I get there," Kee answered. He led the mustang to the water trough, ground-tying him while he followed the old man inside. Kee held his breath. Musty air mixed with rancid smells. The place was a cluttered hodgepodge of blankets and pans, shovels and picks, barrels and boxes.

Kee almost regretted having stopped here, but the nearest place would be a ride to the Silver King Mine or down to Globe, and he felt time was slipping by too fast for Isabel to get her gold to help her grandmother.

While the old man busied himself in the back, Kee opened two buttons on his shirt and took out a twenty-dollar gold piece from his money belt. But there was something else in his belt. A round disk from the feel of it. He wasn't about to take it out here and examine what it was, but he knew he had had nothing like it.

Isabel. She had plenty of opportunity. But why give him...

"Here you go. Only had four potatoes to spare. Just come back from selling off what I had."

Kee opened the sack that Reavis handed to him. The bacon had no rancid smell, and there was coffee and flour. He handed over the gold piece.

"You seen many strangers around these parts in the last day or so?"

"Four or five riders come through about three days ago. Didn't stop. Didn't let them."

"Any Apache?"

Reavis squinted at him. "Them that escape the reservations head south. You run into trouble with them?"

"Not Apache. But I ran into a little trouble. Wasn't anything I couldn't handle, but a man likes to know who's riding his back trail these days."

Kee watched the old man bite down on the gold piece and then he smiled. "Real enough. Don't cotton to most folks. Wouldn't be livin' here if I did. Now, those riders I seen, wouldn't be invitin' a one of them to set at my fire.''

He stared at Kee, scratching at his hairy chest. ''If you want, bring your missus on up. It pleases me some to see a lady.''

''Another time. She's shy as a spooked deer when it comes to meeting folks. Sure appreciate the supplies. Don't suppose you could spare a box of .44s for me?''

With a cagey expression the man waved toward the buffalo gun. ''Know you seen that, saw for myself you know the kind of hole she'd make.''

Kee smiled, but it never reached his eyes. ''You didn't fire that warning shot with the Sharps. Sounded like a brand-new Winchester to me. Like the one on the box covered with sacking. Man wouldn't have a rifle like that without the bullets to use it.''

Reavis stopped scratching and scowled up at him. ''Mister, that'll cost you another gold piece.''

''Now I know why they say you earn more than a miner, old man. Throw in two blankets and you got a deal.''

''Ain't no damn store,'' he muttered, turning back into the maze of stacked goods.

''If you find a spare canteen back there, I'd be mighty grateful.''

''You don't stack up like no greenhorn, mister,'' Reavis grumbled. ''How come you be needing so much?''

''Like I said, I've run into a little trouble. And you keep a sharp eye out, Reavis, those hombres are the killing kind.''

Reavis returned and held out two blankets to Kee. They smelled musty, but were soft, brand-new-soft, army issue. Kee didn't ask where he'd gotten them.

The canteen was battered a bit, but in the dim light Kee didn't find any cracks. He shoved them into the stack along with the box of bullets.

"These hombres got a fine-looking black woman with them?"

"No. An Apache hellcat."

"Didn't figure it could be Julia Thomas. She's been hunting Walz's gold since he died and told her where to find the mine. They ain't gonna find it. That quake changed the look of the land."

"You figure to look some?" Kee asked.

"Ain't looking to die, mister. Best you ride for shelter if you won't stay on. Storm's coming up. Can smell it in the wind."

Kee hadn't reacted when Reavis told him about Julia Thomas, but he smiled now. "That's the best news I've had. Rain's just what I need."

Reavis shook his head, but other than a funny look he didn't ask what he meant.

Outside, Kee sensed the change in the air himself. The temperature had dropped. He mounted and rode back to where he'd left Isabel. Hoping, despite his threat, that she had waited for him.

She came out of the dark holding the rifle. "Kee?"

"None other."

"Something is spooking the horses."

She came up to him, pulling on the lead rope.

"Storm's coming." Kee slid back on his saddle. "Come on, ride with me. It's not that far to shelter." He tied off the lead rope to his saddle, then extended his boot in the stirrup for her to mount.

"You're shivering, Isabel. I'm sorry."

"Not your fault." She had been cold, but now his

body heat surrounded her. "Did you get what you wanted?"

"From Reavis, yes."

She bit her lip rather than respond to the underlying innuendo.

"He told me that still another party's looking for that gold. Julia Thomas. Ever heard of her?"

"She was the last woman that Walz lived with. He supposedly told her exactly where the mine is."

"Yeah, that's what Reavis said. He agreed with me though, about how that quake changed the landmarks. And another thing. That old man's eyesight's failing. He thought he'd seen five riders a few days back. I figure it had to be your cousin and the others. But I didn't see a fourth man."

She leaned back against him, sinking into his warmth and his strength. Weariness assailed her.

"Isabel, did you hear me?"

"I heard you, Kee. There is another man. Vasa. Clarai would not ride without him. I do not know where he was when you met up with her and the others. I saw him. He is a man who kills for sport."

"He wasn't there when I had my run-in with them. Which reminds me—" he leaned close to whisper since the wind was rising "—why did you take off without me? And where did you go?"

"Not now, Kee." She felt the weight of his arm across her stomach, holding her tight against him. "How can you see where we are going?"

"I spotted a place when we rode into the canyon. The moonlight was brighter then."

Kee let his unanswered questions go. He would wait. Right now he used the little moonlight the scudding clouds allowed to light the landmarks he had spotted earlier. The sudden change in Outlaw's gait told him they were on dry sand in the wash he wanted.

He slid from the saddle before Isabel realized what he was doing.

"Wait, Kee. I do not want to stay alone again."

"There's a cave above. I want to make sure there are no snakes."

"Snakes? I hate them."

"Me, too, lovely lady."

Kee walked on. There was plenty of dead wood, left behind by flash floods. He found what he was looking for, a fairly long, straight piece, and pulled some of the dry grass which he wrapped around the wood. Closer to the mouth of the cave which water had cut from the rock, he sheltered his makeshift torch from the wind and lit it.

Inside the place was high and dry. For a change luck ran with him, the cave was long and deep enough to shelter the horses, too.

Luck remained with him as he poked the torch into crevices and found no sign of snakes. A loose ring of stones and one fire-blackened wall told him others had camped here. The sandy floor was dry, leading him to believe it had been a long time since water had flowed through this cave.

The one thing he wanted was a safe place during the storm. He had been caught a time or two on high peaks when lightning leaped from peak to peak and sometimes in sheets of blue flame.

By the time he gathered wood and got the horses settled, the first raindrops fell. Thunder rolled in the great empty halls of rock, but in the inner cave where Isabel had started the fire all sounds were muted.

He saw how she rubbed her arms to ward off the

cold. Taking the two blankets from the sack, he went to stand behind her.

"They're clean, but musty," he said, wrapping first one then the other around her shoulders. She turned to look up at him, a smile on her lips. Firelight bathed her face with golden shadows and somewhere deep inside, his breath caught and held at her loveliness. He felt just like the hard, dry wood catching fire and set to burn for a good long time.

The end of her long braid brushed the earth and he was arrested by the thought that Isabel belonged to this land—wild, free and unspoiled by any man's hand. His gaze held hers. He longed to know if her soft, golden skin gracing her face and neck was the same all over—her breasts, her belly, her thighs, between her legs.

Hunger filled him with a violent rush. Were her nipples the same lush, dusky color as her generously shaped mouth?

His hands clenched over the blanket he had placed around her shoulders, and a low, rough sound rumbled in his throat. Then he looked away. She was a woman meant for some man's marriage bed, and as much as he ached to taste her and show what passion could be like between them, he wasn't about to beg.

She reached up to touch his hand with hers. "Kee? What is wrong?"

He heard the longing in her voice, saw it in her eyes that searched his face. He turned away, and then forced himself to walk around the fire and put distance between them. It was the only way he could keep his hands off her.

Isabel no longer looked at his face, but his hands. She saw not so much their strength but their gentleness when he touched her. A quiver of heat trembled through her that had nothing to do with the warming fire or the soft wool blankets. But she looked up and their gazes clashed. Kee's was suddenly guarded.

"Bet you're hungry. I got two slabs of bacon off Reavis. Flour, too. Might as well eat then bed down."

"Yes," she whispered, taking in the full power of his dark, intense stare. Then she shook her head, as if to ward off the spell of him, and remind herself what was at stake.

"I am hungry, Kee. Hungry for food."

"I know. More's the pity." The corner of his mouth curled up, the smile cynical. But the sadness in her eyes made him turn away with the feeling that he had somehow pushed too hard.

Isabel wanted to be out in the storm. The rain would cool the heat he stirred with his every move and breath. Out there, in the darkness, the wind blew with a wildness that equaled the beat of her pulse. She did not understand why she felt so defenseless. Kee had done nothing to defend against. It was herself. She was fighting herself.

"I will cook. You can make coffee," she said in a brisk tone. And refused to look at him again.

Kee found that he had his own waterspout right outside the cave mouth. Rainwater came down in a steady stream and filled the coffeepot in a few minutes. Wind gusted and sent rain against him, but he welcomed the coolness. It was going to be a long, long night.

When he returned to the fire he found that Isabel was neatly slicing one slab of bacon. He had never seen the knife she held. It was smaller than either of his, about ten inches from tip to handle and she wielded it with a skill that came from long use.

The pan was just hot enough to sizzle when she laid the strips in it.

"Mighty handy with that blade," he remarked, too restless to sit.

"You carry one on your belt and one hidden on that leather thong that hangs down your back. I carry this one in my boot." She wiped off the edge of the blade on the corner of the blanket, then plunged it into the sand and wiped it off again. Knowing that Kee watched her every move, she extended her leg, hiked up her pants and slid the knife into the sheath sewn inside her boot.

He bent down across from her. "Mighty handy, like I said. You have any more hidden weapons I should know about?"

Something in his too calm voice alerted her that Kee was anything but calm. She shook her head, watching him with the instinctive wary sense of prey.

"No? How about this, then?" He opened two buttons on his shirt, slipped his fingers into one pocket of his money belt and pulled out the round piece of metal. It was gold, and pierced with odd cuts. He held it up by his fingertips and examined it. A crescent slice, and what appeared to be a series of narrowing arrowheads and one jagged line that combined made no sense to him.

"It belongs to me. When I left you, I knew that Clarai was close. She must not get her hands on that."

"You're not telling me what this is."

"It belonged to my grandfather, Kee, and it means a great deal to me. I left it with you for safekeeping."

What she did not say, but had thought, was that he would never know it was there. How could she know that he would find a place to buy supplies?

"May I have it now?" She held out her hand for the gold disk, all the imperious arrogance of their first meeting back in her voice and her eyes.

Kee grinned. And it wasn't a nice one. He tucked the disk back into his money belt and watched disbelief spread across her face.

"I'll hang on to this for now. Since you thought it was safe with me and all."

"But there is no reason—"

"You still trust me, don't you, Isabel?"

His dark, intense eyes were waiting to snare hers when she looked up.

"Yes." The word was choked. *Yes, I trust you, but I do not trust myself.*

"What else should we talk about? I know, you were going to tell me why the hell you took off on your own. Especially when you knew those men and your cousin were nearby. Then you might explain why you neglected to tell me about this Vasa. Nothing like the thought of an extra killer riding your back trail when you think you've got all the players figured."

The intensity was all in his eyes. His voice maintained that same infuriating calm. Isabel heaved a sigh and sat back from the fire.

"When I saw that your wound was not serious, I left you so that I could find Clarai. I did not want them to find you and kill you."

"You're so sure that's what she intends to do?"

"Yes." Her voice hissed out from between clenched teeth. Isabel took a deep, shuddering breath. How could she make him understand about her cousin?

"Get back to her later. Why didn't you tell me about Vasa?"

"When I found you again, or you found me, I had just escaped from Alf and was trying to stop you from walking into their trap.

"And when you found me, we did not talk, Kee. We...we..." She looked away unable to put those brand-new feelings into words.

Kee had no such trouble. "We kissed, Isabel." *And I'm still aching from it.*

"Yes, we kissed. And then we rode through the night, until we came to that devil-made trail. There was no time to ask questions, and you certainly were not thinking about anything but—"

"Taking you down beneath me and finding out if your lovely golden skin is the same shade all over."

The words slid out beneath his guard and it was too late to recall them. The hitch in her breathing, the widening of those dark-blue eyes acted like a steel spur raking over his body. Each tiny claw sank deep inside him, and this time he was the one who looked away.

Had he thought it was merely going to be a long night? *Hellishly long* might describe it.

"Something's burning."

"I know," she snapped. She wrapped a corner of the blanket around her hand as protection from the heat and pulled the pan back from the fire. Would that she could so easily pull herself away from the fire in his eyes, and the heat of his voice.

Kee abruptly stood up. "You eat. I'm not hungry."

Having been pushed far enough, Isabel looked up at him through thick, black lashes. "You are a liar, Kee."

Even to her own ears the accusation sounded more like an invitation.

"Sure enough. But we both know what I'm hungry for. Don't we?"

She made a helpless sound. She even bit her lip so she would not answer him. But he stood, tall and lean, all waiting stillness his to command and she whispered the one word he wanted to hear.

"Yes."

He didn't feel like smiling even though he'd won something with her admission. If anything, he felt as if he'd lost something.

Maybe that's why he didn't stop the taunt. "And what is it that you want, Isabel? And don't tell me it's the gold. That's not what I mean. No quick answer. I'll wait. And you can think about it."

Chapter Fifteen

Isabel did nothing but think about Kee while he either stayed in the front of the cave or prowled outside in the rain.

She thought of him wounded and helpless. She thought of how she had touched him, how the dark mat of hair that formed a diamond-shaped wedge on his chest was as soft as it looked. She remembered her fingertips tracing the line of his lips. And later, as curiosity got the better of her, she had traced the small scars on his back and chest.

Truly, Kee was made to be a woman's temptation. His hair was thick, like his eyelashes. She even admired the shape of his ears. And smiled to herself at the very innocence of all her exploration.

She stared into the fire, hugging her knees and saw his smile that invited her to share it. He had asked her what she wanted besides the gold. And she knew the answer. Just as she knew that time was running out before she would give it voice.

Kee stared out at the darkness. The rain slacked off, but the wind remained. He should have his mind on anything and everything but Isabel. How much longer would she deny that wild, hidden sensuality that was awake and growing? He shifted his stance to ease rapidly hardening flesh, but the move was useless. He wasn't going to get rid of this ache alone.

He licked his lips and thought of tastes that were sweeter, hotter and smooth as satin to his tongue. Isabel's taste, her lips.

"Hell," he muttered. "You're a man not a boy. Get over it. You can't always have what you want. She's a marrying kind of woman and you're a roving kind of man. End of sermon, boy."

Outlaw butted his nose in the middle of Kee's back and shoved him outside.

"Damn horse. How come you're siding with her?"

There was no anger, nor heat. The horse had more sense than he did. Someone had to protect Isabel from him, and he was the only one present.

He had to keep remembering that Isabel was not a rain-filled pool to slake his thirst and then leave behind. She was more like a deep, sweet well, that with care, would flow endlessly to give life to a man.

It was thoughts like these that were driving him crazy. He had to stop thinking about her in terms of a forever kind of woman, when he wanted to be a today kind of man.

He reminded himself yet again that she trusted him. Hell of a burden to put on a man who didn't trust himself.

Kee's hand went to his money belt and he pressed against the disk. She'd been as vague about this as everything else until he forced her to answer.

And she never had shown him the map he believed worthless.

The sooner he helped her find the gold, if it was possible, the sooner they could part company.

That was a plan.

The plan of a desperate man, he told himself as he went back to the fire.

She had spread out a blanket for him. Her own, she had placed as far from his as she could and still keep within reach of the fire's warmth.

"Are you sleeping, Isabel?"

She lay so still with her eyes closed that he had to ask.

"I wish I could be."

"We need to talk. Not about us," he quickly added when her eyes flew open and targeted him.

"I want to look at your map now. Even if the landmarks changed, I still might be able to figure out where the mine is. You know that the sooner we try getting to that gold, the quicker we can get out of these mountains. And you'll be safe."

Isabel heard him, but she silently felt his desire to be rid of her. She sat up slowly, drawing the blanket around her shoulders. The damp spots on his shirt told her he had been out in the rain. A few drops still glistened in his hair. She felt his restlessness and the tension that held him so still.

She threw a few small pieces of wood on the fire, staring at the flames.

"Isabel?" Kee stepped closer, and now he could see that she had been crying. Her lashes were wet, spiked together above the sheen of her blue eyes. The thought that he had been the cause sent a pang through him. He could no more stop himself from moving around the fire to her than he could stop breathing.

He dropped to his knees and cupped her cheek to

turn her face toward him. The moment he touched her he knew he was piling up grief for himself.

"If I made you shed tears, I'm sorry. Seems I'm saying that a lot to you. I've never deliberately hurt a woman. I never want to hurt you."

She reached up to touch the errant lock of hair that fell over his forehead. *Tell him!* a little voice demanded. *Tell him about Clarai's obsession. Tell him that your need to protect his life overshadows your desire for him.*

"I know you would never hurt me. I know a great deal about you, Kee. I have never trusted anyone the way I trust you."

"Don't, Isabel," he whispered, then closed his eyes against the truth of her words that he saw in her eyes.

"But I must. You need to know that." *It is so little to give you.*

Her fingertips trailed down the side of his face. To her, even the rough beard stubble that added to his dark and dangerous appearance was pleasurable to touch. Everything about him was pleasing to her eyes, and a temptation to her senses. His scent was of the rain-swept night, and she inhaled deeply, bringing a flush to tint her skin.

Kee noted the slight flare of her nostrils that mimicked his own. He watched her unconscious move to moisten her bottom lip with the tip of her tongue. The wavering firelight played over her face, a face whose changing expressions he hadn't grown tired of watching.

"Talk to me, lovely lady. Talk is safer for both of us."

"Oh, Kee," she whispered still cupping his face, "safe is one of the things I have felt since I met you."

He moved without thought to bring her hand to his mouth and nip the fleshy pad below her thumb. He saw the darkening flare in her eyes and did it again. Then, remembering his promise to himself, he set her hand in her lap.

"Safe wasn't exactly what I had in mind." He could not seem to stop himself from touching her, and smoothed back a few loose tendrils of hair that had escaped her braid.

"But it is true, Kee. Out there you make me feel very safe being with you."

"And in here?"

"In here you present every dangerous temptation that my grandmother, the good sisters and the padre warned against."

"So," he teased, "I'm safe, but dangerous and a temptation to you?"

"And dependable. Trustworthy, too. A man of honor, Kee. That is who you are."

"Quit now, Isabel. You're making more of me than I am."

"No." She shook her head to enforce that denial. "You are all of those things. You are goodness and kindness, too. And you have within you, Kee, a gentleness that is more powerfully appealing than another's strength."

He had to look away for a moment. "Isabel, you can burden a man with words like those."

"I did not mean to. I only spoke the truth. What I feel in my heart."

Kee shifted so they sat with their hips touching. He slipped his hand beneath her braid, cupping the back of her neck as he drew her closer so her head rested on his shoulder.

"Kee, your wound," she protested.

"Doesn't hurt a bit. I just want to hold you. Need to, since we're into truth telling. Can't get into too much trouble sitting like this."

Isabel was not sure about that. He stroked her braid but she felt the smooth move of his hand caressing her back. She wanted and needed this holding as much as Kee. Here there was a peace for her, listening to the faint sound of the dripping rain, the crackle of the fire, Kee's steady breathing. There was warmth, too, from the soft wool blanket, and the fire. But from Kee's body came heat and the strength that silently whispered she could lean against him. For a little while she could mentally shut the door on the worries and fears that gnawed at her.

Kee wanted to talk, and she had told him she knew a great deal about the man he was. She believed it. She knew the man, but not where he had come from, or who were the people that mattered in his life. The ones who had shaped this man who meant more to her than she could tell him.

"Tell me about your family. How did the Kincaids come to adopt you?"

"My real folks never had much. They had spent too many years trying to make worn-out land pay and it cost them what little they had put by. It was too late to join one of the wagon trains, so we headed out west on our own."

"You had no other family to help you, Kee?"

"Nope. Just the three of us making do. But we met up with another family that had a boy a little younger than me and we traveled a good piece together.

"Wasn't far above Apache Junction when they found some color in a stream. They started to pan for gold and the Apaches attacked, killed our folks and left Marty and me orphans. Sagebrush orphans they called kids like us.''

''But how did you survive, Kee, if you were only a boy and with another child to care for?'' She started to lift her head, but his hand held her in place.

''Stay where you are, Isabel. It's a perfect fit.'' He brushed his fingertips over the delicate curve of her ear and barely caught the soft contented sound she made before he went back to his story.

''Surviving wasn't all that hard. My pa hailed out of the Tennessee woods and taught me all he knew. I'd been hunting meat for the table as soon as I could hold up the shooting end of a rifle. And when you're given two bullets to bring home supper, you learn to make them count or you and your family go hungry.

''That's where I was that day the Indians attacked. I was hunting with Marty, trying to teach him a few things. Poor kid had been raised in a city and didn't know the first thing about moving quietly in the woods or setting a snare. The Apache had run off all the stock, and burned one of the wagons. We had a place to stay, had water, and,'' he said with a laugh, ''we discovered this widow who kept chickens. Marty sure had a fondness for chickens and eggs. I bartered fish and rabbit, sometimes venison.

''Truth was, Jesse, who's my mother now, she didn't exactly know we were kids. We kept out of her sight most of the times until the day we found Logan Kincaid. Marty was scared into stuttering so bad I could hardly understand him.''

''You love him. I hear it in your voice.''

''Yeah. I love him. We've become close as brothers although we don't see each other much these days.

Turned out his father came from a wealthy family and with his death Marty inherited businesses and stocks that keep him in Chicago a lot.''

She heard the regret in his voice, and thought of what being loved by Kee would mean to a woman. She would never worry about having her man beside her no matter what joy or troubles were there to be shared.

She was drawn from her thoughts by Kee sliding his hand beneath her braid and rubbing every bit of tension from her back. She made a kittenlike sound of utter contentment and nuzzled her face against his chest. She knew she should move, it would be safer for both of them, but his very gentleness held her there.

''Talk to me, please, Kee.''

''I thought I was.''

She could not help but smile. ''With words, Kee, with words.''

''Anything the lady wants. Let's see…Marty and me were on our own for a few weeks when we found Logan. He had been left for dead by a mean bunch. We figured he was dead 'cause they took everything worth having from him. There we were, two scared kids, and yes, I was more scared than Marty and trying hard not to show it. We were going to bury him so the buzzards wouldn't get him.

''Neither one of us wanted to touch him, so I was using the rifle stock to sort of dig around his body, and Marty was green as grass when all of a sudden Logan started moving. Marty's thinking how brave I am for standing my ground. Truth was, I'd never been so scared. I didn't know what to do with him. I mean, he was hurt bad.

"And then I remembered Pa saying that every woman wants a man of her own." Kee stopped, and then he laughed.

"From that I gather this Jesse was not pleased with your idea."

"I found that out later. Much later. The outlaws Logan had been riding with were still looking for him. Seems their boss wanted to see the body for himself. There were some scary times before Logan took me and Marty home with him. And Jesse. He sure did take to that widow. Wasn't any kin back home, so when he asked if I wanted to be part of his family, what kid wouldn't say yes. Took me in like I was born one of them. Grandmother, uncles, aunt and even a new baby."

"And you would do anything for them?" She knew the answer. This man would give his love and his loyalty to his family. She loved this Kee, with his soft, husky voice, and the smile that curved the masculine cut of his lips. Memories had brought a gleam to his eyes. He was a man a woman could search for and never find. Unless she was very lucky. With a deep sigh she turned her thoughts away from what could be.

"Your family is wealthy, Kee?"

"They have enough. My uncle Conner is a lawman. Uncle Ty and my dad run the ranch and oversee the mines. Aunt Dixie and my mother look after everything else including a brood of children. Reina—she's Ty and Dixie's oldest—is a little hellion in the making. She is always getting into scrapes."

"And you get her out of them?"

"Wise, wise, Isabel. What's a fella to do? She turns her big brown eyes in my direction and I'm helpless as a new foal. Her brothers Justin and James are no better. Trouble is, they're all teaching little Macaria, that's my uncle Conner's oldest girl, every trick they've learned.'' He sighed, and allowed the memories of the years past to flow over him.

''You miss your family, Kee?'' Isabel lifted her head, needing to see him.

''Yes, I've been away almost a year this time and my grandmother grows old. You'd like her, Isabel. She is a truly strong woman. Macaria held her land and her family against a man who wanted to destroy them all. They are a family that stands together and it's a gift I've never taken lightly that I carry their name. When Marty's aunt came west searching for her brother and discovered that he was dead, she believed that Logan had kidnapped her nephew. She really made Conner put his family loyalty on the line and against the badge he wore.

''Marty and I had lied to them and said we were cousins without any kinfolks. It just seemed easier that way. Marty didn't know about his aunt. I told you there was a great deal of wealth involved, and Belinda was ready to use it against the Kincaids if they refused to give him up.

''Not one balked at using anything and everything they had to protect that child. As it turned out, Conner solved the problem.''

''Conner, he is the lawman?''

''That he is, and a man I respect.''

''What did he do to her?''

''Fell in love and married her. They're awaiting the birth of their third child last I heard. Letters have a hard time catching up when a man's on the move. I might even have two new sisters and a brother when

I get back home. Jesse and Logan weren't blessed with children of their own. They adopted these three from an orphanage back East.''

She gently pulled back a little from him, but Kee did not release his hold on her. His hand dropped to the small of her back, fingers tightening a bit to keep her near.

"What's wrong, Isabel?"

"I hear so much in your words and voice. I believe I understand now why the gold I seek holds no lure for you."

"I'm as fond of money for what it can buy as the next man. I just don't like risking my neck to be richer than I need be."

"It is because the Kincaids have money. When there is no need, no desperation, no threat about to seize all you have ever known, it is easy to walk away. But I wonder, if you faced what I do, if you would feel the same."

Her eyes narrowed, but she wasn't looking at him. Kee saw the play of firelight gleam on her lashes and brows, black and thick like a raven's feathers. Her lips appeared darker, redder where she bit them. Someone needed to take her in hand about that habit.

A mouth like hers required a delicate care. He roughly shook his head, a reminder to stop straying into forbidden territory.

"Isabel, I said I would help you any way I can. I can't offer you more than a willing back and my word. I'll find your gold and see you safe home with it. And to that end, show me the map."

"Kee, you have already seen it."

"Seen it? The disk? That's your map?"

"It is worthless to anyone else but me. I told you

my grandfather brought me here once. If you are not standing at the head of the gully and holding the disk up to the rising sun, you will never find the entrance to the mine.''

''That's why you were so upset when I told you about the quake changing the landmarks.''

''Yes.''

There was a world of defeat in that one word. And it touched him in ways that he didn't want to name. Not even to himself.

He caught hold of her arms and dragged her close while he came to his knees and looked down into her eyes.

''I swear to you that whatever it takes, I'll be with you. No matter how long.''

Her hands came up, pressing against the corded muscles of his belly. Her head fell back, throat bared to him.

''No matter what you have to do, Kee?'' she demanded with a burst of fury. ''And will you kill, too?'' She cried out at his tightening grip that pressed through cloth and skin to bone. ''Oh, God, Kee, I am sorry! I did not mean that! I swear I did not mean that!''

She looked into eyes that smoldered with anger, and if she needed confirmation there was his rigid jaw and the savage curve of his lips.

She went still, even her breathing was a shallow draw that barely stirred the air. He was ready to explode into violence.

''Damn you,'' he said through gritted teeth in a hair-raising whisper.

''I did not mean it,'' she pleaded.

"Doesn't matter. We both know it's the truth. That is what it will come down to."

"Kee, please—" He released her so suddenly that she fell back and before she could scramble to her feet he was gone.

Chapter Sixteen

Kee needed cooling off before his temper exploded. The rain-swept night was the best place for him.

He stumbled over rocks until he had put distance between himself and Isabel, but kept the cave's opening in view.

His beliefs were simple. The world was black and white in that there was no evil so petty that it should go unpunished, just as there was no kindness so small that it should pass without thanks.

He wasn't so much angry with Isabel, as with himself. She had only voiced a question he'd been asking himself.

One he didn't have an answer to.

Three years ago the frontier had been declared closed. But that was the opinion of lawmakers back East. They didn't live with cattle rustlers and horse thieves, bank and railroad robbers. Men out here in the territories carried guns. They were more than ready to use them against any threat to families and possessions.

Each year talk circulated about forming up a company of rangers like they had had for years down in

Texas. The rangers were needed to patrol the vast and hostile wilderness that folks back East couldn't or wouldn't understand.

And how could anyone make them understand? They had city streets lit by gas, or homes, like Marty's, lit with electricity. Trouble, call the nearest policeman. Out here, if trouble came to a man, he could ride three days without seeing another soul.

Civilized ways were coming; there never was a way to stop progress. Prescott boasted the first ice-cream parlor in the territory. Fine hotels and fancy restaurants could be found in every city and large town. Churches and schools, what his mother called "the foundations of civilization" dotted the land, even if most were just one room where all grades were taught.

He thought of his family and wished for a moment to be with his dad, his uncles, Conner and Ty. They would understand why he had to think this through.

But he couldn't forget that when threatened, those same men who taught him to never point his gun unless he meant to use it, had done whatever was needed to protect the Kincaid holdings and their women.

But Isabel isn't your woman.

And a little devil's voice answered: *She could be.*

They were both truths. He wouldn't deny them.

Kee raked his hands through his hair over and over. Then he dropped his hands to his sides and stood still, head thrown back as he stared up at the night sky.

Nothing mattered but the fact that he had given her his sworn word. He'd never go back on it.

She was a woman alone in need of his help.

For him, that was the beginning and end of the matter.

He tasted the sweet drops of rain on his lips, welcoming the coolness that the chill of night brought to his temper.

He stood that way for a few minutes more, then thoughts intruded. Thoughts of what had driven Isabel to explode with fury. What other fears did she harbor that she had not shared?

Wasn't finding out the answer part and parcel of giving her his help?

Trouble was, his need to give to Isabel was a fever in his blood and interfered with sane reasoning.

He could understand what it felt like to be a wild mustang caught in a trap.

He had nowhere to run. Nowhere to hide. Nothing to fight but himself.

Isabel proved him wrong.

She came out of the night to stand behind him and with her light touch against his back, Kee knew he might have found control of his temper, but that's all this time alone brought him.

"If you intend to remain a virgin for your precious wedding night get the hell away from me."

The tremor that went through him was felt by both of them. He pulled away with a sharp move.

All she wanted was to smooth the edges of tension from him. All she had done was sharpen them.

"I was afraid you had left, Kee."

"Right. I walked away from my horses and gear. After giving you my word, I walked away from you, too."

"You have every right to be angry with me."

"Damn straight I do."

"Come back to the cave with me. If you will not think of your wound, I will. This damp and cold might bring on a fever."

He spun around only to find her too close.

I shouldn't touch her, he thought.

But he did.

"You're worried about me getting a fever. Let me show you fever, Isabel."

Isabel released a soft, quick breath, then she felt the heat of his mouth on hers. She expected to be overwhelmed by his greater strength in the face of his anger and instinctively stiffened, ready to fight him.

But Kee would never use his strength against her.

He gave in to the need to taste her with a gentle restraint that shocked her with its leashed intensity.

Part cry of denial, part moan of desire escaped her lips, only to be taken by his. Bravely then, she returned his delicate, questing touch with the tip of her tongue.

Kee had taught her that passion had a special taste all its own.

It tasted of him.

And tasted of her.

Blended with heat until it tasted like both of them.

She could no more resist his kiss than a moth could resist the lure of flame.

His lips brushed over hers, sipping at the lush, feminine curve of her mouth. His fingers eased into her hair, finding the warmth beneath the cool strands.

He held her head cupped in his hands, gently directing a teasing dance of the softest touches.

Mouth to mouth. Breath to breath.

Need to desire.

Man to woman.

And Isabel knew she had no guard against this most tender enticement.

Nor did she want one.

She heard a faint, ragged cry. Her own. She reached

for his shoulders, needing something solid to hold on to. Her hands slid upward through the damp thickness of his hair and she brought his head down to end the teasing.

She tasted his kiss with nothing held back, and for long moments lost herself in the dizzying storm of emotion that besieged her.

Kee broke the kiss and roughly held her away from him. "Do you know," he demanded through harsh, ragged breaths, "that a man'll do and say anything when all he's got is seduction on his mind?"

"No. Yes. I—I only know what you make me feel, Kee. I cannot think, I cannot reason. I—I can only want."

"You play hell with a man, Isabel. I'm trying hard to do the right thing here. Go back. Stay away from me. Go," he released her with a small push. "Get."

Confused, she started to run, but she had forgotten the rocky ground, and the rain puddles. She stumbled, tried to catch her balance, slid and went to her knees with a cry. She clawed at the earth in an attempt to pull herself up, and brought up a fistful of mud. She tried to find purchase with her boot tips, but each try only sent her sliding farther down on the slope.

She heard Kee's cursing, but that quickly changed to concern as he called her name.

"Here. Down here, Kee."

She had no thought of pride when she felt his hands close over her wrists. She heard his grunt as he dragged her upward until she could stand.

"You're muddier than a spadefoot toad."

"Toad? You dare to call me a toad?" It was utterly ridiculous for her to feel insulted, but she did. If it hadn't been for him, she would never have fallen.

"Yeah, a toad," he muttered, running his hands quickly over her to make sure she wasn't hurt. "What were you trying to do?"

Isabel took one cautious step away from him. "I was running away. From you, Kee. Running from you and your temper. And your most contrary, confusing, yes, you want me and no, you do not!"

Her voice had grown shrill at the end, but she did not care. She swiped at the mud on her face. And she did not care that she flung a good deal of it at him.

Kee threw back his head and his rich masculine laughter floated on the night air.

Isabel did not think, she acted from the sudden flare of temper. She slapped him.

It was a sobering moment.

Kee no longer laughed.

Isabel instantly regretted what she had done.

Kee rubbed his cheek, not caring that he smeared the mud. *I should walk away,* he told himself, despite the hard, heavy running of his blood.

But once more he ignored the voice of reason.

"You know, lady, you've got one hell of a lot of nerve calling me contrary. You run hotter and colder than day and night in the desert. All I'm trying to do is protect your precious virtue."

"Who asked you to? I can protect it myself."

"Good. Never say I didn't give you the chance."

Isabel felt herself picked up with dizzying speed before she could draw a single breath. The world shifted crazily, and when it settled, she was in Kee's arms, being carried toward the cave. She knew better than to struggle with him on such uncertain footing. She was not about to send the two of them plunging down that muddy slope. But she had to brace herself against the lure to rest her head on his shoulder. And the muscular resilience of his chest was pure temptation to her aching body. She sighed. Kee had strength to spare.

Kee held her a little too close, enjoying the warm and supple feel of her against his body. He shifted her weight, silently urging her to relax.

He paused before the cave's entrance, but it was too dark for her to see his face clearly. He made no move to go inside as the horses stirred restively and his whisper calmed them.

A cascade of water fell to the side and Isabel grew alarmed.

"Kee?"

"Well, it's going to be colder than a miser's heart, but it's all we've got. So hang on."

He plunged them both beneath the icy fall that stung like needles. Isabel bit down hard on her lip not to cry out as every bit of warmth was stolen from her body. It lasted no more than a minute or two before he swung them around and away from the falling water.

"Now what, Kee?" She shivered, and barely managed to stop her teeth from chattering.

"I'm going to show you what happens to muddy spadefoot toads when it rains."

It was a flat, calm statement that belied the heat and sudden tension of his body. He ducked beneath the cave's overhang and everything dipped and swayed for her. She tightened her hold around his neck as he started past the horses.

Her breath caught and held, then came out in a rush just as she turned her face toward his open collar. The water there that touched her lips was no longer cold.

She felt the ripple of response that went through him when her lips touched his bare skin.

"Keep that up and you'll have an even better chance—"

"Of what, Kee?" She wanted it a demand, and heard her own breathless whisper. "Of learning what happens to spadefoot toads when it rains?"

"Yeah."

She shifted subtly in his arms and found him watching her with that dark intensity that arrowed right through her.

"Tell me."

And very, very softly came his husky promise.

"They mate."

Chapter Seventeen

Kee kicked a few pieces of wood on the fire and waited until they had blazed high before he set her down.

She looked like a half-wild gypsy with those dark-blue eyes pinned on him, her braid nearly undone and tangled to frame her face. The firelight tinted her high cheekbones and reddened her lips. His gaze slid down. The soaked shirt and pants clung to her body, concealing nothing from his eyes. The icy water had drawn her nipples into hard pebbles and his breath lodged somewhere in his chest.

"Let's get you out of those wet clothes before you shiver yourself to pieces."

He waited, half hoping she would do it herself, half praying that she wouldn't. He waited, too, for one word of protest, one word of denial. She knew what was going to happen. He'd warned her. And he told himself there was still time. He could still walk away.

But when Isabel made no move to undress, he took the step that separated them. His fingers went to the first horn button of his shirt that she wore. Then Kee knew he had just lied to himself.

A herd of wild horses couldn't have driven him away from her now.

Isabel pushed aside her wet hair. She was shivering, but she was not sure if it all came from the cold bath. Her body still held the imprinted shock of feeling how aroused Kee was. Warmth stole through her, tiny pulses of heat that came from the secret places of her body. She could feel the flush that blazed across her cheeks.

If these last days with Kee had taught her nothing else, she had learned how hard and powerful Kee's body was and how soft her own became when he was near. The weakness melting her bones right now had nothing to do with fear or cold. It owed everything to Kee. A man whose heat reached out to her, surrounding her until she lost all desire to escape. She took one breath, then needed another.

Kee slid open the second button. Her skin gleamed in the fire's light. He thought of bending down and caressing her breasts with his tongue and teeth, drawing out her nipples until they felt like hot, hard satin, and she cried out for release from the passion that stirred between them.

But he knew it was a rare woman who wanted a man like that. Not so deep and hard that she forgot her name and his, and all that existed was the world of fire they created together.

She whispered his name and his fingers shook as he opened the next button. Blood pulsed and gathered hotly, driven by the thudding beat of his heart and his passion for this one woman. Only woman. And that knowledge swept through him with relentless force.

Kee blocked that mental door. He wasn't going to

think about tomorrows, not when she stood before him.

Nearly sheer cotton hugged the small curves of her breasts. Kee touched the backs of his fingers to her chin, lifting it slightly, then he ran them slowly down her bared throat to where the pulse beat with its own maddening rhythm.

Like his heart. And his breathing. Like the blood pooling heavily with a throbbing demand that he no longer could deny.

And he knew how close to the edge he was of losing whatever control he had.

He trailed his fingertips down the open V of the shirt. His gaze followed. Her skin captured the tint of ancient gold. Warm, so warm and teased with dusky shadows.

His gaze flickered upward to catch the prideful lift of her chin and the sultry brilliance of her eyes, but then her gaze lowered.

Isabel kept her eyes locked on his still hand. She was unable to look away, unable to control her ragged breathing or the trembling that beset her body.

She had sought him out. No matter what words were spoken or held silent, she had gone after Kee. She had known what it would mean. He never made it a secret that he wanted her. *No, not you, not all of you, just your body.*

It did not matter. The moment he was gone, she had thought of Clarai wanting to kill him, and then of her desire to see Isabel dead as well. He intrigued her. And she wanted a man for the first time. What if she should die tomorrow? She would never have known what it was like to be loved by him. And she knew he would make love to her and with her, not take.

Was all that reason enough to cast aside every moral teaching and belief? She did not know. She did not care. Some deep, imperative inner urging had sent her out into the night to find him.

And now…soon now…the waiting would be over. The hunger he had created would be stilled.

She stood proud and quiet when he pulled the shirt free of her pants and opened the last few buttons. She could not help notice the slight tremor in his hands. A small core of feminine pride made her rejoice to see that she, too, could stir him so.

She wanted to touch the glistening drops of water on his hair. She was afraid to move. To do, or to say the wrong thing. She watched as he spread the cloth aside and wished she could see what was in his eyes.

At such a moment a woman wanted to be beautiful for her chosen man. She closed her eyes and fought the images of silken sheets and flower-strewn bower that would have been hers on her wedding night. She tried not to see the lace of the bed's canopy, or the flickering of dozens of candles that would have hidden and revealed the joy about to be shared.

And then she realized that there was no true regret in her heart or mind. She believed that no bride could be so cherishingly seduced as she.

The warming blaze of the fire touched her arms as the shirtsleeves slid free under Kee's hands and pooled at her feet.

But thought and belief were one thing. Isabel looked down at herself. Nothing was hidden from his eyes. Her tiny gasp was loud in the silence; her move instinctive to cover herself, but Kee was holding her wrists in a gentle vise.

"No, don't," he whispered. "I was going to bathe you like no lady's maid ever could, lovely one."

"Was, Kee?" Breathless with the last remnant of fear, and hesitant because she was unsure what to do, she barely managed those two words.

"I feel as if I've waited for you my whole life and now—" he looked up and held her wide, dark-blue eyes with his "—now, lovely, I can't wait any longer."

His head dipped, his lips drawn to the velvet shadow between her breasts.

He heard her soft cry as she arched slightly against him.

"That's it, lovely, come to me."

He blew gently, his warm breath feathering over her skin and tasted her tremble with his mouth. He licked the drops of water that fell from her hair. Drops that glistened on her skin and that he tasted like a man who knows the treasured value of sweet, cool water, the only kind that quenched a man's thirst.

He lifted his head and saw that the tips of her breasts had peaked the thin cotton of her wet camisole. Kee barely stifled a groan of raw passion.

"Sweet, sweet hell. You just might burn me alive." His husky voice was filled with emotions he didn't dare name.

"No. Not you." Soft, almost choked sounds. If anyone was burning, it was her. Like a fever had swept over her and deep inside. But she could not tell Kee about the fire that had built and built until she shook from its hot demand. She did not know how to put such things into words for a man.

All she could do was feel.

"Lie down for me, Isabel. I need to get these wet

things off you." *And I need to bury my flesh in yours. I need to rid myself of this ache that's eating me alive.*

He wanted to say them to her, but bit the words back. In her innocence she'd run as if the devils of hell were chasing her. Instead of just one man. Him.

She seemed frozen where she stood. Kee lifted her hands to his mouth and blew warm air over her chilled flesh. Her breath caught and rushed out. He nipped the delicate fleshy pad below her thumb and then raised her hands to his chest.

Her broken breaths acted like a silken caress over his skin. The softer sound she made came from deep inside her when he brushed back the wet strands of her hair and caught her earlobe between his thumb and forefinger. He pressed and could almost feel the heat that spread from her tiny whimper as she pulled back. The sultry darkness in her eyes entwined him in a velvet captivity that he couldn't, wouldn't break free.

He warned himself to keep his hands from her body. Sanity had to prevail. He had to get both of them out of their wet boots and pants or the kind of trembling that they would be sharing wouldn't be coming from satisfying hunger.

She played hell with his good intentions. She managed to open two buttons on his shirt before she curled her fingers into his chest hair.

Kee went still. Her fingertips were cool, but they burned him where they touched his skin, and that made him burn hotter as well.

Isabel looked up. The days of beard stubble only enhanced the rough, masculine cut of his lips. She stared at his mouth with all the hunger that teased her before she knew what intimate kisses tasted like. And what they could do to her.

And she drew her gaze upward to find that he was watching her with dark eyes that seared her to her soul.

Firelight burnished his hair and caressed his face in a way she longed to do. She started to lift her hands but Kee held her away from him. He swept her up into his arms and then lowered her so that her body pressed every hard, muscled inch of him, before he laid her down on the blanket. It had happened so quickly that she did not say a word.

He knelt before her and pulled off her boots, tossing them aside. His hands enveloped her slender foot, gently rubbing warmth into her cold skin.

"Wrap the blanket around you, Isabel. You're still shaking."

"Yes," she whispered and gathered the wool around her, for without his heat she felt the cold brush of air despite the fire's blaze, despite the heat burning inside her.

Kee rubbed until her flesh felt warmer, then he reached up and their fingers entangled on her belt. He let her win the right to open it, but he slid the buttons free before she was done.

"You are very quick, Kee. How many women—"

"Now, lovely, that's no question for a lady to be asking. And never one a man's going to answer." His smile teased one from her. "Lie back, lovely one."

Her eyes held his. She was almost completely covered with the blanket but she had never felt more vulnerable.

"It's all right, Isabel. You know that, don't you? I won't do one thing that you don't want me to do."

His words only alarmed her. Did he expect her to tell him what she wanted? Put these strange needs into words?

Kee leaned back on his heels. Her expression wasn't all he hoped for. If anything, she appeared frightened. What the hell had he said? But he went over every word and nothing he said should have brought an almost fearful look to her eyes.

"What did I—"

"Do you expect—"

They both started and stopped at the same moment. Kee had lost his smile. "Tell me."

"You want me to tell you what I—I—I cannot say this."

"This? What's this? I said I wouldn't do anything that you didn't want."

She shook her head so hard that water splattered him.

"I cannot tell you what to do."

If Kee hadn't leaned forward when she spoke he would never have heard one mumbled word.

"I'm losing my mind and my—" Her quick alarmed look shut him up. "Okay, let's try this again. I know that you've never been intimate with a man." His half-questioning tone was answered by the deep blush that colored her cheeks.

"You don't have to tell me what to do, Isabel. Trust me. I have experience enough for both of us." He wanted to hold her and pet her fears away, but if he touched her right now, he wasn't going to soothe either one of them.

"You don't need to say words. Your body will tell me what I need to know to make this good for you." Oh, hell, she had him so tied in knots everything he said was coming out the wrong way.

She lifted her head and her dark, earnest eyes sought his. She studied his face, feature by feature, until she came back to the smoldering invitation that awaited her. And she drew from her proud, ancient heritage all the courage she needed to speak.

"Will you make love to me? Will you make me a woman, Kee?" Very silently she added, *Your woman?*

For a long moment he held her gaze with a stare of granite.

"Yes," hissed out from between his clenched teeth. For all his fumbling denial that this was going to be nothing more than slaking a lustful hunger, he lied again to himself. He was going to make love to Isabel. He was going to make her a woman. His woman.

And with all the patience he had promised her that he had, he hunkered down before her and waited until she lay back. He could see the desire in her eyes and he fed on that look that approved everything about him. Just as he found favor with all of her.

If her life had depended upon it, Isabel could not have spoken. She lay back. Trust in Kee brought her compliance. She knew men would not have hesitated to name her body as a price for their help. Or they would have taken what they wanted. But Kee was a man of honor. She believed that he was cherishing the growing feelings between them. Each moment they had spent together, the danger, and the laughter had brought them closer.

She was aware of every tug of wet cloth that drew her toward Kee and what he offered. She did not realize he was done until he suddenly shifted. His hands were flattened on the earth on either side of her. He loomed over her, his dark shadow cast against the stone wall.

"If I don't taste you right now, lovely, I'm going to die right here."

But he did not taste. He stroked his forehead against the firm slope of one breast, then the other. His mouth opened and his breath caressed her. His gentle restraint was a lure for all her senses. She loved his voice and his quick smile, loved the rippling strength of his muscles, loved... No! She stopped thinking and saw that all this while he watched her mouth with that dark intensity that left her so weak and breathless.

Kee lifted his head. The faintly alarmed look was gone. In its place was that sensual curiosity that drove his desire deeper, hotter, harder. He shifted slightly upward, slowly lowering his head until all she breathed was his breath, all she tasted was his hunger, all she felt was his heat.

"Kee?" she murmured, nervously licking her bottom lip.

"I'm here. Always here."

His lips settled over hers. And he stole her breath for his own, but so gently, so softly, that she could not say when the kiss began.

Her mouth was a sweet promise of generous, honeyed warmth that made him dizzy with need. The tiny, hungry sounds she made set a blaze burning deep and low. A shudder ripped through him, yet he refused to take and take all that he wanted.

More than his own need, he desired to see and hear and feel hers. He wanted exactly what he told Isabel— her body to tell him what she wanted. And it spoke the ancient language with a heated elegance all its own.

He rocked his head back and forth, teasing her, and teasing himself, until her mouth clung to his in giving and retreat, and he made it all his.

Then he tasted deeply in an intimacy he knew she

had never shared with another man. Minutes later all that was heard was their broken breaths.

He kissed the corner of her lips, then slid to trace the shape of her jaw. The delicate line of her throat invited his mouth to scatter more random kisses until he nipped the hollow of her throat and felt her pulse hammering against his lips.

Kee slipped his hands beneath the blanket to touch her trembling body. His warm, hard palms settled on her collarbone. His long fingers stroked the curve of her jaw. His lips followed each touch, moving again down her bared, arched throat to the small hollow that drew his kiss.

Isabel tossed restlessly under his confinement. She made a plea of his name. All she felt, and saw, and needed was Kee.

She shivered when she felt the sweep of his hands down her arms and only then barely realized that he had drawn the straps of her camisole down to her waist. The wool of the blanket rubbed against suddenly too sensitive skin, and then, then that too, was gone.

Nothing protected her from his smoldering gaze.

He looked at her with half-closed eyes, afraid his control would break if he touched her. He clenched his hands around the blanket. It was pure pleasure to see her lit with the deeper gold of the fire. It was pain, too.

He swallowed, his mouth suddenly dry. "You're all I thought, more than I dreamed," he said hoarsely, then closed his eyes.

For long moments all he heard was the sound of his own rough breathing. Now he had her image blazed in his mind. And he knew that the feminine curves haunting him were more beautiful than those he dreamed about, more perfect than if he had conjured up everything he never knew he wanted in a woman.

"Kee?" She reached up to touch his arm, but he jerked away.

"Don't touch me, lovely."

"But I am dry and you are still wet. Let me help you."

He reared back, eyes open. They were hungry, almost wild and his voice was the same way, stressed to breaking.

"You've got that all wrong. It's going to be the other way around." He spoke hurriedly, stripping off his boots and clothes faster than if the water hole waited at the end of a summer's day of hard work. "Men don't need the same amount of time a woman does to become aroused. Hell, you just breathe near me and I'm hotter than a house afire."

His look was nearly savage as he came to her. "Don't be afraid. I'll give all the time you need."

She could not resist caressing the curve of his jaw as he settled himself beside her. She drew in a long, shaking breath.

"Is that how I will burn, Kee? Like a house on fire?"

He caught her hand and brought it to his lips.

"Hotter."

Chapter Eighteen

Kee lifted her hair and carefully untangled the wet braid. He spread her long black hair out behind her. The long, damp tendrils seemed alive. They curled and clung to his fingers as though pleading for his touch. Like her eyes watching him. An involuntary shiver ran through him. He lifted her hair to his lips and buried his face in the damp strands, inhaling deeply.

Isabel stirred restlessly. She saw his face buried in her hair and breath lodged in her throat at the sharp contrast of his hard-cut features and her wealth of hair. Then she could not breathe at all, for he brushed the hair aside and she saw the passion burning behind his dark lashes. Need exploded softly inside her and brought fever to a heightened state.

If she thought she had any defenses left against him, they crumbled in that moment. With her gaze holding his, she twisted to her side and before she thought about what she was doing, her lips pressed tiny kisses against his thick dark chest hair. She felt the tension that gripped his body, but she was caught in a sensual web. Her lips traced over the sodden bandage and a murmur of regret escaped her.

Kee slipped his arm beneath her, arching her into his body. "Yes, just like that. Closer, lovely."

She felt the incredible warmth of his body all along the length of hers, but the blanket remained bunched between them. Blindly, she turned her face up toward his, wanting to feel his mouth on hers.

And she clung to his muscular strength against the spinning dizziness that took hold of her. Just as his mouth took hers, sweet and hot. She did not mind the roughness of his beard stubble beneath her palm. This was Kee—soft and gentle in the place their lips met, hard as the mountains everywhere else. It was an irresistible combination that made her wish the moment would never end.

She moaned when he broke the kiss. His body tightened as if someone had wrapped barbed wire around him. She came to him with trust and innocence that pierced his desire. Every slow tremor of her body fanned the flames of his. He wanted every untouched secret she held in the feminine grace of her slender body. He needed to possess all of her, to feel her softness yield to his hard flesh. She arched against him once more, her hands on his naked shoulders making frantic petting motions as her mouth sought his. He fought pulling her hard against him and kissing her the same way.

She pulled him closer still in unconscious demand. When she felt the hard edge of his teeth on her lower lip, she opened for him just as he had taught her to do.

Isabel swallowed a cry as a wave of heat swept from the pit of her stomach, heat that was so fevered, her very bones seemed to melt.

Her hands slid to his arms, holding tight. All she

knew was Kee and the penetration and retreat of his tongue caressing her. Very bravely then, she returned the gliding pressure of his tongue with her own. She was lured deeper and deeper into the hotter texture of his mouth, needing his taste, giving him back the same pleasure she received.

When he tried to lift his head and break their kiss, she eased her fingers into the thick pelt of his hair and joined his mouth to hers. Instinct and Kee's own sensual ways taught her what to do. She traced the very masculine outline of his lips with the tip of her tongue, then with her lashes half veiling her eyes, she carefully rubbed the edge of her teeth on his lower lip. When she heard his groan, and felt the tremble of his body against her own, she smiled dreamily and slowly released him.

"So, you like to tease me?" he asked softly, willing to pay the price when he saw the blue depths of her eyes.

"Do men like to be teased?" She touched his lips with her fingertips.

"This man does when it's you doing the teasing." He shifted just enough to catch her earlobe in a delicate vise.

"Kee!"

"Feels good?" He stroked the soft pad of flesh with his tongue.

"Yes," she sighed. "Everything you do feels good. But will you..."

"Kiss you? Yes. All over? Yes. Come give me your mouth, lovely lady. Yes." It was the softest of whispers, just the way he skimmed his lips over her mouth. "More?"

"Yes. Like before."

The soft heat of her mouth, her tongue, drove the thought of talking from his mind. He groaned and took her mouth even as she took his. Like a sudden violent desert storm, passion exploded through him, shaking him with its wildness.

She whimpered softly and tossed her head when his lips slipped to her arched throat. He used his teeth to drag the blanket down, but kept the rest of it bunched between them out of fear of shocking her.

Desire had misted her skin until she shimmered in the fire's glow. He licked her bare shoulder and felt the wild trembling that shook her. He warned himself that he needed patience. But couldn't stop himself from wanting to taste the softness he had just uncovered.

He rubbed his lips against the slope of her breast. She tasted of the night and a wild sweet rain. Kee looked up into her eyes. And still watching her watching him, he caught the edge of the blanket with his teeth and very carefully tugged it across her breast.

Her eyes closed. She moved restlessly, her hands half-curled on either side of her head where the wild tangle of her midnight hair framed her face. He could almost taste the flush that heated her body, could almost see the rush of blood that tightened her nipple. His breath sighed out around her.

And with a delicate care that he didn't know he was capable of, Kee brought his hunger to her and drew the tip of her breast into his mouth.

"Kee!" Her voice was husky with the same desire that was driving him to the edge. He felt her over every inch of his body. Every hammering pulse, every thundering heartbeat was echoed in the rigid flesh straining to be joined with her sultry flesh. The deep instinctive need to mate brought his hips flush against her side. He pinned her legs beneath his thigh, pressing tight, but the folds of the blanket kept her from feeling how violently aroused he was.

And he told himself it was better this way.

Better for Isabel. For his move had only increased the need arrowing through him.

But Isabel felt the fire that kindled in the pit of her stomach when he moved against her. She wanted and desperately needed to ease the sweet ache he created in her body. She knew Kee was strong. His lean body was tense as a drawn bow, hard muscles glistening with sweat in the fire's light. But the feel of him was too new, shocking and maddening and arousing all at once.

She cried out softly and arched against him, yearning to feel that cutting blaze again. His smile against her breast was half savage, half triumph, at bringing the smoldering passion he had sensed in her to life.

But he wanted her hungrier, and so aroused that she would never feel the pain of losing her virginity to a man who made no promises of tomorrow. He stretched his arm up until his fingers entwined with hers and cupped her breast with his other hand. He deliberately held his body away from hers, teasing the velvet peak into a pouting hardness that rubbed against his tongue, begging for more.

She twisted against him, her back arching, trying to free her legs. Each gentle tug of his mouth on her breast sent fire shimmering through her, but never eased the ache of her body. She felt where the fire pooled into unbearable need, and squeezed her thighs tight.

Nothing helped. She was not ignorant of how a man

and woman made love. No one who bred horses or cattle remained innocent for long.

But not one of the whispers that stopped when she came near the village women had hinted of the coiled aching knot that built inside her.

Kee eased her onto her back. He lifted his head, leaving one nipple taut in the fire's glow and bent to take the other in his mouth, to shape this delicate female flesh into the same tight peak. Her every cry was a goad to hurry, and he fought himself, even as the temptation to other sweet, hot flesh lured him.

A low sound of pleasure was torn from her lips and the arching of her body was pure reflex this time as with exquisite care he teased her. He drew cries of passion from her. She clenched his hand and brought the other down to caress his head, pressing him against her.

It was maddening not to touch him as he was touching her. She felt the corded muscle of his shoulder and the shudder that rippled through him. To know her touch could arouse him to the same fever pitch was heady power. And she wanted more.

His hand stroked her from breast to thigh and back again while his mouth gently devoured her supple skin. He traced the curve of her belly with tiny licks and scattered kisses. She pulled free of his hand, and used both of hers to hold his head, crying out his name. Her voice splintered as the first wave of heated pleasure swept through her body.

Her cry was so ragged that he lifted his head.

"Sweet hell. Did I hurt you?" he asked in a voice close to breaking.

"No. Yes. Oh, Kee, I do hurt. Everywhere you are

not touching me hurts,'' she moaned, her short nails biting into his skin.

''I know. It's the same for me. But this happens only once for you. I want it perfect. Like you.'' But her need acted like someone had poured raw whiskey in his veins. Lightning scored through him, stripping his control. He took her mouth as he wanted to take her body, again and again, but it wasn't enough, nothing would be enough.

Nothing would be enough.

He needed more. Much more. He needed to bury his flesh so deeply into hers that there wasn't two, but one.

He felt her move to push aside the blanket. He knew what she wanted with every restless toss of her head, every twisting curve of her body, every ragged-sounding cry. The same thing he wanted. To be covered in a blanket of fire that burned all the way to the bone.

Kee lifted slightly and shifted his body to cover hers. Damp, silken skin cradled his body. She moved beneath him with a hungry twist that inflamed him.

''Sweet, sweet lady, you're going to be the death of me.''

''Yes,'' she cried out. ''I feel like I am dying.''

''No, lovely, not dying. It's a passionate woman being born.'' A broken groan escaped his lips when he felt her nipples nuzzle through the dark mat of chest hair until they pressed against his skin. He tried telling himself she wasn't ready, that she needed more time, more kisses and caresses, but her plea cut him off.

The weight of his hips settled between her legs, opening them. He arched against the hidden core of passion and brought forth a wild cry.

The scent of her arousal drove him crazy, as did her frantic nails biting into his arms.

He tried to speak and couldn't. She had stolen his breath. He braced his weight on his elbows and placed a scalding string of kisses from her mouth to the raven black curls that were softer than down.

He barely heard the way her breath caught and then held when his palm curved over her thigh, kneading from there to her hip and back again until she parted her legs. He caressed the tight curls, seeking and finding silken heat that was moist and smooth as velvet.

Her eyes closed and she bit her bottom lip, rocking her body with each gliding motion of his fingers that made her tremble with the violence of the storm overtaking her.

Every bit of shyness had burned away with each more intimate touch. She did not dare open her eyes for the world was spinning out of control. She knew that Kee was there with her, that he would keep her safe, and bring an end to the ceaseless need that ached. She forgot any desire to protect her vulnerable self. Kee had given her what she wanted, a fever that would shatter her at any moment.

She lifted her hips, her arms reaching for him, both a silent demand that he do something to release the coiling knot that held her in its grip.

She cried out his name for the tension seemed to coil tighter, then tighter still.

He felt her come apart for him. Sweet, liquid heat from within the softness that no man had ever touched. He heard her cry and before he could ask if it was pain or pleasure, she shivered and opened to him, yielding to the sensual storm that consumed her. He had never wanted anything so much as to join his flesh with hers in that one scalding, endless moment when pleasure melted her.

And he was afraid he would hurt her if he did.

He rose up to kiss her with swift, hot reassurance. "It's all right, lovely," he whispered, biting her lip softly. "I told you your body would tell me all I needed to know. You're almost where I am. Trust me?"

"Always, Kee. I— Where are you?"

He almost smiled, but it was beyond him. "High on the mountain, sweet lady. Getting ready to fly."

"I want—I want to be there with you. Take me, Kee. Take me there."

Kee made a hoarse sound, and clenched his teeth. Release coiled tighter than a whip, savaging him, raging to be free. His hand smoothed down the side of her body bringing visible shivers of response from her.

"Once more, just once more, lovely. Share with me. Let me make this easier for you. And me. For both of us."

Once more. Once more the fever swept over her, building and building; each circular caress made her moan until the passion was beyond her and shimmering heat swept through her. Once more. And again.

"Kee!"

"Yes!" he whispered, biting her neck with barely held restraint, soothing the tiny marks he made with his tongue. He settled his weight slowly between her trembling thighs, easing them apart even more to make room for his big body.

"So beautiful." It was all he could manage to say. She was sleek and hot against him and he teased her with flesh that was as hot but hard where she was incredibly soft.

Her nails scored his skin as she yielded to him.

Again he caught her earlobe and bit her, sending fire streaking through her. She arched her hips, easing his way as he filled her slowly, moving very gently by soft increments, retreating then advancing again. Afraid of hurting her, he fisted his hands over the blanket when all he wanted to do was put his hands on her hips and thrust into her, burying himself completely and ending this torment.

But the pleasure that filled her eyes as she watched him forced back his own fever and need.

"I want you," she whispered, offering her lips as she offered her body. Completely, nothing held back.

"Gently, love, gently."

But Isabel shook her head. She did not want his gentleness now. She could feel the power of the storm that shook him, she knew its power over her own body. And it was a wild, untamed thing that sent exquisite lightning through her.

She followed him when he retreated, making a silent demand. Her softness strained against him, begging him to end the last barrier between them.

And when the sweet heated shattering came again, he thrust once, smoothly, holding still as she cried out.

He barely managed to throttle a groan when she rocked her hips against his. He sank deeper, drinking her cry, as her legs tightened and she urged him with frantic touches, and lips that kissed whatever part of him she could reach to lose every bit of control. He reared back and she twisted up to meet him and the rain-swept night came apart around him in deep, wrenching pulses that left him shaking, fighting for breath.

Her body shivered in response, ecstasy flowing

through her, fever burning in bursting pleasure so great she thought she would die. She clung to Kee, passion coiling once more and he held her tight, endless need surrounding them as the night burned its way to dawn.

Chapter Nineteen

Isabel awoke in a cocoon of warmth. She did not move as her eyes opened, confirming what she had sensed. Kee was no longer with her. A folded blanket had replaced the pillow of his shoulder. She rubbed her cheek against the wool, for the moment the scent of their lovemaking blocked that of burning wood mingling with those of bacon frying and coffee perking. There was something else, too, but she could not place it. Not that it mattered. If it was not Kee, she did not want to know.

She stretched very slowly, feeling every small ache. Memory flooded her of Kee bathed by fire while he kept his promise to bathe her as no lady's maid ever could. A deep blush spread from the inside out of her naked body as she remembered those heated minutes and the shimmering moments that followed. Kee's body moving over hers, his mouth as hungry as her own, eager to reclaim the golden fire they built together. And there was that one magical moment when she thought she was dying, that the pleasure they shared was too much, too hot, too intense, and she could bear no more.

It was then that Kee showed her how wild the storm could be. Wild, sweet ecstasy breaking around them, consuming them with its blaze and glory.

She closed her eyes, squeezing them tight to stop the sudden well of tears. She had given Kee more than he had asked for, much more than physical innocence.

With surprising clarity the moment came back to her, their gazes enjoined as were their bodies, her lips forming the word, calling him the name of what overflowed her heart. And with painful clarity she remembered his cherishing kiss, the height they had reached for and found that stripped reality and left a soaring freedom born of flames.

And she remembered the silence afterward. She remembered that most of all.

They had mated, more perfectly than any dream. The two of them joining into a union of one, renewing the cycle of life. Her hand slipped to the slight curve of her belly. The enormity of what she had done without the blessings and vows settled like a leaden weight. She did not know if it was a devil's curse or the Lord's wish, but the women in her family bore few living children. She prayed and made a vow. If she was blessed with a child from sharing herself in love with this one man, no one would ever take that child from her. And she would never burden Kee with her love. That was her secret to keep.

Kee, standing in shadow, watched her awaken, but she made no move to look for him. Nor did he make a sound. For some reason he thought back to his first meeting with Jesse, when Logan forgot to tell her that he and Marty were invited for supper. He had gone hunting, snaring two rabbits to bring as their share, just like his ma had taught him to do when visiting.

hurt in her eyes before she turned away. His curses were vicious, silent and all directed at himself.

"Isabel, I—"

"Would you give me some privacy to dress? I will hurry. I know how impatient you are."

"Is that what I was with you? Impatient?"

"Now?"

"No, not now, Isabel. You know damn well I'm not talking about now."

"Kincaid, obviously you should have one more thing at your door. You should have slept. I have no desire to continue this insane conversation. Leave me." Her voice broke, and she closed her eyes, bowing her head until the tangle of her hair covered her from his eyes. "Please, Kee, just go. I will hurry."

"Isabel, I never made you any promises. But for what it's worth—"

"Will you get out!" she screamed. If there had been anything near enough to throw at him she would have, and done it with pleasure. She could have shot him right then. No, shooting was too good for him. She would stake him out on an anthill and ride away.

The moment he was gone she scrambled to the fire, and sat there, bewildered by what she found. He had made two bark containers, one filled with steaming water, the other filled with rainwater. On his clean neckerchief was a pile of soapberries, the kind Indians crushed for soap. But she wept when she saw the brilliant scarlet candle flower. She lifted the showy flower to her cheek and closed her eyes. He could not have slept at all. He had done all this for her. Care and kindness, food and warmth and a bit of beauty for the eyes and soul.

"Kee, oh, Kee, what a foolish woman I am to need your words."

Sometimes words were not very good when the deepest of feelings were involved. Isabel kept telling herself this when he first brushed aside her attempt to apologize, and thank him for his thoughtfulness, and later, when they rode out toward what was now called Weaver's Needle, and his silence became as high as Iron Mountain between them.

It was painful for her to ride. She did not utter one sound of complaint. She saw how carefully Kee picked their way through this eruption of mountains and ridges and the canyons that drained into the Gila River to the south and north to the Salt River. The desertlike land heated beneath the afternoon sun, a wind from the south bringing with it a dust that coated everything.

When a particularly strong gust left her coughing, Kee rode alongside her, blocking her from the wind as much as he could.

"If this keeps up, we may have to break and camp early."

They were the first words he had spoken to her since this morning, and all she could do was nod. She had used his neckerchief to tie down her hat, now she wished she had it to cover her mouth and nose. They were riding a twisting path through aged, wind-distorted cottonwoods. The air, she could see, was beginning to shimmer with a strange pinkish light as the dust storm increased in power.

Isabel looked at Kee and as he was watching her, she saw worry in his eyes. The blast of wind swirled sand around them and for a moment she lost sight of him.

She screamed his name just as his strong arm wrapped around her waist. With a strength she envied, he lifted her and swept her onto his horse.

"There's not much cover," he yelled to be heard over the rising wind. "We'll try for those boulders."

She could do nothing to protect him as the sand whipped and stung them through their clothes.

The boulders formed a rough three-sided shelter. Kee lifted her down, quickly untying his bedroll and tossing the blanket to her. "Get under that. I'll see to the horses."

He was back in minutes with the canteens, but she had counted every second that he was out of her sight.

Only her eyes showed in the slight opening she had left when she wrapped the blanket around her. It was just enough to see that Kee sat in front of her, quickly covering himself with the other blanket. There was plenty of room beside her, but where he sat, he shielded her from the worst of the storm.

"Kee, how bad is it?"

"Won't last more than a few hours. Then I've known them to last out the night. But no more than that. Try to sleep."

The wind's fury increased to a ceaseless shriek, but the boulders partly protected them from the swirling sand.

Isabel huddled under the stifling wool blanket. And she waited. His continued silence began to unnerve her. Her emotions had already been strained to the breaking point. She hugged her knees and tried to find a comfortable place. The rock poked her no matter which way she turned. A quick peek showed that Kee sat as still as the very stone of this land.

She bit her lip, vowing she could maintain the same cool indifference. But she was not happy about it.

The minutes slipped by slowly. She felt that the silence between them was louder than the storm. Edgy, growing more tense by the moment, she barely stifled a gasp when she felt his hand on her shoulder.

"Lie down facing me, Isabel. The wind's changed. And keep your head covered or you'll cough up dust for a month of Sundays."

She flattened her body as much as she could against the stone to make room for him.

Kee wedged himself into one corner of the rocks, sitting up so he could tent his blanket over both of them. He saw that she watched him, and he nodded, his lips and throat too dry to speak. He offered her the canteen.

"Just a little," he whispered in a hoarse voice.

Isabel lifted the canteen to her lips and just held it there for a few moments. Even warm, the moisture she finally let trickle into her mouth was soothing to the dry tissue. Another sip and she handed the canteen back to him. She watched the spare sip he took of the water.

"Drink, Kee. That was not enough for you." She saw the fine coating of dust on his face and hurried to untie his neckerchief. It was awkward moving under the weight of the blanket. She could barely take a breath without touching some part of him. After last night, it was ridiculous to shy away. But his withdrawal made her do just that. She took the canteen from him, very careful not to touch him, and moistened the cloth. Her gaze pinned to his square jaw, she was afraid to see what she might read in his eyes.

"I did not intend to...oh, it will be better if you use this to wipe the dust from your face."

With one hand he took the cloth, and the other caught her chin. He held her still when she tried to turn aside, and used his wet neckerchief to wipe her skin free of dust. He left a smudge on her cheek and before he could stop himself he bent down to kiss the spot.

Isabel jerked back. "I think you did enough."

"Hell yes, I know." He leaned his head back and closed his eyes. What he had to say would be easier if he didn't look at her expressive eyes.

"You can't call me any more forms of bastard than I've called myself. I don't know how something so good turned to hell so fast. I'm damn sorry for it, Isabel. I never meant to hurt you in any way. You deserved better. You do deserve someone better than me."

"Do not concern yourself, Kee Kincaid. I will find someone better." The words were snapped and cutting, and all she wanted to do was crawl away from him.

His eyes pinned her in place. And in a very soft, but very dangerous voice, he said, "You'll find someone else? Like hell freezing over, lady."

"You just told me—"

"That's what you do to me." He bent over her again, keeping that same low, but intense tone. "Every time I plan what to say to you, you play with my good intentions. The truth is, I was feeling a little trapped this morning. It ain't easy for a man to suddenly contemplate giving up his freedom."

"Is that what you were doing?" Eyes flashing, it took all the willpower she had not to hit him. "And do you think I want to give up my freedom? Do you think I want to trap you? You are a bastard! You cannot be sorrier than I am over what happened between us.'' Her gaze was frantic. She wanted out and there was nowhere to go.

Kee clenched his hands on his thighs to keep from grabbing hold and shaking some sense into her. ''What happened between us was that we made love. And it's never been like that for me with anyone else. I'm not stupid enough to throw that away. Isabel, I swear to you that I'd give anything to steal back time and do it all over again.''

''As would I.'' The words were so softly said that she did not think he had heard her.

''I don't blame you for regretting—''

''No one is to blame, Kee. I made my own choice. I know you would not have forced me. You made no promises, Kee. I never asked you about tomorrows. I am sorry, too. I never had a lover and I did not know what to expect.''

''What are you mumbling about now?''

''This morning. I did not know how to act or what to say or—''

He gathered her close, pressing her head against his chest, stopping the flow of words. ''Hush, Isabel. Just hush now.''

The very last thing she wanted was for him to feel trapped or in any way responsible. She would not take back one word. But oh, it hurt terribly to know that such honesty which should be prized as a virtue, could cut like a sword and she felt the pain that burrowed its way deep inside her.

He rocked her gently, pushing off her hat so he could smooth her hair. He hated lying. He'd done enough lying to her and to himself. But look what happened when he tried to tell her the truth.

He had to try again. "I want you to listen to me. No interruptions. When I said I wish I could steal back time and do it all over again, I didn't mean I wouldn't have made love to you, Isabel. I wanted you like I've never wanted anything in my life. If you wanted me to stop I..." *Go on, tell her. No lies, remember.*

"I would have tried, but I don't know if I could have stopped. That's how much I needed you. And don't be so sure you really made your own choice. You were innocent and I was far from that. I'm not proud of what I did, and maybe I'll burn in hell someday for it, but you were a fever in my blood and—"

"Yes!" she cried out against him. "It was like that for me, too."

"I know. And what's done is done."

She was stunned into silence by the bleak acceptance in his voice. She almost held her breath waiting for him to say something more. There had to be a future for them. There had to be!

But he held her close and rocked her slowly, rubbing his hand over her back. Her thoughts were in turmoil. Perhaps she should tell him first. Some inner voice urged her to keep quiet. She could not press him now. And the feelings she had were too new. Maybe he felt the same way. Time is what they both needed. And time was running out for what she had to do.

"Listen," Kee said, holding her still. "The wind's dying down."

"And that's good," she murmured, reluctant to move.

"Between the rain last night and the sand, our trail

is covered. Soon as I see to the horses, we ride for your gold.''

''Yes, the gold.''

He held her away from him. She didn't know he was whispering silent prayers that they could get out of here. Now. Now before that incandescent sensuality that she was unaware of brought him to his knees. He had wanted her, but thought the fever would abate. Not true. He wanted her more.

But even in the gloom created by the tented blankets he saw the tears glittering on her cheeks. His mouth was over hers, sealing any words about to be spoken.

The taste of him swept through her, making her shiver. He stroked her over his hard body, telling her how perfectly they matched, male to female, hard to soft. She gave herself to his kiss as she had given herself to him. Nothing held back.

All too soon he broke away. She did not know what it cost him to leave her. Or that he never wanted to leave at all.

Chapter Twenty

They rode through a land that was denuded of firewood by the Cornish miners that used the fuel for the Silver King Mine to the east. Kee told her he'd heard stories of those same miners walking nearly twenty miles across the desert to Globe on Friday nights to drink away their pay and then make the same walk back on Sunday.

She did not care that the name had been changed. To her, it would always be what her grandfather had called it…the Finger of God. There were always stories being written for the territorial papers that related wild tales of this haunted area. She had no sooner thought about it, when Kee spoke of the very same thing.

"Any sane man or woman would run the other way if one or all of the stories are believed, Isabel. I've heard of swinging rocks that turn out from walls of a canyon and crush the rider, or trees whose branches can reach out and entangle you. I've heard crazy notions about wild animals that come out of the rocks when you sleep and fishes with legs that crawl out of the streams and upper lakes and drown everything living within their reach. Scared yet?''

''Is that why you told me? To scare me? Not that it matters. I need to go in there and find my grandfather's legacy. I believe this is a dangerous place for many reasons, and maybe it is a haunted place, too.'' She glanced over at him, at the easy way he sat his horse as if he were an extension of the animal. His eyes were never still, always moving, searching out the land before them as they rode toward her goal.

''I'll share a story with you, Kee, of how the first Indians went *into* Superstition Mountain.''

''Into?'' A quick look caught her nod. ''You mean they physically went into that mountain?''

''So the story goes. There is a Pima who works for my grandmother who told us the tale of the great chief Montezuma who ruled over thousands. A vision came of a great calamity about to befall him and his people and he brought them to the plain adjacent to Superstition Mountain, and then he used his magic to open a side of the mountain. When they were all inside and safe, he closed the great stone gateway. To this day many believe he and his people still live within the mountain.''

''Why do I get the feeling that this story has something to do with where we're going?''

Isabel smiled at him. ''You are right. Before Jacob Walz died in Phoenix two years ago, Kee, he made a deathbed confession of where the mine was. He said there was a great stone face looking up at his mine, and that if you pass three great hills you have gone too far. He lied when he said the rays of the setting sun shone on his gold. And you cannot climb on his mine to see the Finger of God.''

"Finger of God...Weaver's Needle. And you said that you need the first rays of the morning sun to find the entrance."

"Yes. Tomorrow. Tomorrow I will show you more gold than you could spend in three lifetimes."

"And you want it all?"

"No. I will try to find my grandfather's bones. I will keep that promise to my grandmother. As for the gold, I will take only what we need to keep her home secure."

"Not a greedy woman, Isabel?"

She refused to rise to the taunt in his voice. But moments later she did answer him. "Yes, I can be as greedy as anyone else about something that really matters to me."

They came upon Weaver's Needle in the late afternoon.

Kee pulled up, shoved his hat back and stared as the slanting, red, dying rays of the sun shone on the strange, phallic finger of smooth, black basalt rock.

He couldn't tell if the devil had shoved it up from below as a warning, or if the good Lord had hurtled it down from above for the same reason, but that black rock rose perpendicularly from the plateau and towered hundreds of feet in the air.

"The Finger of God," Isabel whispered as she drew her horse alongside his. "It seems to stand as a sentinel and warning all in one."

"But a strangely beautiful one in a way," Kee murmured. He looked up as he heard the soulful cries of the mourning doves and a chill shivered down his spine. He glanced over at Isabel and saw that she, too, went still, a visible trembling taking hold of her when the cries were repeated.

"They mate for life," she said without thought. "And their cries are for those who have lost their heart mates."

He sensed she hadn't meant it to be a spur against his nerves, but it acted like that. "I'll ride ahead and scout out a place to camp."

"I want to come with you, Kee. Please, I do not want to be alone here."

"You feel it, too?"

"Like a faint whisper of warning to stay away?"

"Yeah, something like that."

"But I cannot stay away."

"I know." He slanted the hat to shade his eyes. "There is something strange about the place and I don't really want you out of my sight. Just because we haven't caught sign of being followed, your cousin and those hombres don't strike me as the sort to give up easily."

"No. She will not give up easily."

There was a remoteness to her now that he couldn't understand, and he had no time to probe.

"Just so we understand each other, Isabel. If I say to stop, you stop without arguing. I'll see you safe or die trying."

He rode off before she could tell him that was the last thing she wanted, but the one thing she feared most.

But the approach to the black needle of rock proved to test even Kee's temper. They had to backtrack due to deep crevices that could not be crossed, or the sheer cliffs that offered not even an old game trail to climb.

The ravines were no better, choked as they were with thick clumps of catclaw or the low-growing prickly pear and the giant saguaro cactus, and ocotillo.

She enjoyed the sight of the blooming paloverde trees whose leaves were the brightest of yellow. She had two such trees near the stone courtyard outside her bedroom.

Isabel gasped. Ahead were the spectacular rock formations she remembered from the time spent here with her grandfather. Her spirits lifted. If this was the same place, the earthquake could not have destroyed the landmarks she needed. Once there had been a large herd of bighorn sheep flourishing in this craggy terrain, but they had been hunted for food until most were killed.

They were close. She felt the excitement build, and its flush chased some of the chill from her body, for there was an eerie quiet suddenly broken by the trickle of sliding gravel as the horses labored up the talus slope.

She knew what Kee searched for, a camp where they could watch if anyone approached. But she needed to be close to the gully that split the Finger of God in half.

She was about to call out to him when he veered off to the left. A few ponderosa pines grew in a straggly cluster and he headed the horses straight for them. She remained mounted, admiring his effortless grace that took him from horse to ground in one smooth move. He ducked beneath the low-growing sweep of pine branches, only to reappear a few moments later.

"Someone's been camping here. Fairly recently, too. And they didn't want anyone to know how many there were. The ground's been swept clean around the fire ring."

"Do we go on, Kee? I need to be at the start of that gully between the needles when the sun rises."

"You need rest, Isabel. We'll eat here and make a cold camp down below."

She could see he was not happy about what he had found. She wondered if Clarai was already here, waiting for them. But there was no sense of being watched, and she was sure she would feel her cousin's presence. It was such an evil thing.

She wondered if it was to be this easy. She would find the opening in the morning, and by this time tomorrow she could start for home. And leave Kee.

Distracted by the sudden emptiness that spread inside her, she never saw the way he watched her... hunger and longing in his eyes.

A lost moment, for she stopped thinking about what tomorrow would bring, and he moved to help her dismount.

He coaxed her into his arms with a gentle voice that soothed, and there was not one ounce of pride in her when she felt the caressing glide of his large hands closing around her waist to lift her out of the saddle. Held against his body, she snuggled close to him.

"As bad as I figured?"

"More." She felt boneless sinking into the warmth of his body. She ached and was not ashamed to admit it.

"I have never had trouble riding for long hours before, Kee."

"You never had a lover, either. Hang on."

It was all the warning he gave as he swept her up into his arms. His masculine scents filled every breath she drew, horse and leather, and something more that she could not name. But the blend was heady, and she thought that she could find him anywhere in a crowd of men.

She thought he would hurry to be shed of her, but he walked slowly and the longer he held her, the more her senses came alive with a curious weak feeling that overtook the pain of blood flowing again to numb, aching body parts.

"What you need is a soak in a hot spring—"

"Oh, yes. We have a small one near our hacienda and bathe there often. My grandmother claims the water holds many cures." Her head rested on his shoulder with a deep, longing sigh.

"You never told me where you live."

"To the west, close to Bosque."

"Maricopa Mountains."

She tilted her head to see his face. "You say that with a fondness of knowing them."

"I've done some horse hunting around there. Might have stopped and taken a cold drink at your well."

Her arms tightened around him. "Never. You were never there, Kee."

He stopped just short of the trees. He wasn't mistaken about the intensity in her voice. One look and it was there in her lovely blue eyes.

"How can you be so sure?" He was unaware that his voice had become a husky whisper. Her lips were too close and all he could think about was covering her mouth with his and sliding his tongue inside for a taste of wild honey. And this time he wouldn't wonder if there was a passion to match. He knew. Desire surged through him, shocking him with its speed and fierceness. From one pulse beat to another he was hard, aching and hungry for her.

Isabel kept her eyes on his throat. She could see his pulse and she ached to put her lips there. Desire filled her. The strong cords of his neck drew her eyes and she licked her bottom lip, then bit down hard to stop herself from doing something foolish.

"You never answered me."

"What?" Her gaze lifted to his; smoldering fire lit their brown depths. She clung tighter when he shifted her and slowly released her legs, letting her hips slide down his body with an intimacy that left her shaken.

"Are you ever going to answer me?" he asked with a crooked smile.

"They would be dead."

"Who?"

She shook her head, and tried to step back only to have a rock roll beneath her boot. Kee's quick move caught her up against him.

He felt the trembling that beset her, but he had his own unruly reaction to her to deal with. She did nothing and proved all over again how little control he had with her. And tonight he needed a sharp eye and clear head.

"Can you stand on your own now?"

She reacted to the sudden sharpness in his voice by jerking free. "Yes. I—I can stand on my own. And I know you have never stopped at our ranch. The women would have talked about you. Or they would be dead not to notice. Since that did not happen, you were not there."

The words were a rushed tumble that ended as she backed away from him.

"I will gather wood for the fire while you see to the horses."

With her back toward him, she did not see the regret in his eyes, or that his hands clenched at his sides not to reach out for her.

It was better this way, he told himself. Bitter, but better for both of them.

He stripped the saddles and his packhorse with a speed and energy that should have taken the edge off his building frustration, but didn't even come close.

He heard a cut-off cry from Isabel and shucked his gun, searching for what alarmed her. He started to circle the trees when she called him.

"Come and see this, Kee. I will not touch it."

In a moment he was beside her. He saw what she stared at. A roughly carved owl sat in the crook of the tree.

"The Apache," she said in a deadened voice, "believe the owl to be a warning of death."

"And it could have been put there years ago, Isabel. But you don't believe that, do you? You think that Clarai was here."

"Yes."

He stood behind her and placed his hands on her shoulders. He rubbed them, feeling the chill that shivered through her.

"You're stronger than she is, Isabel. Her beliefs aren't yours. And I'm with you all the way. I won't let her hurt you. I certainly won't let her stop you."

"I am not worried about myself, Kee. It is for you that I fear."

He turned her around. "Look at me." And he waited until that dazed look left her eyes. "If you want me to find another place to camp, I will."

"Kee, you cannot ignore her. She is a very real threat."

"Honey, I'm no damn hero. I intend to be very careful if I run into that cousin of yours again. I also intend to take care of you, Isabel. All right?"

She nodded; there was not anything else to do. He knew the danger as well as she did. And if it came to making a choice between saving Kee's life or the gold that Clarai wanted...no, it would never come to that. Isabel rubbed her arms when he went back to the horses and cast a fearful look at the wooden carving.

It was a death omen. And she could not ignore it.

Kee found a narrow stream to refill the canteens and let the horses drink. He couldn't see any smoke and hoped that Isabel wasn't still brooding about that damn owl. He should have explained to her that he took every sign and warning seriously, but right then he didn't think she needed to have her fear increased.

He staked out the horses in a dry wash that held a few puddles from the recent rain. There were some wild oats and grasses for them to feed. When he hiked his way back to rejoin Isabel he was surprised to see that the fire she built could be covered with his hat.

Bacon sizzled in the pan, and she poured out coffee before he sat down beside her.

He took the cup with a grateful murmur and sipped the hot brew. "I swear I'm going to have a thick steak and potatoes when we get back to civilization. And cake. Drizzled with honey."

"*Sí, empañadas* and *capirotada,*" she said, then grinned.

"So you've got a sweet tooth, too? My Sofia still makes the best bread pudding to be found in the territory. It's a favorite of my uncle Ty's. His wife tried to match Sofia's but no one can. And no can watch her, either. She has some secret ingredient she adds when no one is looking. Even her husband, Santo, can't tell."

"Are they part of your family, Kee?"

"They came with Grandmother Macaria when she left Mexico to marry Justin Kincaid. They must be in their seventies now, but that old man still puts the fear of him and God in us. It's a combination of love and respect that we have for Santo and his wife. She still rules the house with her wooden spoon. I felt it a few times on my backside when I tried to steal cookies before supper."

She laughed, as she was sure he meant for her to do, then turned with a wistful sigh. "I would have liked to have known you then, Kee."

"No, you wouldn't. I was a smart-mouthed kid, who delighted in pulling little girls' braids and sticking them into inkwells if I could get away with it."

"What happened to that mischievous little boy?"

"He started growing up, Isabel. He learned that little girls smelled sweeter than his friends, and he found better use for long braids. But all this was before we headed west. And afterward, well, I guess I had to grow up so fast in the weeks after my folks were killed that I lost that boy trying to survive."

"No. I do not believe that, Kee. I do not think you really believe it, either. You have laughter in your voice and eyes when you speak, so the memories you kept are good ones. That is all that matters, that you remember those good memories of happier times."

And she was going to make this brief interlude with him one of her good memories, when everything but easy talk and laughter were forgotten, a memory she could recall and savor when Kee was no longer part of her life.

They ate as they talked of their childhood. When done, she scoured out the pan with loose sand, and he buried their fire, then swept the area beneath the trees with a pine branch to wipe out their tracks. Keeping to the rocks, they made their way to where Kee had left the horses.

Isabel found a dry spot where thick layers of sand would make a softer bed. She spread out his bedroll and after a moment's hesitation, she opened the other blanket next to it. She rocked back on her boot heels just as Kee approached, carrying his rifle. She noticed he wore a tanned hide jacket, and knew from her search of his pack that it was soft as butter and just as supple.

"I'll be up there, keeping watch."

She followed his gesture to the rocks above. "You need to sleep, Kee. You cannot keep watch all night."

"I've done it before, night riding a herd, and you're the one who does all the work tomorrow."

"No. I will share keeping watch with you. Two hours? Is that all right?"

He knew he wasn't going to get by without arguing, so nodded and walked away. But if one night's sleep was all he could give her, she was getting it whether she wanted it or not.

"Two hours, Kee," she called out softly. She did not know if he heard her, or if he would wake her. She wrapped the blanket around her shoulders and sat on the bedroll, leaning back against the earth bank of the wash. She would not sleep, but only rest. It was time he started treating her as an equal, and not a woman who needed his coddling.

But the night without sleep and the long ride and emotional turmoil took their tolls and her eyes closed. Sleep claimed her just as the brilliance of the stars laid claim to the night sky like hundreds of lanterns suddenly lit into light.

Kee barely glanced upward at the display. Tired as he was, he had no mind to sleep. His breathing was soft and easy as he began to check on the sounds around him. Night-prowling animals like the kangaroo rat or the night lizards or the black-tailed jackrabbit that was feeding down below. Every place he camped, the sounds were different, from the rubbing of dead branches when the wind blew, or the grasses rustling as the breeze cooled the night.

If his own senses weren't always alert, he had his mustang. Outlaw would warn him if he heard something strange. He glanced back and down the wash to where Isabel was. He knew he shouldn't let his thoughts stray to her. But she was there, in his mind and...he stopped himself.

If there was a move made by Clarai, it would be tonight or right after Isabel found the opening to the mine. He had to stay alert.

But even the best intentions can be overcome by the loss of blood, and exhaustion. Kee fought to stay awake. He shifted positions, putting more of his body into the open, exposing it to the cold desert night.

He wished for coffee. He could swear that the scent of it and tobacco were teasing his nostrils.

Then the night exploded.

Outlaw snorted, then whinnied.

Kee caught a flash of light where there shouldn't have been anything. He rolled and sighted his rifle, but a report went racketing through the night just before another hit him a wicked blow on his skull and he felt blood trickling to the sand.

Chapter Twenty-One

He knew he should move. Every instinct screamed at him to do it. But Kee couldn't move. He was fully awake, yet not one limb responded to his mind's command.

He heard someone scrambling up and close to him. He lay there, helpless and alert, unable to get one finger to move.

Eyes open, he stared at the starlight gleaming along the barrel of a rifle. His rifle, and thankfully it wasn't aimed at him.

Then he saw and heard Isabel.

"Clarai! I know you are out there. You know that I am a better shot than you. If you do not leave now, I will fire and I will not miss."

"Isabel! Cousin mine. Listen to me. He is a liar and a thief. We have come to rescue you."

Fury bubbled in Isabel's blood. She was sure that Kee was dead. And to stand there and hear lies about him snapped whatever control she had. She laid a careful and measured field of fire around them, warning everyone off, keeping Clarai and her men away.

A broken cry split the air, following swiftly by falling rocks. Someone had been hit or killed. She did not care which, they had to pay for what they had done to Kee.

"We'll wait, Isabel. Find the gold. And when you do, we'll be there to take it from you. You're alone now. All alone."

Isabel shivered as a loud war cry broke the night. She was afraid but held her ground. She prayed that they would retreat. She had to get to Kee. Maybe there was a chance.

Kee was very much alive. He could hear them, and he could see, but he was paralyzed. He knew if Isabel hadn't arrived when she did, he would be dead. But the idea that he could have all his senses but touch, and call himself alive, sent a stream of terror through him. The thought that he could never touch Isabel again, or feel himself become a part of her, and she of him, never to ride the wild trails he loved flashed in his mind. Better the shot should have killed him.

He must have passed out, for he came to with the hot wetness of her tears falling on his lips. He tried to speak and tried again, only to hear a weak sound pass his lips. He attempted to move, begging his body to act to the strength of his mind's demand, but only a spasm shot through his body and nothing responded.

He made another sound, desperate to attract her attention, but she was sobbing so loudly that she couldn't hear him. He knew if they had pulled off, it was only for a while. They would be back and hunting her. He had to get both of them out of here. But how? A scream of pure rage welled in his throat and went no farther. He must not let Clarai or Benton or anyone else know that he was alive.

"Kee, *querido*...oh, beloved, I swear on your soul

and mine that I will make them pay with their lives for this.''

Kee croaked. He licked her tears from his lips and managed her name.

She reared back as if she were the one shot.

''Merciful God! You are alive!''

Not quite, he thought, but I'm trying to get there.

''Kee, speak to me. Tell me where you are hurt.''

If he had been able to speak, he couldn't. She was smothering him in kisses, her hands moving frantically over his body trying to find a wound.

''Get...'' The word took an unbearable effort. He had to make her understand that they had to get out of here.

''I will not leave you, dearest one. I will not. Do not ask that of me. Only talk to me. Tell me where you are hurt.''

He wanted to shake her, just grab hold and shake the daylights out of her, or hold her so close that fear could be halved.

The good Lord took pity, for her sobs quieted, and she realized how still his body was. For a moment terror held her in its grip. She knew he was alive. But he was not moving. He was not talking.

''Kee, I need to get you down below. Can you help me? If I...'' She stopped herself, and slipped one arm under his shoulders, but Kee was a big man, and her strength was not enough to lift him.

''Horse...get.'' He nearly sobbed aloud in frustration and then she was gone.

Sweat glistened on his face, he could feel it break out all over his body as he attempted to move. More of those knifelike spasms shot through him. But he realized that his head moved. Just a little, but it gave him hope.

He beat back the panic that threatened him. For a man who made his living as he did, using his skill and his strength, this was the most terrifying feeling.

The dull throbbing in his head grew painful in its intensity. Still Kee attempted another move. He curled his fingers into the earth and tugged. Then again. They responded, but left him weak as an hour old calf. Maybe he wasn't hurt badly, maybe he was stunned. He tried to remember how he fell, tried to recall the placement of the rocks. Maybe it wasn't a bullet that laid him low, but that he had hit his head.

He was grasping at straws and knew it, but just as he couldn't seem to stop himself from pushing his body to move, he couldn't stop the thoughts from coming and going until he felt sick to his stomach.

He prayed. Something he hadn't done in too long a time. But he prayed and begged for mercy. Not only for himself, but that he could be strong enough to protect Isabel. They would kill her once she found the gold.

He didn't want to live in a world without her.

It was a stunning moment to realize that tears were scalding his cheeks. His tears. For that endless moment he ceased fighting, almost stopped breathing, but he did not stop praying, for his fingers curled over the edge of a rock and its very ragged sharpness pierced his palm.

He blinked his eyes and a groan torn from deep inside his chest escaped his lips as he tugged and pulled on that rock. Forcing his body, forcing his mind to concentrate on that pain, feeling it grow to bladelike keenness, he moved his body.

He moved! Hot tears blinded him. Tears of humble thanks.

Maybe he wasn't crazy. Maybe this—whatever it was—was only temporary.

Excited by that small move, his heartbeat thundered in his ears. He managed to wrap his fingers around that rock. He knew there was no real strength in it, but he wasn't giving up. Babies crawled before they walked. And that is what he felt like, a baby trying to crawl. He bit through his bottom lip, tasted the hot salt of his own blood and fed on the rage that was building inside him. Those bastards weren't going to win. He'd made the one careless move that put him on his belly, but they'd made a deadly mistake not to kill him.

Sweat dripped and stung his eyes, but he kept on. He used the fingers of his other hand to push his body and was rewarded by coming to the rocks. He only had to focus on the image of Isabel, alone and at their mercy, to find the strength to pull harder. The dull throbbing in his head grew to a roar but he gritted his teeth and managed to draw his other arm around. With both hands on the rock he tugged until he swayed on one knee. He threw back his head, panting and weak, blood running down the side of his face. A guttural moan escaped him.

Helpless. She depended on him and he was useless to her.

And that's how Isabel found him, braced on one knee, head hanging and so still she feared that this time he was dead.

She could not utter a sound. Not screams of rage for what they had done to him. Not sobs of despair to see his strength cut out from under him.

But there was nothing wrong with her strength and Kee needed her now.

Outlaw snorted when he smelled blood and she turned to soothe the horse, knowing how much he was needed to help Kee. Inside she was shaking, but all that was visible was the fine tremor in her hands as she reached out to touch Kee.

"Horse," he grunted.

"Right here."

"Close."

She withdrew to grab the reins, and brought the mustang closer to him. It was a test of will to hold the horse and murmur soft words to steady him as she watched Kee's struggle to move.

He tried to catch the stirrup and missed. She shifted so she could hold it out to him. Then, realizing the mustang would stand, she left him ground-tied and went to help Kee. She slipped her arm around his hips to aid his attempt to stand. It did not work. She took his hand and placed the stirrup into it. With him holding on, and her using both her arms around his waist, he managed to stand.

But the mustang sidestepped and Kee almost went down to his knees. Only Isabel's firm grip and sheer determination kept him erect.

"Kee, you must hold on. Do you understand? I need to get the rifle, Kee. I cannot trust them to stay away." Twice more she repeated this as she inched herself away from him to grab the reloaded rifle from its leather scabbard. She breathed a little easier with the weapon in hand.

Back at Kee's side she slipped her arm around his waist while he held on to the horse. It was awkward moving off, for Kee's feet were dragging. But every step forward was a celebration to her, for it moved them out of danger.

But she knew they were leaving a trail, and she could not leave him to use any of the tricks he had shown her to cover it. She had to get him someplace safe and care for his wound. His clothing was soaked with sweat; she felt it seep into her own. Sound suddenly penetrated her thoughts.

As she spun around and brought the rifle to her shoulder, she saw Kee grab hold of the saddle with his other hand.

But there was no time for Kee. The looming silhouette of a man was on the top of the wash and she could not wait, could not think. She fired. And fired again.

A bullet spat in the earth near the mustang's feet and he trotted off, dragging Kee with him.

Kee heard Isabel return fire, but they were shooting at him. Two more shots came close and Outlaw shied, but Kee hung on as the horse headed down the wash to where he had been staked. There, Kee's strength failed him and he fell into the soft sand.

Isabel knew she had missed. The man was shooting at Kee. Rage, white-hot rage fed her. She found cover, and waited until she had something to shoot at. She had a general idea of where the man had taken cover. He had to shoot upward, and she down. The advantage was hers and she made the most of it. Each time he tried to aim his shot, she fired. But her concentration was not total. She was torn with wanting to follow Kee and care for him. She prayed he had not been hit again.

And she had more to worry about.

Where were the others?

She believed she had wounded or killed one. One man had her pinned down while Kee was below and helpless.

Where, then, was Clarai and the other man?

Circling around.

It had to be.

They would come at Kee first in the dry wash, and then up here for her.

Firmly convinced that she was right, she fired a wild volley in the shooter's direction. Dropping down, she crawled backward until she was well below the rocks and could turn safely to make a run toward Kee.

The horses were milling about, shying and pulling at the stakes, snorting when they got too close to him and smelled blood.

She dropped to her knees beside him. The sweat and fine trembling of his body told her he was still alive. But she had to move him. They were too exposed here.

And the shooting had stopped. That sudden and very ominous silence chilled her blood. She could see them in her mind's eye, wary, circling round, rifles aimed at the two of them.

But only if they were here.

There was no time to go back to get his bedroll. She had to use his saddle rope. Not daring to let go of the rifle, she used the stock and her shoulder to lift him a little. She was drenched by the time she managed to get the loop around his chest. And she prayed very hard that he stayed passed out as she slapped the mustang's rump to get him started down the wash.

She did not dare chance sending the horse up one of the banks. The rocks would injure Kee when she was desperate to save his life.

She had to chance making a run deeper into the dry wash. But she needed more cover for both of them.

With savage strength she yanked up the stakes and sent the horses flying ahead of them. Dust rose in a choking cloud as the horses ran from the smell of blood.

The only sounds Isabel heard came from the soft thudding of the animals' hooves, the pounding of her heart and her own panting breaths as she ran alongside Kee's body.

She could not see. Running harder she grabbed hold of the mustang's mane with one hand and let him guide her. The wash narrowed. At any moment she expected to feel the slam of a bullet.

Where were they hiding?

Kee groaned. But there was no help for him. She kept on with her bold move to use the horses as cover and urged Outlaw to keep up with the others. She could no longer see over the top of the banks. The ground sloped and started twisting. There were more rocks. She stumbled over them and her thoughts flew to Kee and what he must be suffering.

Brush snagged her shirt. And the dust cloud had dissipated. She jerked free and wiped the sweat dripping down her forehead and stinging her eyes.

For a moment she did not understand why the horses had stopped. Then she realized they stood at the edge of a pool of water. The rocky banks were a good five feet over her head. She could not drag Kee free of this place. This, then, was where she would make a stand.

But the night silence was now broken by the whisper of the wind and the small rustlings of prey and predator. Relief flooded her as she saw the horses dip their heads to drink, including Outlaw.

Kee trusted the mustang's instincts. She would, too.

She fought her intense need to go to Kee. She had to make sure they were safe. One careless moment on her part could mean their lives.

She was not going to let that happen.

Despite the trembling of her legs, she crawled up the bank. Something slithered away at her approach, but she paid it no mind. She hunted something larger and far more deadly.

Danger had heightened every sense. She held her breath, released it slowly, and searched with eyes that tried to probe every shadow.

Nothing.

Kee would go out there and make sure. But she was not Kee, and she would not leave him.

Maybe she had lost them. Or perhaps they had pulled back to wait until morning. The horses had calmed, a few of the mares were feeding on the grasses.

One last look, and then she hurried back to Kee.

She used her boot knife to cut away her sleeve. Everything had been left behind. They had Kee's rifle and his Colt. But the only bullets were looped in his gun belt.

Anxious as she was, Isabel first reloaded the rifle before she ran her hands over Kee's prone body and determined that the only wound he bled from was a graze on his scalp. Wetting her torn-off sleeve, she washed him carefully and thought with longing of their gear.

She gently rolled him over and saw that Outlaw

moved to stand over him, his muzzle dripping water on Kee's face.

Kee sputtered and coughed. The mustang lowered his head to nudge Kee's shoulder.

"Easy boy, easy," Kee said in an almost normal voice.

"Thank God," she whispered, leaning over him.

"Amen," he whispered.

Outlaw stamped his hoof and then blew on Kee.

Isabel pushed the mustang's nose out of her way. She fought the tears that burned her eyes. "I thought they had killed you."

"Me, too." The words were slurred. He knew he'd lost blood, and that dull throb remained in his head. If he concentrated hard, he could move. At least his hand, and he needed to touch her. Needed that contact as much as he needed water.

"Can you move at all, Kee?"

"Try."

"There is water. Help me, and we can get you a drink. I washed off the wound. You bled so much, but I think it was just a bullet graze. I was so..." She bit back a sob as her voice broke. Kee needed a strong woman now, not one who gave way to the fears and terror that had governed her every breath.

He managed to get up on one knee. Isabel went down beside him. She lifted one arm and put it over his shoulders.

"Lean on me. Let me help you."

It was agonizing how slow the moments were until they made headway and reached the edge of the water. There, Kee sprawled on his belly, drinking until his terrible thirst was quenched. His vision blurred. He pushed himself forward and rolled his head back and forth in the water. Isabel was pulling on his arm, calling to him, but the coolness soothed the throb in his head. He just didn't care what it did to the wound.

He gave in to her urging and reared back as she yanked his arm. He turned onto his back and lay there panting.

"Feel…like a mule kicked…me to hell…and gone."

"Stop talking. Save your strength, Kee." She threw an anxious glance around, knowing they could not stay there. His clothes were muddy and wet. He needed a fire and food.

"You? All…right?"

"Never mind me. I shot one of them. Wounded or dead, I…it does not matter." She shrugged and saw that he had closed his eyes.

"Kee, we cannot stay here. I do not know where they are. But this is too open."

"Take horses. Get our gear."

"I will not leave you alone."

"No choice. Helpless to move much. Up to you."

While he struggled to speak, he was tensing and then relaxing his whole body, the numb feeling slowly receding. Whatever had paralyzed him seemed to be passing, and he once more thanked God for it.

He lifted his arm, increasing the throb in his head. But it seemed to satisfy Isabel that he would be all right.

"Can you use your gun, Kee?"

"Help me to sit up."

She half pulled, half shoved him over to the rocks where he could rest.

"You go. Now."

He saw her snatch up the rifle, heard her, and then

the night's natural quiet seeped into him. He worked the thong off his Colt and slid it out of the holster. He kept watching the horses, but they showed no sign of alarm. He laid the gun on his lap and wiped his hands dry on his shirt. He kneaded the muscles first on one arm, then the other. His head still ached, but the throbbing was almost gone.

He heard the rattle of trickling gravel and snatched up the gun, afraid to have it out of his hand. He threw quick looks to the top of the banks, and then back to where Isabel had disappeared. He hated her being out there alone. But then he remembered her steady and measured fire, and heard her telling him that she had either killed or wounded one of them.

He caught himself as his eyes closed and shook his head. Images of Isabel swam in and out. She would be all right.

She had to be.

He felt on edge. He didn't like the quiet. He didn't hear or see a sign of Isabel. His gaze went to the horses. They appeared calm enough, but something was nagging at him.

His mouth was dry again, his throat parched for the water within easy reach. Yet he made no move.

He searched the rocky bank across from him. His hair was prickling on the back of his neck.

Kee wasn't sure if he really heard something above him, or if he sensed it. But he saw Outlaw's head come up. The mustang's nostrils flared wide and he was looking at Kee.

Buried in shadow, the move Kee made to tilt his head back and look up wasn't seen. But Kee could and did see the glint of a rifle barrel edging out over the rocks.

Whoever was up there was looking for him.

Or lying in wait for Isabel to come back.

Kee's hand clenched around the gun. He couldn't see who was up there, and he couldn't shoot unless he moved. And he knew that right now, he couldn't move quietly even though his life and Isabel's depended upon it.

If he gave himself away by the slightest noise, the other man had the first shot. All he could do was sit there and wait.

But he couldn't let Isabel walk into a trap.

Whoever waited above had a clear shot at her long before Kee saw her. He wouldn't be given a chance to warn her away.

She would be brave despite her fear, and in a hurry to get back to him.

Or maybe she wasn't coming back. Maybe one or more of those bushwhackers had waited for her. Someone like the mysterious Vasa that he hadn't yet seen. Or maybe— He stopped, suddenly sick of his speculations that stacked all the odds against them.

Whatever hand he'd been dealt, he'd play out the cards as they fell.

Outlaw stretched his head toward him, then his head went up, ears pricked, nostrils flaring. The horse didn't like the scent wafting his way.

Kee didn't put it past that crazy horse to charge right by him and up the bank. He was desperate enough to wish he could communicate that very act to the mustang.

His musing ended. He saw the spill of moonlight on the earth in front of him. All night, only bright stars had shone while a thin cloud cover floated over the moon. Now, he could see the tips of his boots. With bated breath, he inched them back into the deeper shadow that hid him.

One chance. That's all he had. He had known it all along. He had told Isabel another half truth. He had patience for her, and for working with horses, but none at all when it came to waiting to die.

Chapter Twenty-Two

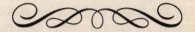

He had surprise and would use it. They all had to know that he was wounded. Someone would have been smart enough to check and find his blood.

But none knew if it was a serious wound.

Kee leaned to the side and tilted his head back. He saw the full extension of the rifle barrel above him.

Now or never. The gamble was his life.

Kee thought his bullet home. He would have one good shot. He inhaled, then exhaled slowly, his finger gently squeezing the trigger.

He rolled out into the open. He couldn't make out who was the man up there, but there was a frozen moment of time when Kee knew the man questioned what he saw.

And that moment was all Kee needed to fire his shot, for a bullet hit the earth at his side, and it was the last shot the man would fire. The rifle clattered down the rocks and lay there as the man fell forward, sprawled facedown.

Kee held his gun on the still figure, ready for another shot if needed. The fingers of his free hand worked feverishly to poke the empty shell from the gun's chamber and replace it.

He listened, every sense alert, but he heard nothing.

Biting back a groan, he managed to sit up, realizing that he moved a little more easily. His body could respond to his needs. He worked his way back to the deeper shadows and used the rocks to pull himself high enough to reach the rifle. Isabel had taken his, and he'd felt the empty loops on his gunbelt. Every weapon counted. He knew he didn't have the strength to climb higher and see who it was he shot. He wouldn't mind having the extra gun belt, either. He forced himself to make one lunge, but the man was too far above him for him to make a solid grab at his arm.

He climbed back down slowly, telling himself to be satisfied that he had cut the odds by one. On solid footing he swayed, leaning back quickly against the rock for support.

They all had to hear those two shots, but no one came, no one called out.

Isabel had to have heard them, too.

There was still no sign of her.

His head ached and his hand went to his skull. He probed gently beneath the cloth Isabel had tied around his head. There was a long furrow over his ear that had cut his scalp, but it wasn't bleeding.

And he had no time to rest. He had to find Isabel.

He flipped the rifle, holding the still-warm barrel in his hand and used the stock to support his weight as he hobbled out of the shadows.

Outlaw swung his head toward the milling mares, and then trotted after Kee.

Seeing the animal beside him, Kee grabbed the

horse's mane. He wished he could ride; he swayed like a drunken cowhand after a payday binge. But to ride meant he would be more visible to anyone who watched. He was getting damn tired of being used for someone's target. He needed to go hunting on his own.

And find Isabel before that.

Good common horse sense kept telling him to get her and pull out. They could come back for the gold, but not if they were dead. And that crazy, poison-mean cousin of hers seemed to want that more than the gold.

The good, the dangerous and the desperate all flocked at a hint of gold. It never stayed secret. And people were always ready to kill to possess it.

And he'd made a vow to Isabel that she would have her gold and her life or he'd die trying.

He caught the faint smell of smoke as he worked his way through the narrow, twisting path of the dry wash. He pulled up, his hand tight on the mustang's neck to keep him quiet.

If he didn't have to take every step with caution he could scramble up the rocky bank and scout ahead.

The way the wash formed, he had to go on blind.

He felt that his muscles had loosened up from that paralyzing shock, but his head still throbbed with a dull ache that wouldn't quit.

To tease him, a slight breeze blew the scents of coffee brewing and bacon frying. His supplies. And he couldn't believe that Isabel was cooking for him.

In seconds he realized that it was still quiet, but the night had a different feel to it. He thought he heard something, not a clear sound, but something was moving out there where he couldn't see.

He thought of drawing his knife, that was quiet, too, but he didn't want to lose the rifle.

There was a faint whisper. Something rubbing and working a few stones loose to fall on the ground.

Kee moved to the side, once more using the deeper shadows for cover.

He waited there in the darkness, every inhaled breath bringing the stronger smell of a campfire and cooking. He killed one, Isabel thought another was dead. That left Clarai and one other...no, no, he kept forgetting this man Vasa that Isabel swore was with them.

His leg muscles grew shaky, but he didn't dare move around.

Then he saw a shadow where none had been, and heard the soft footfall. Every muscle in his body tensed.

Down that narrow trail came his packhorse and Kee reacted with a quick move to grab the horse's nose.

"Easy boy, easy now," he murmured. He felt the quiver that ran through the animal, and it matched the shudder that passed through his body.

Isabel had taken this horse with her and the one she'd been riding. Someone had turned him loose.

Someone waiting for him.

The one thing no one could figure is what he'd do. They might expect him to ride off and leave Isabel to them. He knew there was trouble, killing trouble up ahead. He could figure what the men would do. But that Clarai...he just didn't know if she'd go for him or hurt Isabel.

He took stock of what he had. Guns, knives and horses. And no one else but himself to depend on.

There was barely room for him to lead the packhorse past Outlaw. He had to depend on the mustang. He hated tight places as much as Kee did.

Securing the rifle under his left arm, Kee drew out his belt knife. He ran his hand over the mustang's back.

"Forgive me, boy. But you'll be saving lives."

He didn't have the strength to slap the horse's rump hard enough to get him running. He used the blade to make a small cut, but its sudden sharpness piercing the hide was enough. Outlaw reared and his hooves thundered down before he bolted. The other horses ran with him.

And Kee hurried to follow them. They were his cover, and his distraction.

He heard it in moments, the commotion of horses and shouts and then a single shot that made his heart stop and start. He hoped it was a warning shot to turn the horses as he loped forward, keeping to the side of the wash. He could make out men's voices, and a woman's cry. He wanted the mustang to take the horses out of the wash, even if it meant that he was on foot.

He had the rifle up and cocked and took Benton by surprise.

The horses were gone. He heard them still running.

"You make mighty free with a man's possessions when he ain't around," Benton said.

"Kee, leave us."

He didn't spare a glance toward Isabel. Nor did he understand her saying that to him. He kept the rifle on Benton, didn't see a sign of Muley Cotton or Alf Dennis.

But Clarai was there, lit by the firelight and he never blinked but he wanted to rub his eyes since he wasn't sure that his vision was clear. She was Isabel's near spitting image. Same height, same slender build, same raven-black hair. Isabel sat beside her. He didn't see any ropes holding her there.

He couldn't drag his eyes away from her cousin. There was a difference in the features: where Isabel's were finely drawn, Clarai's appeared coarse. And the eyes, that's where a man could really tell them apart. Clarai's were as black as her soul. He'd faced eyes like that before, usually over gunsights.

"Come away from the fire, Isabel."

"No, Kee. My cousin and I have talked. We are going to share the gold."

Benton stuffed his mouth with bacon, and paid Kee no mind. But then Kee got that hair-prickling sensation that he was being watched.

"Tell this Vasa to come on down. Time we met."

Kee knew he was in no condition or position to dictate terms to any of them. If Benton and Clarai tried rushing him together, he'd have a hard time shooting one and keeping the other off his back. But he held his ground, trying to silently communicate with Isabel who had not made one move to leave her place.

She just watched him with those blue eyes filled with more secrets and shadows than he could fathom.

He didn't understand. Had everything she told him, everything they had shared been nothing but lies? But why? That made no sense at all, no matter how quickly he ordered his reeling mind to make sense of this.

And that Vasa still had not appeared. But no one said that Kee was crazy for mentioning him.

"Vasa!" Kee yelled, "show yourself or this woman of yours is going to die."

"You gonna shoot a woman?" Benton stopped chewing long enough to ask.

"No, Kee," Isabel said. "Just take your saddle and leave us. There is nothing here for you. I will say it again. My cousin and I will share the gold when we find it."

But Isabel couldn't find the gold in the morning or at any other time if he left. He still had the gold disk and without it... What the hell was that woman trying to do? Offer herself as hostage and then sacrifice so he could get away? She had to know that Clarai wasn't about to let him ride out of here knowing about the gold.

"Please, Kee. Just go."

And then Kee's eyes shifted to the man walking out of the shadows. He topped Kee's height by a good two inches and had about thirty pounds on him, but there was nothing to suggest that the man wasn't a fighter. This had to be the missing Vasa. He wore his gun tied low on his thigh. Butter-soft buckskins, the kind the Apache made for themselves, clung to a powerfully built man. His skin was dark; a scar ran from his eye to his jaw.

Kee took this in with a quick glance, for the man stood directly behind where Isabel sat. And he felt the surge of his blood at the way Vasa looked at Isabel not Clarai.

Right then and there, Kee knew this was going to end as a shooting matter between the two of them.

Thumbs hooked in his gun belt, Vasa stood with his legs spread, waiting for Kee to make the next move.

And his heated blood cooled rapidly when he saw Vasa lean down to whisper something that made Isabel pale.

Kee damned his luck to catch that bullet graze. The man's cruelty gleamed in his eyes.

"I'm not leaving without Isabel. Gather up our gear. We'll ride out together."

"She won't go with you," Clarai said. "We're cousins, blood, family. That's important. Not you, a stranger. And you only want the gold."

"Kee," Isabel called quickly, "I know I promised you a share if you helped me, but I do not need you now. They will get their reward."

"The lovely señorita speaks the truth," Vasa added in a slightly accented voice. "We are the ones who will help her and she is gracious with her promised reward."

If Kee hadn't known Isabel, he would have missed the flare of fear and rage that showed in her eyes. But she said nothing to contradict him. And she said nothing to ease Kee's mind about the kind of reward she had promised Vasa.

Clarai had heard him, too. She hissed something in Apache at him, but Vasa merely shrugged and smiled.

"Well, now, I figure we all deserve a share of that gold. So I'll just help myself to some coffee and we'll sit here until morning."

Benton looked at Kee as if he were loco. Clarai put arrows in him from her black, snapping eyes. Vasa smiled and Isabel stared at him with dismay.

Kee didn't care what they thought of him. He was laying out the scene in front of him. Benton wasn't about to get himself killed. He might stay out of it, figuring he'd end up with the gold and a woman no matter if Kee did the killing or Vasa did. What worried Kee was that Vasa hadn't moved. He had Isabel to grab as a shield. Nor could he dismiss the threat of Clarai, although he couldn't see that she held a gun. His horses were gone, not far, he hoped, but theirs were staked up the short bank of the wash. Not far from where he stood was the pile of saddles. His own and Isabel's were on top.

As if she had followed his every thought and knew he would be making a move, Isabel jumped up and ran around the fire toward Kee.

"You must go. I insist. We had a bargain. I hold you to your word." She came forward with every word until she stood in front of him. "Kee, go. I beg you."

This last was so soft that he barely heard her. As she meant it to be, for her voice rose with the next words.

"I used you. Are you too stupid, *gringo,* to understand that? I have no more need of you. Take your horses and get out of my sight."

Her eyes pleaded with him to do as she said. But he was torn. What threat were they holding over her head? He had only to grab her and put her behind him. Once more she seemed to divine his thoughts and divert him from acting.

"Is it the gold that you want? I will make sure a share is sent to you after the sunset tomorrow. We wait for that."

"Enough!" Clarai rose from her place near the fire and Kee saw the glint of the knife that she held. The blade had almost cut him once, and she must have been holding that against Isabel. He thought there was still a chance, but Isabel had already turned her back and was walking away from him.

And Isabel had hidden something else from his view. Vasa and Benton had drawn their guns and were holding them on him.

"If you kill him now," Isabel calmly stated, "I will

never show you where the gold is. He will ride away and none will stop him. Call them again, Clarai, and tell them that. And remember, cousin, we speak the same language.''

Kee expected to hear Apache from Clarai, but it was a Mexican dialect mixed with English that ordered he go free.

Isabel was not done. "Tell them to come to the fire. I want no bullet in Kee's back.''

Kee, more confused than ever, saw that Clarai was going after Isabel, then she stopped at a gesture from Vasa. And she called in three more men. Mixed breeds, Kee thought, when he saw the men. Renegades and outlaws from the other side of the border. One wore double guns slung around his hips, the others held rifles. New ones.

"Guess this is where you expect me to say *adiós*." But Kee made no move toward getting his saddle. He wasn't about to set down the rifle he had taken from the man he had killed, and he wasn't about to put his gun hand on anything but the butt of that gun. Yet he knew the odds were stacked too heavily against him.

Vasa seemed to weigh his decision before he motioned to one of his men. "Carry the saddle for him. Do not worry, Pedro, he will not shoot you. The *señor* is a man of honor, *sí?* Unlike you," he added.

"Hold up. It's not that simple. There's the little matter of having my own rifle back. You understand that, Vasa. A man's gun is like his woman. She only responds to his hand. And then there's my pack. Cowhand works too damn hard for his money. Gets real possessive over what he owns. Don't figure I'll be leaving without those things.''

Kee did care about the family gifts, and some of his

possessions, but right now he wanted hands busy on anything but guns.

"Where the hell is Muley?" Benton asked. "That sure looks like his rifle."

"He is dead, courtesy of the *señor,*" Vasa answered.

So Vasa had found him, and Kee knew that Vasa had been watching him work his way up the dry wash to here. But why hadn't he killed him? Isabel was the only answer.

He saw that they had raided his packs and taken most of the supplies. But he had gotten what he wanted—two men carrying his gear and his rifle.

He went up the short, soft slope of the bank at an angle to them. He whistled for Outlaw, and as he had hoped, the mustang had not gone far. He trotted up, but shied from the strange man who tried to grab his bridle.

"Just leave my gear and get back to the fire where I can see you," Kee ordered.

The men moved fast, but not so fast that Kee didn't manage to throw his saddle and pack over the mustang's back. The horse wasn't happy with the additional burden but he stood still. Kee didn't attempt to cinch the saddle. He wasn't riding out and giving them his back.

From below, he heard Isabel call out to him.

"*Vaya con Dios,* Kee. Remember the ledge."

The man had been in such a hurry that they had left his rifle and forgotten to take the other one. He walked out into the night beside his horse, steadying the packs and Isabel's words replayed over and over in his mind.

"Go with God," she had said. A common enough

goodbye in the Southwest. He needed the good Lord and a host of saints and angels to help him out of this.

But what had she meant about remembering the ledge? He'd almost gotten the two of them killed there. Was she warning him? Or sending him a message?

Chapter Twenty-Three

He worried and worked over her words as he made his way with a slowness and caution over a leg-killing talus slope so steep that even the horses had trouble with it.

"Go with God," he whispered, stopping to rest and wondering why that bullet he'd been waiting for never came. He leaned against one of the mares who butted her nose against his shoulder demanding some attention.

As he absently stroked her neck, Kee stood up straight. Isabel called Weaver's Needle the Finger of God. Was she telling him to go there in the morning and use the disk to find the gold? But when he added her words to remember the ledge he drew a blank.

She said something about a gully and nothing that he recalled about any ledge. And his head ached again.

She had done everything but physically shove him out of there. His lips twisted into a bittersweet smile. Clever and lovely. She had made sure he knew there were three more men to deal with. And that Vasa had some hold on her.

Kee glanced down to where their fire had burned to

coals. He couldn't see the guards they posted, but he knew they were out there, likely waiting for him to make a move to rescue her.

Isabel was safe enough with them tonight. There wasn't a man down there that didn't want his hands on the gold.

And her. He couldn't forget the possessive cruelty in Vasa's eyes. His stomach churned with sickness.

He searched and found a pebble that he brushed off on his jacket. He placed it in his mouth to generate moisture. He had no canteen, and no coffeepot even if he would risk a fire.

He took the disk from his money belt, and held it up. This was the key to the gold. But how? And where?

He had the strongest feeling that Isabel had bought him time to get there first. That had to be why she lied to them and said she couldn't find the gold until the sun set.

Her message at the end had to do with one of those black basalt towers. All he recalled was something about standing at the head of the gully and holding the disk up to the rising sun. Somewhere a ledge came into play. A ledge that was as dangerous as the one they had come down.

It had to be that. Nothing else made sense.

The moonlight played over the needles and the deep shadows hid the crevices and ravines that guarded it. He couldn't stand here and look, he had to get down there. He had to block the thought of Isabel from his mind, and fight off every weakness that threatened to put him down.

She was counting on him, and he'd made his vow to her.

He needed more time. Time to scout the land, time for Isabel to tell him everything her grandfather had told her. He couldn't forget about the earthquake that happened here almost six years ago. And in May, too.

The thought went round and round as Kee worked his way to that one gully. He rested for only a few minutes at a time, cinching Outlaw's saddle during one period.

Moonlight helped him find his way. The horses found him water. A hollowed-out stone nearly his height across and about ten inches deep held enough for him and his animals to drink. Kee rested there, drinking every few minutes after he recalled something Logan had taught him. The Apache could go for days without water because when they had this precious liquid of life, they drank and saturated their bodies until they could not hold another drop of water. But as he lay there, the awareness of time slipping quickly by came with his notice of stars beginning to fade from the night sky.

He took one last drink of water, which he held in his mouth as he started off once more. Outlaw trailed him, the mares and packhorse picking their way close on the path the mustang chose.

He reached the gully between the towering rocks just as night faded into that dark grayness that preceded dawn.

Exhausted, and afraid if he sat down he wouldn't get up, Kee just stood there, head hanging like that of a played-out horse. Isabel! Her name was a silent cry in his mind.

He removed the disk once more. Studied it with his fingertips. When he held it up for the first sun rays, whatever it pointed to would be behind him. Then he realized the utter impossibility of what she wanted him to do.

If he held the disk with the open crescent moon in proper position, the graduated cuts of arrows pointed toward the west. If he held the disk so that he had the curve of Isabel's sweet smile or reversed it like the arch of her brow, he'd either have to climb or dig.

Or go east, he added, turning the disk over and over in his hand.

He turned and faced west. A hundred places and all dangerous. He did that with each direction, one more deadly than the next. He could search here, like Julia Thomas and others who had hunted for the Dutchman's gold, Peralta's mine, and all the other stories, for the next thirty years and never find it.

Isabel depended on him to figure it out. He was missing something. And he had too little time. He was counting off the seconds in his mind when that sky would change to its painted colors like the bunting hung for one of his grandmother's fiestas.

But this was a party of one. Until sunset.

The calluses on his fingertips had thickened them, so Kee used his lip to test the edge of the disk. At first he dismissed the slight indentation as a chip. After all, the piece had age to it. But when he chanced lighting a match he saw that wasn't true. The pointed notch was so tiny that it was easy to miss. It had to be the sign he prayed for...the way to hold the disk to find the mine's opening.

And he was going to test that belief, for the color spread over the sky welcoming the sun's rise.

"You are all fools to believe her," Clarai whispered as she stirred the fire with twigs, then added a few sticks. "He will not go as you believe. He will hide and wait his chance to get to her." She glared at Vasa. "You should have killed him when you could."

On the opposite side of the fire, Isabel fought to keep her breathing even and her eyes closed as she strained to listen to her cousin's low voice. But as the seconds ticked by in her mind, Vasa's continued silence worried her. She knew he was not asleep, not as Benton was, snoring and mumbling on his bedroll a few feet from her. The three other men had melted into the darkness minutes after Kee had disappeared.

She prayed they were not following him.

There had been no real chance to give Kee more of a message. She had to trust him to figure out what she meant. She sent her prayers out to him as the darkness slowly began its fade and the world took on a grayish cast.

Minutes, only minutes more and the sun would rise.

Doubts plagued her. Kee's head injury could prevent him from getting there in time. And she had never showed him the key to using the golden disk her grandfather had made.

Trust him, she told herself.

She had. And she still did trust him. No questioning doubts lingered, and no regret for loving him. Love...

Even silent, the word, the thought, the very strong feeling behind it, sent shock waves through her. How did it happen? When? She needed to know the moment love for Kee had come to her. But she could not afford to allow her wary guard to drop and daydream of the time spent with him. She had to remain alert.

She discovered a truth and now found regret. She had never told him. So she sent her silent message on the edge of a prayer. *I love you, Kee Kincaid. God keep you safe for me.*

She was jerked from her quiet by the sound of a slap and Clarai's hissed accusations. Isabel could no longer pretend to sleep, for even Benton awakened to groggily ask what the hell was going on.

Isabel looked across the fire. Vasa held a struggling Clarai on his lap, whispering to her, but his eyes were pinned on Isabel, and she could not stop the cold shiver that crawled up her spine. Only the thought that she had to stay here and lull them into the belief that she would show them where the gold was, and buy time for Kee, kept her from running.

That, and the fact no one had searched her. She still had her boot knife.

Her stomach turned over when she saw that Vasa was kissing Clarai to silence. Kissing her with those dark eyes open, staring at her. Isabel hoped disgust showed in her eyes as she rolled over and turned her back on them.

The thought flashed into her mind that she had felt vulnerable and alone at times, but never like this. It was like watching a mountain storm, the black clouds gathering in strength, knowing there was nothing she could do to prevent it, nothing but to hang on and pray she would survive until the storm had passed.

Out of the black despair that encompassed her at that moment, the image of Kee's face appeared. She saw that dark intensity in his eyes and knew he thought of her, too. Her fear for him was his for her. Reaching out across the distance that separated them were his arms to enfold her in their loving warmth and strength. And she let that feeling of love grow, until its heat and power filled her mind and heart and body.

She protected him by staying there and he kept her vow by going after the gold.

Somehow, someway they would be together.

The wind rose up suddenly, blowing over the land, swirling dust clouds and a long, low wail came with it.

Isabel did not hear it, did not see it. She put herself with Kee, whispering what he needed to know, guiding him to the exact place as the first blinding rays rose to pierce the gully between the towering stones. She saw his hands holding the disk up. Those long, strong fingers that moved over her body with such passionate gentleness, delicately held the golden circle between them. Now, lift it slowly, center that tiny notch until you see its open points touch each of the black stone fingers. Look up to the first small arrow. The sun is nearly there. Turn, Kee, turn. But watch the crescent. Slowly, ever so slowly comes the sun and there! There, Kee, it is waiting for you.

But hurry now. You have only minutes to get to the crevice.

The sudden clamp of a hand on her shoulder brought her scream.

"Get up! You can make yourself useful. Cook for us."

Isabel stared into Vasa's dark eyes. With quiet determination she removed his hand, daring him silently to object. She had lost her precious moments with Kee.

It was all up to him now.

Kee couldn't believe how intricate and yet simple the disk proved to use. It was almost as if some unseen hand had guided his every move. But when he started for the dark crevice lit by the sun's rays, a knifelike pain pierced him and sent him to his knees. He saw where a snake had crossed a small sand bed, and a place where a covey of quail had raced along in a wide group. But no other tracks of any kind. He labored up the slope toward the opening, sliding on the loose talus.

He had a sudden prickling along his scalp. Ahead in the rocks there was a faint stirring, the kind of sound settling timber made. He didn't like it. He couldn't stop the wild tale of swinging stones from entering his mind. Logic dictated that rocks loosened by a fall or an earthquake could, when wind and sun and rain had worn away support, suddenly fall and crush someone.

Made perfect sense to him.

But when he reached the tall, narrow opening, he knew the horses wouldn't be coming with him. There was barely room for him, and only if he turned sideways and squeezed through.

He rested his hand against the rock face and it came away, crumbling as it fell. Kee stepped back and as he did, he saw the same signs as on the disk cut into the face of the rock.

He had found the way to Isabel's gold!

He went back to Outlaw, and untied his nearly empty saddlebags. Kee forced himself to think of nothing but Isabel. Those stories of mysterious deaths and vengeful gods were trying to crowd his thoughts.

The opening was seamed with ancient cracks. He thought he could make out a few more cuts in the rock, but they weren't clear. He prayed the opening didn't crumble when he entered. Once again he heard that faint stirring within the rocks. He ignored it, for a little voice told him to hurry.

He didn't know if the warning came because of the gold or because Isabel needed him.

He entered into a dark space. Rock overhung the opening, and appeared solid when he lit a match. From above, the deep crevice couldn't be seen.

His mouth went dry, yet he was breaking out in a cold sweat. The thought of Isabel trying to work her way through this sent a chill through every fiber of his body.

There was a smell of dampness in the air, and that was hot and close. He didn't like the feel of it; he didn't like anything about this strange, haunted place.

And it seemed there was no end to this tunnellike crevice cut so deep into the rock.

Kee's boot sent something rattling ahead. The sound stopped immediately and there were no others. He didn't think it was a snake, but he hated the thought that it just might be and lit another of his precious few matches.

A skull gleamed on the sand. He swallowed, went past it, and the match blew out.

Cool air brushed his face and with it he heard what sounded like a storm wind blowing. The piercing and heartrending cries were followed by unearthly shrieks and howlings. They combined to soul-wrenching sounds that seemed to come from everywhere at once.

He dropped the saddlebags and covered his ears. Stumbling forward, he felt the space around him and once more he lit a match. High above was a hole in the rock. That explained the sounds. Not the sudden silence. He examined the rock wall closest to him. His eyes went to the gleam below. A small rock, a little larger than a bullet, but it was gold. The real genuine high-grade gold. The kind he'd seen a few samples of from one of the Kincaid mines.

No matter who had come here first, it was a gold mine and now all he had to do was figure a way to get the gold out.

He tucked the rock into his jacket pocket, and pushed on. Within minutes he had come to the end. He felt the walls, and there was no opening. The dark wasn't complete, but it didn't let him see too much, either.

Stripping off his jacket, he used his knife to cut off his shirtsleeves. Using the cloth for light was dangerous, but he had to know if there was anything there. He wasted precious moments in the dark, cutting off the water-shedding fringe from his jacket and using it to tie the twisted cloth in place. When he was done, he had an awkward torch, but it lit up the space where he stood.

And above, about shoulder high he saw the ledge and the notched opening above that. There was a gleam of gold there, brighter and larger than the small rock he'd picked up.

But Kee admitted to himself that he was afraid of going up there. The whole place seemed unstable. One wrong move on his part and he'd be buried alive.

You're crazy, the sane voice of reason told him.

"Isabel needs this gold," he whispered.

He tossed the burning cloth up onto the ledge. Then he carefully placed his hands on its edge and tested the rock. It seemed solid. Nothing crumbled beneath his grip. He heard again that faint whisper, both to hurry and of the rock stirring. Taking a deep breath, he swung himself up, getting one leg and half his body on the ledge.

The burning cloth wasn't going to last much longer. He had no time to check out the notch, only to toss down what loose rock he could lay his hands on. The chunks of ore were bright. Jewelry store rock, miners called this. And they were heavy, even the smaller pieces.

The notch had streaks of gold, not thin hairlike seams, but wrist-size bands of it. And the quartz was rotten. He was breaking off chunks of it with his fingers; some crumbled but he kept on throwing them down.

The shrieking wind began again, and the cloth was burning down to almost nothing. Kee looked at what had accumulated below. All that gold. A man could go anywhere, buy anything and come back here for more. He could understand the fever that got into men's blood over the search and the find of gold. But some things weren't worth it. Isabel's life.

He eased himself down and dropped the rest of the way. Using his jacket as a pack, he gathered the chunks and then went and filled his saddlebags. This had to be enough for whatever she needed. That prickling was back and it wasn't running over his scalp now, but his whole body.

He wanted out of here. And he wanted out now.

He sweated and panted, hauling his load and had to slow down to where he crawled and pushed the bundles in front of him.

And he found himself whispering to Isabel that he was coming, she had to hold on a little longer, but he would be there for her.

Because he crawled, he felt the vibrations as if the earth shifted beneath him. He had passed the skull. He couldn't have much farther to go. And no god of the mountain, or the devil himself was going to stop him from getting out.

But he knew he had challenged the mountain and its secret. When the stronger vibrations came from the ground beneath him, Kee wondered if he would survive.

Chapter Twenty-Four

Isabel kept her eyes away from the gully and never once looked up at the tower of rocks. Her skin crawled with the way Vasa watched her every move, from the moment she rose to begin cooking until now when she returned with an armload of firewood. Clarai also watched her. She sat above with a rifle across her lap.

Benton had taken the horses back to the end of the dry wash to water them. Of the three men, Isabel had not seen them since they came one at a time to the fire this morning, ate, had coffee and just as silently returned to guard them.

"Your little cousin does not believe that you must wait for sunset to show where the gold is."

"She can believe what she wants, Vasa. I told you the truth. And I would not lie and cost Kee his life."

She needed to turn his thought away from Kee, but for a moment nothing came to mind. She did not want to talk to him, or be near him. She could almost feel her cousin's jealous rage reach out to touch her.

Desperate to get away, and desperate to distract Vasa, she snatched up the coffeepot.

"I will get fresh water."

"Wait. I go with you."

The shot into the sand at Vasa's feet made him and Isabel jump apart.

"Stay away from my man, Isabel. Or the next bullet will be for you. A broken leg or arm won't stop you from showing us the gold."

Isabel barely glanced at Clarai. She knew her cousin meant what she said. Clarai would shoot her. Benton came in at a run leading the horses.

Isabel saw that he had drawn his gun. Vasa started to claim it was an accident, but two of his men entered the wash. Isabel paid no attention to their excited questions. She stood off by herself, trying to think of another way to get out of Clarai's sight.

Then she heard the question that made her step closer to them.

"Where is Luis?" Vasa asked his men.

She saw the two glance at one another, then shrug.

And she thought of Kee first. Had Luis followed him? No! She could not, would not accept that. Kee had to be all right. She had willingly given herself over as hostage to keep him safe. No god would be so cruel as to let that be in vain.

The air was hot and still, not a hint of a breeze stirred in the dry wash. Isabel could not hear their whispers. Clarai had not moved down to find out about the missing Luis.

The horses, including her two packhorses, milled about.

It was the chance she had been waiting for.

Isabel moved slowly, trying not to call attention to herself. She had put one horse between her and the four men. A quick look showed that Clarai still watched outward, away from her. She wished she could slip her boot knife free. Having a weapon in hand would make her feel more confident that she could escape.

But no one was watching her. Vasa and Benton both were looking to where the other men pointed. Telling them where they had last seen Luis? She did not care.

A few more steps. She lightly slapped the rump of one of the horses blocking her way. They would expect her to run down the twisting path of the wash. She intended to climb the rocks and find Kee.

She was about to make her run when she heard the man's shout. The others had heard it, too. And it was the one word she prayed not to hear.

"Gold!"

She ran behind the others and saw Luis's stumbling figure weaving a drunken path toward them while he shouted the word over and over in a hoarse voice.

Her assumption had been right. Luis had followed Kee. Vasa and Clarai had never believed her lies. Had Luis hurt Kee? Or...no! If Kee had been killed she would know. She strongly felt that to be true.

Then Vasa, impatience stamped on his face, grabbed the mane of one of the horses and swung himself up to ride bareback. He urged the horse up the slope, sand flying as Benton, with a loud whoop, followed suit. The other two men were trying to mount without saddles when Isabel passed them and raced to the top of the wash.

Clarai ran beside Vasa's horse. He reached out his arm and stretched out his leg. Clarai grabbed hold and in seconds she was mounted behind him.

The two men raced each other, wanting their share. She saw how hard they kicked their horses to catch up to the others. All running toward the towering spires.

Isabel stood there forgotten by all of them. But she no longer was necessary. They had found the gold.

And desire to possess its riches would fire their blood until nothing else existed.

She shaded her eyes with her hand, searching for a sign of Kee. A haze enveloped the sun, but did not lessen the heat that baked the land. Still, she stood and watched for long minutes while hope grew dim that Kee had survived. Yet she could not drag herself away. She had to be sure.

Slowly, she lowered her hand, cold seeping through her. He was not riding, walking or even crawling back to her. Nothing moved out there but the shadow of a hawk. Despair turned her erect stance into slumped shoulders and spread a weakness in her legs. She caught herself swaying where she stood.

She was being a fool to continue to hope and wait. But she knew the man she longed to see. Unless he was dead, he would come back for her.

Then the wind came up, whispering over the rocks and sand, faintly wailing as it swept through the ravines, and she felt it shed the tears she could not, tears for finding a man she loved and having him taken to give her her dream.

Suddenly she turned away from the sight of the desolate land, jamming her fist against her mouth to stop the cries. She fought to control the emotions tearing through her. She had been strong for so long, she was not coming apart now. She would gather up the horses they had left and strip the camp of everything they had stolen. But she could not say goodbye, not even a silent one to the man who had filled her heart.

As she turned, she heard the wail that rebounded from the rocks and echoed through canyon and ravine into crevice and was lost only to rise again.

''Where?''

It sounded like Clarai's and Isabel smiled a bitter smile, looking up at the fully risen sun. The haze had burned off and now the mine's entrance would once more be guarded, its secret safe within the darkest of shadows.

And Kee...

Kee was a flame burning inside, a dream and sweet memory she would keep alive. As for the gold and the land that would be lost, perhaps her grandfather was telling her it was time to let it go. Without the golden disk she could spend years searching for the right place, just as her cousin...

The earth tremored beneath her feet, cutting off her thoughts and sent her back down into the dry wash.

Get out! Get out! sang a silent litany and she hurried to do just that. She flung saddles on the horses that were rolling their eyes and tossing their heads. The animals sensed the danger and she fought not to allow their panic to infect her.

She left nothing behind her as she rode out.

But she did not ride far. The mountain had claimed one life she loved; it would not claim Kee as well.

Kee couldn't see the sunlight as the ground shook beneath him. He moved like lightning the last few feet, choking on the clouds of rock dust that had loosened. He was desperate for air, clean and untainted, to fill his lungs. But there was more than a natural shadow hovering near the entrance. A dark, more dense shadow of a man.

He pushed his packs ahead of him, swearing under his breath at the scraping noise they made, that he could do nothing about. Someone was waiting to kill him.

And that thought slipped into a quickly laid plan of what he could do.

"Gold," he croaked. "I've found the gold."

He felt the packs pulled free from the crevice, and then, surprisingly, strong arms gripped his wrists and helped pull him clear of the dust.

He came up in a rush, knowing full well the limits of his strength, his knife at the young man's throat.

His move worked because the man's eyes were glued to the gold bursting from the saddlebags.

"Lose the rifle and the gun belt," Kee ordered.

Like a man in a trance, he obeyed. Licking his lips, eyes lit with greed, the young man called Luis finally pulled his gaze away, and realized that he had lost his weapons.

"This is all?"

Kee smiled. "Take a hundred men a hundred years to clean out that vein. Makes a man drunk just to look at it. Just lying there, easy pickings. And you're going to get a share. This is what you have to do...."

With Kee holding his own rifle on him, Luis ran as he was bid. The man was more stupid than he'd been told. Crazy gringo! Telling him to call the others to share in the gold. So much. He thought of the fine horses he would buy, and the saddle trimmed with silver conchos. The finest whiskey and the women...

And the fever spread as he shouted louder and louder, Kee and the rifle forgotten, his mind bursting with thoughts of what he could buy.

He infected the others as they raced to where he

stood. Telling them what he had seen of rich golden rock, and what waited for all of them. Yes, he told of the riches, but not of the man with the rifle.

Luis mounted behind his brother, and they all drove the horses to get there. The fever high in eyes that held every greedy dream known to man.

In the ravine where he had hidden his horses, Kee watched them. He watched as Luis turned in half circles, his eyes frantically searching the face of the rock.

"It is here! I tell you I saw it! Here, in this place—more gold, rich, rich gold."

"Where?" Clarai screamed at him, her hands curled into claws, ready to attack him and force him to tell.

"Where?" Benton shouted, moving like lightning to search himself as the other two men took up the cry.

Only Vasa remained silent as he, too, hunted the opening.

Kee knew one of them would find it. There hadn't been enough time for him to conceal the opening. A shout alerted him. And one by one, he watched as the mine drew them in, swallowing them up.

A haze floated over the sun. Nothing moved, not even their abandoned horses swished a tail on the talus slope.

Until now Kee had used his strength of will to keep away thoughts of Isabel.

But not a moment longer.

She had not been with them. He chased the thought that she was dead. He would know. That truth planted itself inside his heart and his mind. Somehow he would know if he'd heard the last whisper of his name from her lips.

Then the wind came up, whispering over the rocks

and sand, faintly wailing as it swept through the ravine.

It was time for him to go and claim a far richer treasure than gold.

As he rode out, he saw the haze lift and the shadows that fell hid the crevice. He knew it was there, and exactly where, but he could no longer find it.

The mare's whinny was followed by more from the other horses. He felt Outlaw's fear as the earth seemed to tremor and rocks fell clattering into the ravine behind him. He thought of that faint creaking within that hellhole of gold. The mountain guarded its secret well.

He set boot heels to his mustang's sides, anxious to get out of this strangely haunted place. He fought off the exhaustion that swept over him, a whisper of other dangers drumming up from the racing hooves of the horses.

And he had to find Isabel.

One minute he rode alone, and the next Vasa raced alongside him, shouting they were all dead. Vasa drove his horse into Kee's, trying to cut him off with every swipe of his knife.

Kee blocked the thrust of the knife with his arm slamming into Vasa's wrist. He kicked free of his right stirrup, balancing his weight on the left as he swung his leg flat on the running mustang's back. There were other evasive moves he could make, and the shifting weight would never alter the mustang's stride, but they required strength and concentration and this wasn't a show for an appreciative audience, but death waiting in that slashing blade.

He spied the bed of soft sand ahead, whispered to his horse, then suddenly jerked the rein. The mustang responded by veering off and turning in an ever tightening circle, leaving Vasa racing past them.

But the man had survived his own share of fights and reacted quickly to his sudden lack of target. He brought his horse around, using the strength of his knees and his hands as he twisted the animal's mane and sent the horse running at Kee.

But Vasa didn't know Outlaw or his instinctive need to fight and protect his rider. Kee slipped off and the mustang reared, screaming his challenge like a wild stallion born. Teeth bared, head down, Outlaw charged Vasa's horse.

And Vasa's animal reacted with like instincts, rearing and screaming his own challenge. Vasa clamped his legs around the bay's barrel, his strength fighting the animal's need, for he had sighted better prey.

Isabel.

And Kee saw her ride closer and closer to Vasa.

He ran for his horse, stumbling in the soft sand. Vasa was driving his animal into hers and Kee saw her fall. It took him precious seconds to mount and race to where Vasa held his knife to her throat.

"No! The gold, Vasa. You can have the gold!"

"I'll take both the woman and the gold and see you dead. You planned that. You led them there to die. And so you will die. And she will watch. And when she lies beneath me, I will laugh at her tears."

Kee rode closer. He felt every tense muscle of the mustang rippling beneath him. His own body was as taut. He met Isabel's terrified gaze.

"I thought it was you, Kee."

He slid from his saddle and drew his belt knife. "Me and you." He saw Isabel strain against the arm

that Vasa locked around her waist. Any pain Kee felt
was lost as Vasa's blade nicked her bared throat.

Soft, chilling laughter came from Vasa as he
watched every breath that Kee took.

Outlaw distracted all of them for a moment. He
reared, teeth bared, hooves hitting the earth with thunder as he went after Vasa's horse. There was no sign
that the saddle hindered him, for the mustang was wild
again, protecting his band of chosen mares from a rival
and he would fight to the death.

Kee could do nothing to stop the battle between the
animals. His eyes were locked on Vasa's knife and
Isabel's eyes dilating wide until the blue disappeared
and black terror watched him. He shouldn't be looking
at her eyes at all. His breathing went shallow, his
heartbeat drummed like a stampeding herd. A slightly
oily feeling lined the pit of his stomach. His legs tremored with the need for him to be absolutely still yet
his blood raced with the primitive urge to act.

He felt as wild as his mustang, his need to protect
overpowering in its intensity.

"Let her go, Vasa. Fight me like a man. Hiding
behind a woman is a coward's way. Let her go." Soft,
so soft he made his demand as his hand clenched the
handle of his knife and slowly brought its point up.

Kee knew he had to end the fight quickly.

Suddenly Vasa laughed and flung Isabel toward
Kee.

Kee swung his arm out and away from his body to
avoid stabbing her as she fell against him. But she
knew the danger as well as he and fell and rolled out
of his way.

But Vasa had moved, too. Like a snake he struck

from Kee's blind side and the point of his knife bit into Kee's hip.

Kee backed away. White-hot pain exploded from his leg to his shoulder. But the pain gave him an edge. It reminded him what he was fighting for, and what would happen if he lost.

They circled each other, neither man watching the other's blade, only the eyes. For the eyes would tell the other man's move before the hand and knife thrust.

Kee willed his mind to empty. He willed his body to absorb the pain and lower its intensity. He curved his body to avoid another slash, waiting, and using those precious moments to force the pain to lose its hold on him. Blood soaked his pants, but the weaker the pain grew, the more his mind controlled it, and he felt stronger.

He'd gotten himself out of tight spots before and that ability, combined with the white-hot rage of what Vasa and his band had done, and what Vasa planned for Isabel, brought the surge of power he needed.

He crouched and spun to avoid the knife. Vasa's laughter grated on Kee's ears. The small rocks could easily roll under his boots and trip him. Kee cautiously moved back, drawing Vasa and his wickedly sharp knife with him.

"How can you fight for a woman who shed no tears at her cousin's death? She has a heart of stone, that one."

Kee wouldn't answer the goad, or the ones that followed as Vasa's taunts vividly drew Isabel's fate at his hands.

Kee darted forward, then sucked in his belly as he slashed down twice in quick succession and left Vasa bleeding from his arm and leg.

"Careless, Vasa," Kee goaded, sweat stinging his eyes from the relentless sun. "A man gets that close, it's killing close."

"Come again, *gringo*. Come again."

Vasa lunged at Kee. The tanned skin jacket bore a long slash that was meant for Kee's skin. Vasa closed in again, as if he sensed a weakening. Kee stomped hard on Vasa's ankle, knocking him back. They tightened the circle, their harsh breathing almost blending. Vasa came in low, his knife flickering back and forth. Kee bent to avoid the thrust, his own knife held point up to stab. But Vasa leaned quickly to the side, kicking hard at Kee's arm and Kee lost his knife.

A handful of sand blinded Vasa. Kee came to his feet, his almost numb arm bent to block the knife that Vasa thrust at him. He had Isabel to thank for the flung sand, and it bought him the second he needed to reach behind and throw his other knife.

Vasa loosed a howl of rage. He dropped his knife to clutch Kee's, frantic to pull it free and stop his life's blood from pouring out to the earth.

Kee staggered and picked up the knife he had dropped. Vasa was on his knees when the unholy scream froze him and Isabel in midstep to get to Kee.

She cried out. Staggering out of the blinding sun was a torn and bleeding Clarai.

"You will never have him!" she yelled.

Both Kee and Isabel saw the rifle come to bear on them. Kee dived for Isabel, taking her down beneath him. He saw Vasa jerk as the shot rang out, then another and one more before he sprawled facedown.

The wind came up, blowing hard, swirling sand around them. Kee covered Isabel with his body, his face buried against her hair. But he couldn't shut out the sounds of the soul-piercing howling like some great beast dying or crying out in rage.

Minutes only, he was sure of that, for the silence was as sudden as the dust storm. He dragged himself to his knees, and lifted Isabel from the earth.

"Hold me," he whispered to her. "Just hold me."

It was Outlaw who nudged them a long while later. His velvet-soft nose worked over Kee then Isabel before he seemed satisfied and tossed his head.

Isabel took Kee's face within her cradled hands. "I must try to find her, Kee. No matter what she has done, I cannot leave her here."

"Together. We'll go together."

Arms around each other's waists, needing the support as much as they needed the closeness, they walked to where they had last seen Clarai. Kee found the rifle half-buried in sand. But of the torn and broken woman there was no sign.

"We can search," he offered.

Isabel was silent, tears streaming down her cheeks.

"You know she meant to kill you and not Vasa," she said after a few minutes.

"I'm not so sure. When you were in their camp she saw how he looked at you. I wanted to kill him then."

She turned to him, her lips seeking his, and she cherished the warmth of them on her own. Here was life, and the promise of love.

And here was the passion that had flared to life from the first, igniting the hunger each knew the other would feed and satisfy.

When Kee lifted his lips from hers, it was to murmur, "He was damn wrong. There's not one cold or hard thing about you. Let's go, lovely lady. I want us gone from this place."

"What happened back there, Kee?" She tilted her head back to look into his eyes and saw only dark shadows.

"Someday I'll tell you. Someday when I sort it all out. I'm not really sure of everything."

He took her hand and started to walk.

"Wait, Kee. Tell me where it is that you want to go."

"Home. I want to take you home. That is—" he drew her into his arms and held her tight while a few deeply taken and released breaths helped him say the words that would change his life.

"That is if you want yourself a cowhand with a smart mustang and four mares—"

"Yes! Oh, merciful God, yes!"

"Let me finish. You're getting a little bit more. Four prime mares and a breeding stallion—"

"Kee, I love you. I love you."

And this time the kiss was not a promise, but a seal of two lovers while a soft wind sighed through the canyons and ravines, and whispered into the deep crevices of the mountain that had endured men's hunting for a treasure of gold.

They rode away in the late afternoon and as Kee topped a rise he saw that Isabel had lagged behind. She was looking back, and he thought it was with regret that she could not keep her promise to her grandmother and bury her grandfather on his land. He was going to call out to her, but stopped himself, remembering her strange reaction when he showed her the gold.

She had kissed him briefly, and said that she knew.

He found the patience to wait for her, letting her mourn her loss.

But Isabel was not mourning any loss. She whispered silent thanks to her grandfather who had led her to a treasure far more enduring than gold.

She had found love, and a man worthy to be called the hero of her heart.

Epilogue

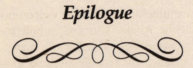

The autumn wind blew through the willows on Queen's Creek as Kee led Isabel from their night camp. They were north of the Rocking K now, and he had turned their packhorses over to one of the men who had gone ahead to tell the family they were there.

Kee had sent a telegram, asking them to wait at the house for him. He had places he wanted to show Isabel, just as she had shown him every inch of her ranch.

But the closer they rode to the big Spanish-style house surrounded by ancient cottonwood trees that helped keep the thick adobe walls and tiled roof cool, the more nervous Isabel became. He made her laugh telling tales of swimming in the pond before Santo would allow them to try the swiftly moving current of the river.

He drew up for a moment to study the sprawl of buildings. At the back of the main house, he pointed out the adobe wall that encircled his grandmother's pride and joy, her garden. He told Isabel stories he had heard of Logan and Ty climbing the thick wooden gates to sneak into the house without their mother, or older brother Conner ever knowing. And she laughed then teased him that she knew he had done the same.

"It is beautiful, Kee. Larger than my home, but everywhere my eyes see the loving care given to land and the herds of cattle and horses."

"You feel it, too?"

"The peacefulness, yes. It is a welcome feeling." She saw that the windlass turned to pull water from the center courtyard well. There was a man in the low tower who watched them with his field glasses. Kee pointed out where Santo and Sofia lived in their own smaller house.

"I wish you could see the rose garden in the spring. And in the summer, when the sun is very hot, we would lie beneath the lemon trees and drink lemonade that Sofia cooled in the springhouse."

"You missed all this and never said a word."

"I had you, Isabel. It was enough and always will be. Where you are is my home. I need no other."

"Kee, I—"

"You're still very nervous about meeting them, I know. I swear to you, my lovely bride, that no one will bite. Well, I might, but only when we are alone."

"Then be very careful, *caballero,* for I will bite you back."

Kee threw back his head and laughed. "I can't wait."

It was Isabel's soft laughter that floated down to the impatient crowd. They could see the two coming along and twice Logan had to restrain Jesse from running out to meet her adopted son.

Kee saw his family gathered, and crowded Isabel's horse. He lifted her hand to his lips. "Remember, I love you. And they will love you, too."

She rode beside him on one of her palomino mares whose dark liquid eyes and flashy, long silver-white mane and tail had captured Outlaw's heart as surely as her rider had captured Kee's.

Her trembling hand clenched his. And once more he whispered, "They will love you. Like me... passionately, and hopelessly."

But one slim figure broke from the group to run toward them. And Kee knew who it was. Long brown hair flying with glints of sun trapped within its thickness. Her mother's hair, but as she came close, those gunmetal-blue eyes were Ty's own. Kee pulled slightly ahead, leaned down and swept the young girl into the saddle before him. They had been doing this since she was boot high. He held his horse to a walk and Isabel caught up with them.

"Princess," he said when she was through smothering him with kisses, "you've grown half a foot taller and twice as pretty."

"I've missed you so. No one else calls me pretty. And I've needed you. Mother has been horrid. She wants to send me East to school. Aunt Belinda even found a place. Miss Armbruster's Academy for Young Ladies. I don't want to go. There's nothing they could teach me that's of any use. They'd have me gussied up like today, in a gown that's impossible to run in."

"Whoa, princess. You're dressed up to make a good impression on my wife. And that's respect for me. So stop pouting and let me introduce you. Isabel, love, this is my oldest niece, Reina. Thoroughly spoiled and a brat to boot."

"Kee!" Isabel warned him to stop with a sharp look. And to Reina, "You are as lovely as he said." Kee received a warm smile and Isabel a cold shoulder.

But she understood. The young girl was in love with Kee. He was not of her blood. How could her astute husband be so blind?

Isabel could see his family. A very large crowd whose impatience surged toward them as they turned into the courtyard through the open gates.

"Family party tonight, Kee," Reina informed him. "Fiesta for everyone else. The invitations have been going out for weeks. You must promise me a dance."

"Only if you mend your manners, little witch."

Reina had no chance to pout or reply for Logan lifted her down, and then had Kee in a bear hug. For a few mad minutes Isabel was forgotten as Kee was passed to Jesse, then his aunt Dixie, little ones squirming between adult bodies, his uncles holding him close with an open display of male affection that at first surprised, then warmed Isabel toward his family.

Kee was calling out names and she tried hard to keep matching faces to them, but there were so many, for men came from the bunkhouse and corrals, and women from the house.

Then her gaze found a woman who stood alone near the massive doors of the house. She needed no introduction to Macaria Kincaid. She was just as Kee had described her, stately, gray in the thick crown of braids she wore, and her smile of welcome so warm that Isabel dismounted and went to her.

She wished she had worn something more fitting. Her split leather riding skirt and creamy linen shirt were of the same quality as Macaria's lilac silk gown, but at her insistence they had ridden here, and a hot bath was something she missed. She removed her hat and her gloves, all the time knowing she was being studied and judged. It was no different from the way her own grandmother had greeted Kee. But she had not found him wanting, and loved him dearly.

"Kee came to us, Isabel, half-grown. To me he is more son than grandson, but most of all, he is a blessing to our family. I see in you a woman of strength, and one who loves with an open heart. I hope my family will find a place there. Now come and greet your husband's grandmother properly and I will forgive you for marrying him without us being there."

Over Isabel's shoulder, Macaria smiled at Kee, and then her gaze went to each of her tall sons ranged behind him, their wives at their sides, and the little ones crowding close.

And she silently offered a prayer, and a whisper. "See, Justin, another good match. We have done well by them. And they have brought love and children to the land we loved, dearest."

First Kee, then the others besieged them, and swept them into the house.

Later that night Isabel placed her hand on Kee's heart, her head resting on his shoulder. She loved this quiet time after their passion burned bright and hunger was stilled. The soft creakings of the old house settled around her. They had talked far into the night, and ate, and drank, his family close by, taking her in as Kee claimed they took him in, into their home and their hearts. There was pride in the eyes that watched him as he told of making the men back down from trying to take her grandmother's land and reselling it to the new rail line.

Only one spot marred the evening: Reina and the sadness in her eyes as she realized that her hero was hers no more. She was young, too young to think of love, but she would find someone as special as Kee when the time was right for her.

Kee was Isabel's, lover and husband, keeper of her heart and dreams, hero of her soul.

And soon, very soon, she would tell him that he had another role to play. One that required great patience and stamina, and love, a great deal of love.

She snuggled close and sighed, contentment in every deeply taken breath.

In the darkness Kee shifted his body a little, waiting until his wife was asleep. Only then did his hand curve over the soft swelling roundness of her belly.

He smiled. He couldn't wait to tell Logan he was going to be a grandpa. Maybe tomorrow Isabel would tell him about the child she carried.

Or the next day.

It didn't really matter. He would only love her more.

Author's Note

Strange happenings, mysterious deaths and bogus maps continue to circulate, adding to the legend of the Lost Dutchman Mine. It is over one hundred years since Jacob Walz died. Unexplained deaths have occurred, some bodies recovered but their treasure maps were missing. Was the mine ever real? There are those who claim gold could never be found there. Others say the earthquake truly destroyed the most important landmarks.

Was Walz crafty? Did he choose a site where the very ominous name of the mountain range plays into the legend? Was there nothing more than a hoard of gold that he and Ken-tee stole from the Vulture Gold Mine in Wickenberg?

Truth? Legend?

Gold-hungry adventurers have been searching for years. Adolph Ruth believed he had the map that came from the early Peralta family. He was murdered, but his possessions were not found until a month later, far from his body. His map was missing. But he had a little book where he had written of thirty-six other deaths and claimed that the mine was within five miles of Weaver's Needle. In 1964 Glenn Magill, a private investigator, set out on his search. He and his men were shot at, threatened by Apaches and rattlesnakes, tricked by swindlers, lied to, warned in letters, sabotaged and beset with accidents. They kept on until 1967 when they found a pit above a tunnel. There were signs that fit Walz's clues but no gold.

The laws passed in 1983 protect all National Forest Wilderness Areas including the Superstitions from any mineral exploitation. So the Lost Dutchman Mine may remain just that—lost.

But the legend lives on.

And who can say if one or two of the hundreds of hikers and horseback riders that visit the site annually, do not have gold fever, do not have a carefully hoarded map, and are not still searching?

And if they are counted among the missing—does that mean they died mysteriously or that they found gold...?

*Take a trip to Merry Old England
with four exciting stories from*

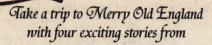

In January 2000, look for
THE GENTLEMAN THIEF
by **Deborah Simmons**
(England, 1818)

and

MY LADY RELUCTANT
by **Laurie Grant**
(England, 1141)

In February 2000, look for
THE ROGUE
The second book of
KNIGHTS OF THE **BLACK ROSE**
by **Ana Seymour**
(England, 1222)

and

ANGEL OF THE KNIGHT
by **Diana Hall**
(England, 1154)

Harlequin Historicals
The way the past *should* have been.

Available at your favorite retail outlet.

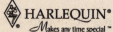

HARLEQUIN®
Makes any time special ™

Explore the American frontier
with these rugged Westerns from

Harlequin®
Historical

On sale May 2000

THE CAPTIVE HEART
by **Cheryl Reavis**
(North Carolina frontier, 1750s)

TANNER STAKES HIS CLAIM
by **Carolyn Davidson**
(Texas, 1800s)

On sale June 2000

BANDERA'S BRIDE
by **Mary McBride**
(Texas, 1870s)

MOLLY'S HERO
by **Susan Amarillas**
(Wyoming, 1870s)

Harlequin Historicals
The way the past *should* have been.

Available at your favorite retail outlet.

HARLEQUIN®
Makes any time special ™